Pat,
All the best!
Ana Bane

|||| | ||| ||||||||||| | |||| ||||
D1607674

THE STRANGERS SAGA
BATON ROUGE
Book One

Ana Ban

Strangers Saga: Baton Rouge: Book One by Ana Ban

1.Romance 2.Police Procedural 3.Mystery

First Edition

Printed in the USA

ISBN 9781697609769

For my dad.
Thank you for your unending love and support.

Acknowledgements

FIRST AND FOREMOST, I WOULD like to recognize the infinite encouragement of my love, Julio. With your support, I'm able to follow my dreams.

A big thank you to my family, for always being first in line to read my books. None of this would have been possible without your belief in me.

And finally, to Christopher Granczynski for editing this work and pushing me well past my comfort zone. You helped me dig a little deeper and bring these characters to life.

CONTENTS

Chapter One

S tanding in the shade of a willow tree, Sadie looked to the house and worked on finding her calm. She'd gotten the call late last night, drove in first thing that morning. She knew this would be the right move for her. More importantly, the right move for the little girl on the other side of that door.

If nothing else, Sadie Nichols was no coward. She strode to the door, knocked. Waited for the owner to answer. Locks turned and a weathered face peered out. "Sadie? That you?"

"Good mornin, Auntie May. May I come in?"

"Of course, darlin. You're here to see Eva, I'd imagine."

"If that's all right," Sadie said, stepping inside and slipping off her shoes. "How's she doin?"

"Well as can be expected. Quiet. Poor girl. She's through here." Sadie followed Maybelle through the small rooms and to the sunporch. Eva huddled on a bench in the corner, her dark hair shorn at uneven lengths but still long enough to hide her face. "Eva, your cousin Sadie has come to visit. I'll get you both some lemonade."

"Just a water for me, Auntie May. Thanks." The older woman bustled out, left them to speak. Sadie appreciated the gesture. Settling across from the preteen, Sadie folded her hands on her lap and tried a smile. "Eva, do you remember me? I'm Sadie."

No response, just that same listless stare.

"That's all right. I came to see you a few months ago, when your mama was sick. I'd been livin in Lafayette—do you know where that is? Just an hour's drive from here. Big city, lots of people. I loved it for a long time, still do, but I thought it was high time I moved back here. Gonna open a store, find a house. If you'd like, you could come live with me." Eva twitched, just the smallest sign that she'd heard. Showed interest. Sadie sat forward, careful not to frighten her. "I'd love it if you did, but only if you'd like it, too. If you would, I'll need a sign from you. Just a little nod, maybe a smile."

Sadie paused, watched. Maybelle hovered at the doorway, afraid to interrupt. Prayed that the girl would agree. They both waited with bated breath. Eva didn't move, didn't speak. Sadie's heart began to break.

Then Eva's gaze lifted and met Sadie's for the briefest of moments. In that split second of time, a connection sparked and a vision turned Sadie's eyes hazy. She saw a clear picture of Eva, working in the store alongside Sadie. Wrapping up an item for a customer, paint smears on her arms. Smiling. Happy.

In a blink, the vision was gone. Sadie had known. Had known that this was the right move, coming back to Baton Rouge. Had known it was time to open her store, lay down roots. She had known it in her gut.

Now, she knew it in her head, her heart. This had been the right move not only for her, but Eva as well. Sadie and Maybelle watched Eva nod her head and they both let out sighs of relief. Maybelle went in, set down the two glasses she'd poured. "It'll all be all right now, darlins."

"Yes. It will." Sadie stuck her hand in her pocket and brought out a keepsake for Eva. A promise. "This is for you. It's a reminder that I'm here for you, and I'm workin to keep you with me. It might take some time, Eva, but it'll happen. Trust me."

Sadie set the locket on the table, the small inset amethyst sparkling in the morning sunlight. Eva looked at it, reached out but didn't grab. So quietly Sadie had to strain to hear, she said, "It's purple."

"Your favorite color. I remembered." Eva nodded, picked it up and looped the long chain around her neck. Sadie had left it long enough to hide under her clothes. "When you need a reminder that someone's out there, fightin for you, take it out and know I am."

Eva didn't smile or speak but she did hold up the chain, watching the locket as it twirled slowly back and forth. Sadie and Maybelle shared a look, an agreement on what had to be done. "Drink some of your lemonade, Eva. I'll walk Sadie out."

"I'll see you soon," Sadie said. "I promise."

Maybelle waited to speak until they reached the door, stepping outside with Sadie. "You'll do right by her."

"This can't be easy for you."

"Watchin my Justine battle drugs? No, darlin, that'll never be easy. But doin right by my granddaughter? Didn't take a second thought."

"I've already got my storefront, and I'll be meetin with Carolyn about a house this week. I'll find a good lawyer, see what's what."

"Have you told your family?"

Sadie looked away, let out a sigh. "No. But it's time."

Δ Δ Δ

3

When Sadie made the call to her parents, they set aside the time to see her right away. Her brother was able to do the same, thanks to his unusual work hours at the news station. She headed straight to her childhood home and let herself in. Diana had that strained look in her eye that any mother would get when her child called a meeting. Instead of telling Sadie to sit and demanding she spill, Diana poured sweet tea and organized a plate of cheese and crackers. Seth walked in a few minutes after his sister, his hair still damp from his shower. "What's this about, Sadie?"

"If you wouldn't mind," she said, gesturing to the dining room where their father already lounged in his chair. Sadie sat at the table scratched and nicked from years of use, waiting for Diana and Seth to join them. She looked at the faces she'd gathered and decided to just lay it on the line. "I'm gonna adopt Eva."

The air pulsated with tension, as she'd managed to render the room speechless. Diana recovered first. "Eva? Evaline Wentworth, Eva?"

"That's right."

"You can't."

"I have to." The words hung there as three stunned faces attempted to come to grips with their meaning. "She needs a home. I can give her one."

"What the hell happened?" her dad asked.

"James." Diana's disapproving tone had more to do with his choice of words than his question. She laid a hand on his arm, rephrased. "Justine went through rehab. She's been better."

"She was. Maybelle called me last night—she'd gone to pick up Eva for a sleepover, found Justine high."

Diana stood with tears welling in her eyes. She looked out the window, unable to meet anyone's gaze. "Even still, Justine will never agree to you adoptin her."

"She's an addict, rehab or not. No court in the world would deny Eva'd be better off with me," Sadie answered.

Having composed herself, Diana sat back down. "She's a teenager, you're practically a teenager yourself."

"All the better to understand her."

"She'll be a lot of work," her dad said.

"She's family." Sadie delivered this firm, harsh. She'd had enough. "Look, thank you for listenin and tryin to do what's best for me. Right now, I need to do what's best for Eva. This is happenin. I'm adoptin her. It may be the dumbest thing I've ever done, but it would be the worst thing if I just sat idly by."

Diana reached out and clasped her daughter's hand. Dark, gentle eyes studied her youngest, recognized the unyielding set to her jaw. "Well, darlin, I know that look in your eye. You're as stubborn as a mule and tougher than a goat. You're gonna do this whether or not we agree. I have some concerns, and I hope you'll listen to them, but you're right. Eva needs a better home. You can give that to her. I'm still gonna worry, but you'll have our support."

Her parents shared a look, and Sadie watched as her dad's eyes softened from steel to gray. He ran a hand through his pale hair and sighed. "You'll have our support."

Seth, six years her senior and looking more like their dad every day, didn't move, didn't speak. Sadie was the baby, a late and unexpected addition to the family. She knew they all still saw her as a child; she intended to prove otherwise. "I can do this."

Her mother nodded, one glistening tear escaping before she stood and left the room. Sadie understood her heartache. This wasn't just her family—Justine was her niece, her godchild. Diana felt guilt about the choices Justine had made, even knowing she couldn't have done anything to stop her. Diana felt like she'd let Justine down. Her hesitance had less to do with Sadie's plan and more to do with her own perceived shortcomings.

James stood, squeezed Sadie's hand once and gave her an encouraging nod before going to console his wife. Once they were out of the room, Seth cleared his throat. "This is really why you moved back here."

"It is."

"You're positive it's the right thing?"

Sadie pressed a hand to her stomach, nodded. "I'm sure."

"All right. What do we need to do first?"

Sometimes, her brother could be so remarkable. With a wry smile, Sadie answered. "I need to get the store open, so I have the money to fight for Eva."

"You know my schedule. Anythin you need, just tell me when and where."

"Thanks, Seth. You're the best."

Sadie left the house, taking a deep breath of the late winter air, that strange, southern combination of cool and humid. As she approached the driver's side of her SUV, a pickup pulled to a stop behind her. At one time it had been fire engine red—but, like many things, it had seen better days. Peering at the figure as it emerged from the driver seat, her eyes grew wide. "Declan?"

For a brief moment Declan paused, studying the full-grown woman that used to be his best friend's little sister. Her pale blonde hair shone brightly in the sun, her wide, stormy eyes—so familiar to him even after all these years—watched him as he watched her. When her lips curved, displaying that little dimple in the bottom right corner, his thoughts quickly turned wayward.

Reeling himself in before he did something embarrassing, he settled on an easy smile. Sadie ran and practically leapt into his arms, wrapping herself around him in a bone-crushing hug. It took him off guard, but not because of her exuberance—that was a holdover from her younger years—but by the way her body felt pressed so tightly against his.

He took a step back to balance them out, wrapping his arms around her and trying not to notice how she smelled of jasmine and lavender. "Hey, Sadie. You've still got that endless amount of energy, I see."

"It's all the manual labor," she replied, pulling back just enough to look up at his face. It seemed further away than she remembered. "Goodness gracious, did you get taller?"

"Maybe you've shrunk."

The door to her parent's house opened and Seth emerged. Declan stepped away from Sadie, guilt settling low and fast. Seth raised an eyebrow in their general direction before clapping Declan on the back. "Hey man, good to see you."

"You, too. I was gonna call you later—I've found a place."

"A place?" Sadie asked.

"I've moved back."

"Really? When?"

"Couple of weeks ago. Been stayin with my folks, started with the BRPD. Movin in this weekend, if you're free," he added, looking to Seth.

"You know I'll do most anythin for a free beer."

Sadie still stared at him. He ran a hand through his dark hair self-consciously. "What?"

"I'm just surprised."

"Why's that?"

"Thought you liked the big city."

"It was time to come home," Declan replied, his eyes hooded as he scanned her features.

Sadie swallowed once, her throat unusually dry. Declan had never looked at her in quite that way before. She took a step back to give herself some breathing room. "I better get goin, I'm checkin out the store today."

"Store?"

"The first official location of Sadie's Things," she said with a smile. "I'll catch you guys later."

With forced casualness, Sadie strolled to her car and slipped inside. One last glance at the boy next door left her fingers trembling as she started the engine and drove away.

Chapter Two

Arriving at the dingy storefront that would soon be filled with handmade, vintage, and refurbished items, Sadie unlocked the door and flipped on all the lights. As of now, the store consisted of a giant room that had been split in three; the front half would be the store, while the back half would be her workshops. A small loft upstairs, which would eventually be converted into an office with a utility kitchen for breaks, would serve as Sadie's home for the time being.

She would be on the lookout for a house, something that would be perfect for her and Eva. She'd be meeting with a realtor later in the week, but her focus now was reserved for her current project.

With the space being officially hers, she began with scrubbing every inch of the area. She wanted to start sleeping there that night—she'd already brought an old futon up for her bed—so she made sure the loft passed for livable.

After an hour of cleaning and rearranging, Sadie decided to take a break. Lighting a smudge stick containing sage and lavender, she allowed the powerful smoke to drift through her new home. Letting that settle, she headed out to the grocery store for essentials.

Since she had a mini fridge in the loft, she grabbed lettuce for salads and steaks to cook in the toaster oven. She couldn't wait to have a full kitchen again, but for now she would make do.

Back at the loft, she threw a steak in on broil and headed down to the bottom level. Tomorrow, she would move her first items out of storage and into the empty space. She had a very specific idea of what she wanted; her plans were all drawn out in her sketchpad.

Making a mental list of where to start with the main level, Sadie went upstairs to flip the meat and toss the salad. After a few minutes, the center glowed a healthy pink and she set it on a plate to rest. She'd only brought one box with her, which included a pot and one pan, dishes for two in case she had company, and her coffee pot. Her clothes were in a suitcase, which she would unpack later. The rest would be placed in storage for the duration.

Scarfing down the meal as soon as it was ready, Sadie went back down and set to work on the main room. This space proved infinitely easier to clean than the loft had been; it sat virtually empty. She planned to leave the walls the same bright yellow but gave them a good wash. The cement floors were covered with dark strips of laminate to look like wood. The overall impression of the space felt cheery, bright, and clean.

In the very back of the store, she'd decided to leave the concrete floors. Since a lot of her work consisted of sanding down furniture and painting, the concrete could withstand anything she threw at it. Long sheets of pegboard that she'd had delivered the previous day were stacked along one wall in the bigger section. Double-wide doors separated the store front from the middle room, which would house her sewing equipment, while another set led into the workshop where the furniture refinishing would take place.

After scrubbing down the space, Sadie lit another smudge stick and gave the herbs a boost with words. "Into this smoke, I release all energies that do not serve me or mine. Be gone, all negativity, so that I may shine. Only positivity and light may enter here. Banished are any evil spirits that linger near. This I ask, one by three. As I will, so mote it be."

Satisfied with that, she hauled in her first load from her SUV—her basic tools, along with a ladder.

She hung the pegboard along both shorter walls in the workshop. One would be for organizing her tools, while the other would be used to sort her art supplies. Beneath the pegboard, Sadie would be building low shelves to store larger items.

Against the wall that separated the two work areas, Sadie had plans for a long workbench to hold her table saws. The rest of the space would be open for working on the projects.

In the sewing area, Sadie wanted a large cutting table, which would double as a work space for other crafts, and another long work area for her various sewing machines to rest. The open wall opposite the machines would be shelving of all sizes, to help organize the vast amounts of material and notions that were required when refashioning clothes.

She'd asked the contractor to paint the same cheery yellow on her workshop walls, and included the same laminate flooring in the sewing area. She saw the space as a blank canvas, and Sadie couldn't wait to fill it with her vision.

Exhausted physically, Sadie trudged up the stairs to test the small shower in the tiny bathroom. Though only a stand-up deal that barely fit one person, it would suffice until she found a more permanent home.

Even with every part of her body aching, Sadie's brain refused to shut down. Slipping into comfortable pajamas, she curled up on the futon with her sketchpad, drawing out new ideas that had come to her during her cleaning spree.

It would be helpful to have a washing machine, which she should have thought of before. And a sweet little coffee and water station, to offer her customers while they browsed. Another work space in the shop itself, as she wouldn't have any employees to begin with and would like to be able to create during business hours.

While she concentrated on her work, thoughts of Declan came unbidden to her mind. With a sigh, she paused in her sketch to gaze out the window.

Declan Park had been the ultimate boy next door. He and Seth had been best friends since before they could walk, and he'd always treated her as the sister he never had—which meant a lot of torturing and teasing, along with the more pleasant activities such as teaching her sports and how to defend herself against unwanted advances.

Even through all the torment, Sadie had harbored the biggest crush on Declan through most of her childhood, including when he took off after graduation and she didn't see him every day. He'd come home on holidays with stories of the police academy and his first cases on the force.

After that, he'd stopped coming home. The last time Sadie had seen him was during her own graduation from high school. He'd shown up to support her—with a lanky brunette on his arm. That day any hope of catching Declan's eye, as more than his best friend's little sister, had been finally crushed.

She'd left just after graduation—her idea of selling vintage items online as a class project had exploded, and she'd decided to continue growing her business in the larger city of Lafayette—and hadn't seen him since. Now, six years later, they'd both decided to move back to their hometown and he'd given her a look that she'd been wishing for since she'd been old enough to understand her feelings.

He'd looked at her not like a kid sister, but as a woman. Sighing with frustration, Sadie closed her notebook, fixed the futon into a bed, and did her best to push Declan from her mind so she could fall asleep.

$\triangle \; \triangle \; \triangle$

Tapping her phone against her palm, Sadie hesitated before pushing send. Savannah White had been her best friend since grade school. Surely, she would understand Sadie's need to speak with Grant. He was the only lawyer she knew. Still, it didn't feel right without Savannah's permission.

He'd been Savannah's first love, after all.

"Hello!" Savannah said, her reliably cheery voice loud and clear.

"Hey, Savannah," Sadie replied. After a long pause where she checked to make sure the call had connected, she asked, "Hello?"

"I'm sorry, who's this?"

"Savannah, it's me. Sadie."

"Who?"

"Sadie. Your best—oh, you brat."

Savannah's light laugh made Sadie grin, even when she was being a pain in her butt. "It's been so long I'd forgotten who you were. How the hell are you, sweetheart?"

Through a fresh wave of guilt, Sadie told her friend about what she'd accomplished since moving away from Lafayette. Savannah had moved to the bigger city two years after Sadie, though they'd stopped being roommates once Savannah had met her boyfriend, Branson.

Not that Sadie could blame her. Branson was a sweet, loving fireman. That was the dream.

Sadie skipped the reunion with Declan. Savannah would be able to pick up on every nuance in Sadie's voice, and she'd spend the next hour describing each micro expression on Declan's face. Sadie didn't feel prepared for that conversation.

As it was, Savannah knew Sadie hadn't gotten to her true point yet. They'd known each other too long for Savannah to let her slide. "That all sounds well and good, but what did you really call for?"

There was no more beating around the bush. "I—well, I need to call a lawyer. I was going to call Grant."

This statement was met by complete and utter silence. Savannah finally answered after several beats of silence. "My Grant?"

"Yes."

She heard a heavy sigh, and Sadie could all but see Savannah nodding over the phone. "I get it. He might not be able to help you, but he could point you in the right direction. Of course you should call him."

"Thanks, Savannah. I know it's not easy." That was an understatement. Grant had been Savannah's first love—and until she'd met Branson, she'd been convinced he was her only love. Emotion ran deep for the both of them.

And since they'd been together so long, Sadie felt as if she'd also lost a good friend when the split happened. Talking to Grant felt like a betrayal, even though she'd known him as long as Savannah had. They'd spent so much time together as teens, and even with the years that had gone by, she knew Grant would help her now.

After a few more minutes of catching up, Sadie said her good-byes and scrolled to find Grant's number. She felt confident he hadn't changed it since they'd last spoke.

Only one ring sounded before he picked up. "This is Grant."

Twirling her fingers into the material of her overalls, Sadie tried to smile through the nerves. "Grant, hi. It's Sadie. Sadie Nichols."

"Sadie?" She heard genuine pleasure with an equal amount of bafflement. "How are you?"

"I'm good, really good. I've just moved back to Baton Rouge. How have you been?"

"Good," he answered just as generically. "I passed the bar last year, been workin for Carter and Munger since."

He let the conversation lull, knowing Sadie would ask what she'd called to ask. "That's great to hear. I always knew you'd be successful, whatever you chose to do. That's actually why I'm callin. It's kind of a long story, but I need a lawyer."

Concern edged his tone. "Are you in trouble?"

"Oh no, nothin like that," she said with a nervous laugh. "I'd like to adopt my cousin. Well, technically my second cousin. She's in a bad situation right now, and I want to give her a home."

"That... that is big news. I've got an hour free this afternoon, we could grab some lunch and catch up."

"Oh, Grant, that'd be amazin. Thank you."

"Sure thing. Tony's, one o'clock?"

"Perfect. See you then." Disconnecting, Sadie blasted oldies music to motivate her while she built tables and shelves for her sewing space. By noon, she'd completed the cube shelves and had worked up a sweat—and her appetite.

The shelves would need a few coats of paint, but she would start that after her lunch meeting. Running upstairs, she showered off the fresh grime and dressed comfortably in a pair of jeans with a shirt the color of cornflowers. The dolman sleeves would keep her cool while the jeans would offer protection for where she knew they'd be sitting for lunch.

Jumping in her SUV, she headed across town and made it to Tony's a few minutes early. Grant already waited under the bright blue awning, his fingers running across the screen of his phone. He wore dark gray dress pants and a white button down with the sleeves rolled to his elbows. Sadie would have placed money that there would be a discarded tie in his front seat.

He looked good, she decided. He'd filled out some in his chest and shoulders and had topped off just under six feet. His wavy, light brown hair had been carefully styled to look like it'd been no fuss. When he looked up from his screen, the brows that had been furrowed cleared and he offered her a bright smile.

"Grant!" With her characteristic enthusiasm, Sadie wrapped him in a hug, which he returned with a soft pat on her back.

"Hey, Sadie. It's good to see you." Stepping back with his hands on her shoulders, his hazel eyes studied her face and found the girl that had once been his friend. "Hungry?"

"Starved," she answered, leading the way into the small deli.

They ordered the fresh catch of the day—Grant with a side of gumbo, Sadie with a baked potato—and took their food containers across the street. Tony's had the best location, along the bank of the Mississippi. The owners went out before dawn each morning and hauled their load to the restaurant by cart. While they served other food, including their famous gumbo, the catch of the day had always been the go-to.

Grant found an unoccupied bench and sat, turning so he faced Sadie instead of the river. She copied him and for a moment, it felt as if the last several years disappeared and they were back in high school. "Haven't been to Tony's in a long time."

"What? At least I had an excuse, not livin here. But I always made a point to stop when I was home visitin my parents."

He looked out across the sparkling blue water as it flowed gently south. "Too many memories, I suppose."

"I know. I do. And I'm sorry for not keepin in contact."

"I understood. There were no hard feelins, Sadie. Then or now." She nodded, though she still felt the guilt of being a poor friend. Spreading butter over the potato, she waited for it to melt as she tried a bite of large-mouth bass. "Tell me about your cousin. What's goin on there?"

Thankful for the change of topic, Sadie delved into the story. "Her name is Eva, she's twelve—about to be thirteen. She'd been livin with her mom and whatever crackhead man she had hangin around. Her mom's addicted to meth, and it's a horrible situation. Justine had a bad night a few months ago, wound up in detox. Child services were called and Eva was taken into custody."

"My God, Sadie, that's terrible," Grant said, laying a comforting hand over hers. "How long was she in custody?"

"She was in for a night, then stayed with her grandma for a week. As soon as I heard, I made the decision to come here, to fight for her. Started doin my research on a place to open my business, tyin up loose ends in Lafayette. She's such a sweet child. Then, two nights ago, her grandma called me. Maybelle went to pick Eva up for a sleepover and found Justine high on somethin or other. Yesterday mornin I went to see her, asked if she'd like to come live with me. She said yes. I can't... I just can't leave her there, in such an unstable environment."

"Of course not. That would go against every fiber of your bein."

Smiling in spite of the seriousness, Sadie marveled over the fact that Grant seemed to know her better than her own parents. "Thanks for that. However, I have no idea where to go from here."

"Family law isn't really my area, but I do know someone who's amazin at it. Her name is Clara Kent."

"Any relation to Clark?" Sadie asked, grinning as Grant chuckled.

"Unfortunately, no. Because that would be awesome." He hesitated, and Sadie knew he'd left out an important piece of information. "There is somethin you should know. She's not just a lawyer—she's my girlfriend."

"Oh," Sadie said. It's all that would come to her.

"I'm not sure if that would be awkward..."

Waving away his concern, she did her best to smile. "Why would it?"

Quiet again, Grant fidgeted with his hands, looked anywhere but at Sadie. "How is she?"

Sadie knew who Grant inquired about without needing to say Savannah's name. "She's good. Happy. She's datin someone, too. He's a really good guy. She's been workin at the museum, teachin classes here and there."

"She always loved museums. I'm happy for her," he said, his tone bittersweet. Checking his watch, Grant sighed. "Sorry to eat and run, but I've gotta head back to work. I'll text you Clara's number, let her know to expect your call. Don't be a stranger."

Sadie stood, hugged him again. "I won't, I promise."

Chapter Three

Sadie dressed bright and early for her meeting with Carolyn O'Dell, one of her mom's closest friends and the best realtor in Baton Rouge. Her office, located in what had once been a family home, greeted Sadie with cheerful flowers overflowing from window boxes against the lemon-yellow siding. A little bell dinged when she entered, announcing her arrival to all in the office. A young brunette with a bright smile welcomed Sadie to O'Dell and Associates.

"Hi there, I have an appointment with Carolyn," Sadie said.

"Why, if it isn't Sadie Nichols," Carolyn's booming voice called out from a doorway.

Turning with a huge smile of her own, Sadie closed the distance and slipped her arms around the petite woman. "Hey, Auntie Carol. Goodness, you look amazin. Did you make a deal with the devil?"

Carolyn's bleach-blonde hair, a perfect puffy coif, framed her heart-shaped face and wide hazel eyes. And though Sadie towered over her, Carolyn remained the strongest person Sadie had ever met. Laughing, Carolyn squeezed Sadie's hand. "Bless your heart, darlin. Come on back."

"Thanks for squeezin me in."

"Of course. You're the closest thing to a niece I've got, after all." They sat beside each other in comfortable brown leather chairs. After studying Sadie for a moment, Carolyn said, "My, my, you've grown so much in the last six months. Responsibility suits you."

"You don't think I'm makin a mistake?"

"Heavens no, child. Besides, even if I did, you've always been too bull-headed to listen."

They both laughed, but Sadie took Carolyn's approval to heart. She'd grown up with the woman—called her Aunt Carol— and considered her opinion one of the most important in her life. "My mom's worried."

Carolyn shooed this away with a wave of her hand. "Mom's worry. That's what they do. You'll know, soon enough. Doesn't mean she doesn't support you."

Blowing out a breath, Sadie nodded. "I know. Thank you."

"Now, onto fun stuff. I've got several houses lined up for us to have a look-see. You ready?"

"I'm ready," Sadie answered. She'd already dropped off her pre-approval letter from the bank, and she trusted Carolyn to find her an appropriate house with the requirements they'd talked about over the phone. Three bedrooms preferably, one for her, one for Eva, one for an office. Two full baths. A decent kitchen, space for a garden. Those were her main points.

And character. Sadie couldn't live in a cookie-cutter home.

They drove together to the first house, a two-story colonial that had white paint and a blue trim, complete with a white picket fence. The yard had been meticulously cared for, with gorgeous roses blooming along the front edge.

It looked nice, but didn't give Sadie butterflies. She needed butterflies. Still, they walked through, made small talk as they looked. As they walked out, Carolyn asked her thoughts. "It's nice. Really nice. But…"

"Not the right one. I get it. On to the second!"

Sadie liked the second more, as it boasted an overgrown garden with a stone well. She delighted in finding a working retrieval bucket, but still the rest of the home didn't speak to her.

Sadie tried hard not to feel defeated. Home buying could be a long process, and they were only on the second listing. Carolyn had done a good job checking off all her boxes, but the homes so far were just missing something. As they drove through an older neighborhood with tree-lined streets creating a tunnel effect, Sadie sat straight up with a gasp. "Pull over."

"What? What is it?" Carolyn asked.

"That house, right there. I love it!"

Baffled, Carolyn slowed and came to a stop against the curb. The house Sadie gushed over sat empty, lawn overgrown and tangled, shingles falling off the roof. Most people would dismiss the home at first glance, but—and while Carolyn wouldn't have picked it for a young woman like Sadie—the realtor could see beyond the wreckage, to the whimsical tower in the front and the arched roof that guaranteed the same for ceilings inside. The yard, once cleaned up, would be huge and give the owner plenty of privacy.

"Let me make a call," Carolyn said, knowing that they'd found the one.

While Carolyn spoke to the agent listed on the sign, Sadie got out and wandered through the yard. The wrap-around porch needed to be redone. Sadie could see a swing there, or perhaps in the back. Why not both? The rickety fence that lined the property needed to be fixed, painted. Trees along the edge gave even more privacy, and Sadie delighted in discovering them to be heavy with fruit.

Plenty of room for a garden, an outdoor entertainment area. As she went back to the front, Carolyn made her way to the door. "Careful honey, one step is out, other spots are rotted. I've got the code so we can go in and take a look. It's foreclosed, so it'll come as-is."

"Can't you see the potential?" Sadie asked. The screen door needed to be replaced, but the front door had some gorgeous stained glass she hoped to restore. "Is this crazy? I love it already."

"Not crazy, darlin," Carolyn said, maneuvering the key into the lock. "Sometimes when you know, you know."

Sadie knew. The butterflies she'd been missing took wing as she brushed her hand over the detailed wood trim. Her vision blurred and suddenly she saw herself there, in that swing she'd already imagined, rocking softly with Eva at her side and tall, cool glasses of iced tea in their hands.

The vision dissipated as she stepped inside. Sadie ignored the dust and gloom, saw the wide-open living room and hardwood floors throughout that would easily return to their former glory with a little bit of buffing. The ceiling in there arched high, the wooden steps with a hand-carved railing leading upstairs to a little loft area that could be a cozy reading nook, or an area for Eva to handle schoolwork.

They wandered through the decent-sized dining room and into the small kitchen, where Sadie paused and plotted. Carolyn pursed her lips, did the same. "It's a bit small. But knock this wall down, take a little away from the dinin room, and you've got a lot to work with. Back here is a half bath, in decent shape. And the master bedroom."

Walking through, Sadie fell in love with the large space and ensuite bathroom. Though not arched, the ceilings were high and begging for bamboo fans. Upstairs, Sadie found two decent-sized rooms with a full bath in between. Perfect for her office and Eva's room.

"It has good bones and gorgeous details," Sadie said. "Apart from the kitchen and the outside, I don't see a lot of major work that needs to be done."

"If you're sure, let's order an inspection, see what we've got."

Sadie nodded decisively and beamed. "Let's do it."

△ △ △

Too excited to do anything else, Sadie went to her little loft and began sketching out ideas for her home. For she knew, deep down in her soul, that the house would be hers. Since it had been foreclosed, Sadie could pay for it outright with the money she'd saved for a down payment. Then, she could still get a loan for repairs and manage to come out ahead.

An inspection had been set up for that Friday. Tomorrow, she'd meet with Clara about taking over custody of Eva. She still had quite a bit of work to get her shop in order before she could officially open for business.

Her growing to-do list made Sadie go a bit cross-eyed, but with everything falling in line so nicely, she knew finding the energy to finish all these tasks would be a piece of cake. It had to be.

Though she went to bed late that night, falling asleep with her sketchpad still in her hands, Sadie woke bright and early for her appointment with Clara Clark. Her intense curiosity about Grant's girlfriend nearly overshadowed her purpose for meeting with the lawyer. Nearly.

She found the office with ease and walked inside with her head held high. She'd dressed appropriately in a black skirt and blazer, though she had to add a splash of color with a bright pink shirt beneath. For luck, Sadie had added her favorite turquoise jewelry.

The office had a surprisingly homey feel, which put her a bit more at ease. Giving her name to the smiling receptionist, Sadie sat and clutched her purse to her lap while her fingers and thumbs squeezed together. She still didn't know which she worried about more—meeting Clara or finding out she somehow wouldn't qualify to adopt Eva.

When the woman emerged, the first thing that caught Sadie's eye was the bright red hair pulled halfway back and flowing over her shoulders in gentle waves. Big brown eyes softened with a friendly smile as Clara held out her hand to shake Sadie's. "Sadie Nichols? Welcome. Come on back."

Sadie pursed her lips. So far, she certainly couldn't hate this woman on her friend's behalf.

Following Clara into a cozy conference room, Sadie took a seat and set her purse on the table, her thumbs tapping nervously. Clara pulled out a folder and had a clean notebook beside her, pen at the ready. "All right. Tell me about Eva."

"She's twelve years old. Her mom is addicted to meth, and I believe she does other drugs as well. We didn't realize how bad it was until Justine—that's Eva's mom—got arrested and placed in detox. She was only there for a week and when she went home, Eva did too."

"Is there a father in the picture?"

"None of us know who her father is. Justine might, but she's never said."

"The week Justine went into detox, where did Eva go?"

"She stayed with her grandma Maybelle after one night with the state."

"Would her grandma sue for custody?"

Sadie shook her head. "Maybelle is gettin on in years—she's my mom's oldest sister of five. She had Justine pretty late in life, after havin no luck conceivin for many years. She's not doin well health-wise, either. I've spoken with her about Eva, told her my intentions to make sure she'd be all right with that. Visited with Eva while she stayed there, too. She was so quiet. I can't even imagine what that poor girl's been through.

"Justine stayed on track for a couple-three months. Maybelle called me a few nights ago. She'd gone over to pick up Eva for a sleepover and Justine was toked out. The next mornin I went to visit, asked Eva if she'd like to live with me. Eva said yes. When Maybelle brought Eva back home that mornin, Justine swore up and down she'd change, get back on the straight and narrow, but Maybelle is worried about Eva. Auntie May knows Eva would be better off with me."

"Maybelle would attest to that fact? If it comes to a fact-findin hearin?"

"I believe so, yes."

"That's a boon for our case. All right, here's the deal. Right now, your best bet is to sue Justine for bein an unfit parent. Once we win—and, from what you've told me, I'm pretty confident we will—you can apply for custody."

Swallowing hard, Sadie nodded. "How long will that take?"

"I'll do everythin in my power to push this through, but it still can take months. I'll ask for a home inspection, but if Justine shows a livable space that won't do much. In the meantime, your odds for gettin approved for adoption would improve if you're also licensed to be a foster care parent. Approval for adoption can take anywhere from four to twelve months, so we're gonna do everythin in our power to speed up that process."

Sadie took a deep breath, let it out. Steeled herself for what was to come. "Thanks, Clara. I'll do whatever it takes."

Chapter Four

I f there was one thing the south took seriously, it was Mardi Gras. If there were two things the south took seriously, the second would be food. Crawfish, to be more specific.

Declan hauled the fourth fifty-pound bag of crustaceans over to the hose, rinsed them off, and dumped them into an ice chest. His parents' barbecues were considered legendary, and they had cornered the market for both Fat Tuesday and Fourth of July. He'd been helping with this particular boil since he could walk.

Joining his dad and James Nichols at the boiling pot, he looked over to see his mom and Diana securing plastic tablecloths to several long tables. They would then cover those with newspaper before dumping the cooked crawdaddies and all their fixins on top.

Accepting a cold glass of lemonade, Declan looked longingly at the beer in which the older men partook. He, unfortunately, was on call for that night, which meant no booze for Mardi Gras. It was almost sacrilege.

"Should I light er up, sweetheart?" Joe called out.

Madeline turned, grinned. "Sure as peach pie in the summertime."

"When is everyone supposed to get here?" Declan asked.

"Five or so. Why? You lookin for someone in particular?" his dad responded.

"No." Scowling, Declan turned, headed to the kitchen. "I'll go help Mama."

Joe chuckled, nudged his oldest friend. "Seein Sadie again really did a number on my boy."

"Those kids'll figure things out eventually. Seth, on the other hand—"

"Just wait. He'll meet the right girl and be whipped upside down in ten flat."

Leaving the men behind, Declan found his mom bent over the oven. The scent of apple pie filled the air and made his stomach grumble. Diana stirred a giant bowl of coleslaw and offered him a warm smile. "Well, look at that. Not every day we get such a handsome man joinin us in the kitchen."

"What can I do to help?"

Madeline took out two pies, placed another two inside. "Let's see your choppin skills, darlin. We need potatoes—lots and lots of potatoes."

Happy to have something to do that took his mind off the stormy-eyed girl that would be showing up at any time, Declan set to work scrubbing and peeling twenty pounds worth of spuds. He chopped and tossed chunks into a container while beside him, Diana diced onions, swiping at the occasional tear escaping her eye.

"You know you can cut out the core, prevent the cryin," Declan pointed out.

"Nothin wrong with a good cry now and gain."

He didn't respond. He'd learned long ago not to argue with the logic of women. Once he got through his pile of potatoes, Declan lugged the container outside and set it beside the now-boiling pot of water. A few guests had arrived, huddling around Joe and James as they expertly maneuvered the first batch of crawfish into the pot.

Declan gave a half-hearted greeting before heading over to two bushels of corn and set to work peeling husks and setting them on one of the plastic-lined tables. He became so engrossed in the work that when he heard Sadie's soft voice from behind, he started then felt his cheeks warm from embarrassment.

"Sorry!" She grinned, not sorry at all. "Need some help?"

"Yeah, sure," he replied, annoyed with himself for being so unobservant. He did notice she'd pulled her long, pale blonde hair into a braid. His fingers itched to dive into the plaits, muss it up. She wore casual jeans rolled at the ankle with a tie-dyed purple, green, and gold shirt, the same color beads draped over her neck. Her scent hit him next, right in the gut. "Want to peel or chop?"

"I'll help you peel for a bit first. Choppin won't take long."

They worked with the ease of familiarity. Sadie had been coming to these cookouts her whole life, too. "How's the house hunt comin?"

Her unbridled excitement lit her eyes to soft gray, and for a moment when their gaze met, Declan forgot his own name. "Absolutely wonderful. I found a fixer upper, got an inspection done last Friday. Put a bid in that same afternoon. There's still quite a bit to do before closin, but it'll be mine."

"That's great. Congrats."

She did a little happy dance. "Thanks. My dad's offered to help, got me in contact with some buddies that are willin. Seth too."

Declan made a note to stop by, see what he could do to assist. "And everythin else?" Sadie looked at him in surprise. He felt inclined to explain. "Seth told me about Eva."

Her joy diminished, determination taking its place. "I met with a lawyer last week. We're takin Justine to court as unfit. The lawyer recommended I apply to be a foster parent—I won't actually *be* a foster parent, but the process will help prove I'm a good fit to adopt. She gave me a few other things to do, so at least I feel like I'm makin strides instead of just sittin on my gills waitin for a court date."

"Let me know if you need any help. I have a few connections in the law, bein a cop and all."

"All these years and I'm still not used to that," Sadie said. "Detective Declan. Has a nice ring to it."

Their eyes met again, and the intensity in his took Sadie by surprise. She stared, unable to look away. Her mouth parted to suck in a breath. His gaze dropped to her lips, and he found himself wondering what they would taste like. Wanting to find out.

"I—I'll start choppin now," Sadie mumbled, darting around the table to start cutting the corn in thirds. Taking a moment to rein in his unruly emotions, Declan grabbed another husk, ripped the silk off. He looked up, watched Sadie. Her own gaze snuck a peek but, finding him staring, focused quickly back on her task.

"We're needin some corn over here," Seth called out.

Sadie sent her brother a glare. "Then you best get your lazy butt over here and help."

Sauntering over, Seth greeted his longtime friend before grudgingly pitching in. Deciding they needed another knife, Declan headed into the house to grab one. His dad and James were dumping the first batch of boiled crawfish into a cooler. They'd steam in there while the potatoes, corn, and onions cooked in the flavored water. Once that was done, they'd start the whole process over again, until all four batches were done.

He took several deep breaths once inside the kitchen, forcing himself back under control. This was Sadie. His best friend's little sister. She'd been the closest thing to a sister he'd ever had. What the hell was he thinking? He could keep his hands off her for one blessed night.

With a straight back and a decisive nod, he rejoined Sadie and Seth, making sure to keep a bit of distance between himself and Sadie's tempting mouth. Pep talk or not, he didn't fully trust himself around her. Fifty people or better now roamed the backyard, kids playing on an old swing set, adults catching up over cold beer and lemonade. After the vegetables cooked, it all got dumped onto one of the tables.

"Remember, don't eat the dead ones," Joe joked, as he did every year. Everyone gave him a pity laugh before diving into the first course. Most of the adults dug the meat out with no more trouble than tying a shoe—both skills learned as children and practiced often. The younger kids, however, needed help, while the older kids seemed determined to do it themselves.

Declan grabbed a plate and piled on the sides he'd painstakingly prepped before going for his own crawfish. As he twisted the first one open, he spotted his cousin Virginia pulling up with her new husband, Travis. She wore a sweet peach-colored dress that hid the smallest baby bump he'd seen on someone five months along.

"Ginny, how are you, kid?" Declan greeted her with a hug. "And how's the little one?"

"Oh, just fine. Still gettin mornin sick, but I'm told that'll go away anytime."

"Virginia Montgomery," Sadie called out sternly. "I've got a bone to pick with you, lady."

She bounded over, but held herself in check as she wrapped her arms around Virginia's back. His cousin still looked startled, but returned the gesture. "Why're you mad at me?"

"I had to hear about your baby from my brother. My *brother*." Virginia laughed, clasped Sadie's hands. She had an apology on her lips, but Sadie's eyes went hazy with a look Declan recognized. One that made his heart squeeze like a vice. She blinked up at Virginia, all traces of humor gone. In a low voice, she said, "Ginny, go see your doctor."

"What?"

"Go see your doctor. Somethins wrong, but if you go, they'll be able to fix it."

Virginia's eyes went wide, terror clouding her vision. She latched onto Travis. "Honey, we need to go. Now."

Sadie stepped back, worry clear on her face. Declan approached her side as Virginia smiled apologetically to his parents and the rest of the party, then slid back into her car. She looked back to Sadie one last time, who gave her an encouraging nod and smile.

"What was that about?"

"Everythin will be fine," Sadie promised.

"She said she's still been gettin mornin sickness. It's not just mornin sickness, is it?"

"No," she said quietly. "I don't think so. But like I said, she's gonna be fine. As will the baby."

Declan looked down at the top of her head, opened his mouth to speak. But then she looked up at him with her large, stormy eyes. Damp eyes that had seen too much. He shifted his line of questioning. "Are you all right?"

"I'll be fine." He reached in his back pocket and produced a handkerchief. Sadie stared at it before quirking a smile. "Who carries hankies anymore?"

"My mama raised me right."

His intense gaze and unexpected tenderness left Sadie with a tumble of emotion swirling around her belly. Handkerchief still in hand, she began stuttering. "I—I gotta go. I mean, I'll be back. Later."

Declan reached out to touch her arm, but she'd already stepped away. Whatever she'd seen had rocked her to her core. He watched as she raced across the lawn and to her parents' house. She just needed a few minutes to herself. He could give her that.

"What's happened?" Madeline asked, moving closer to her son.

"Ginny wasn't feelin well. She's gonna check in at the doctor."

Madeline's gaze switched to the house where Sadie had disappeared. She nodded in her easy, knowing way. "Make sure she eats when she comes out."

"I'll keep an eye on her, Mama."

Madeline squeezed his arm. "I know you will, sweetheart. I know you will."

Declan picked at his food, caught up with family and friends he hadn't seen much in the last several years. When he'd followed his career to New Orleans, the visits home had become fewer and farther between. He'd missed being home, close to everyone he'd grown up with. And even though it only took an hour and a half to travel between the two cities, he'd put his job first. He'd been so focused on moving up, advancing in the force—taking night classes to get his degrees, picking up extra shifts whenever they were offered—he'd forgotten the other things that truly mattered.

Like his family. And the girl that walked out of the neighboring house, looking decidedly less pale than she had ten minutes earlier. Her eyes met his across the lawn, and he felt his heart stutter in his chest.

Yes. Some things were more important than work.

"Well, if it isn't Detective Hot Pants."

Declan turned with a wide grin, wrapping his arms around Sandra and, much to her delight, spinning her around in a circle. "Always good to see you, Sandra Dee."

"You know no one's called me that since high school. How is it that you got paired with the sexiest detective in Baton Rouge?"

"Just lucky, I guess," Declan answered, clasping Kevin's hand in greeting. "Glad you made it, Wise."

"You've not met all the rug rats yet, have you?" Sandra gestured to three munchkins that had expressions varying from suspicious to cheeseball. "The oldest here's Elizabeth, then we've got Scarlett and Finnegan."

Declan knelt. "And how old are you? Twelve?"

Elizabeth giggled and held up four fingers. "I'm this many."

"What about your sister and brother?"

"I'm three!" Scarlett cut in. "Finn's just a baby. He's only one."

"About to be two," Sandra added. "And you're all more trouble than you're worth."

The girls grinned at Declan like the angels they were while Sadie made her way over. "Kevin and Sandra? Long time no see!"

"Why Miss Sadie, aren't you pretty as a peach? Does this mean your troublemaker of a brother is here too?"

"Just missed him. Hot date."

"Isn't it always?"

Sadie smiled at the smaller girls. "Would you two like to see a real live tree house?"

Jumping up and down with pleas in their eyes, Sandra agreed, scooping up Finn in the process. "Let's all go, leave the men to the manly talk."

"Tell me somethin," Declan said as he watched them walk away. "How the hell did you manage to convince Sandra to marry your loser ass?"

"I knocked her up," Kevin replied without missing a beat.

△ △ △

The party began to dwindle as evening turned to night. Most families with kids went home—Mardi Gras might have been a southern holiday, but it *was* still a Tuesday. A decent group remained, lighting a bonfire and toasting to another successful boil.

Madeline convinced Kevin and Sandra to stick around even after the kids began to drop. They'd been carried into the house and slept peacefully in Declan's old room.

Late in the night, Travis called Madeline to let her know that Virginia would be kept in the hospital overnight for observation. On hearing the news, Declan immediately sought out Sadie. He found her near the fire pit, sitting alone on a log, watching the sparks fly up into the air. Declan joined her, keeping his voice low. "We just heard from Travis. Ginny had abnormally high blood pressure and is bein kept overnight. As long as it goes down, she'll be released tomorrow."

"It'll go down."

"Travis thinks her job caused it. She planned on quittin once the baby was born—she wants to stay home. But it's a high-stress job, and even more so since she knows she won't be there in a few months. I have a feelin this'll force her to leave earlier than expected."

Sadie nodded, looking equal parts concerned and relieved. "I'm glad she went in."

"She knows you. Knows not to question you."

"She's always been a good friend."

Declan understood Sadie's meaning. When you were a kid and knew things you shouldn't, other kids could be downright cruel. Virginia didn't have a mean bone in her body. On instinct, Declan clasped Sadie's hand in comfort. He knew how worried she was for his younger cousin. Sadie didn't look at him, but she didn't pull away, either. She squeezed his hand as her way of saying thanks.

Though he wanted to do more, say more, his phone had other ideas. With a muttered apology, he dug out the offending device and barked a greeting. "This is Park."

"Detective, we need you at the governor's mansion."

Instantly clicking over to work mode, Declan looked at Kevin and motioned him over. "What's happened?"

"There's been a murder."

Chapter Five

Twinkling lights covered every available surface of the mansion, interspersed with cheap plastic beads in an array of colors. Drinks flowed easily and food graced every available surface. It was Mardi Gras, after all—a night for revelry; a night for gluttony; a night for sin.

Declan took in every detail with a practiced eye. Being first on scene after the initial 9-1-1 call always felt a bit surreal. Uniformed officers had already cordoned off the area and gathered all guests in the main room. Before the harsh overhead lights had turned on, he felt certain the partygoers had been enjoying the magical ambience; now, their bloodshot eyes and alcohol-laced veins turned the whole scene garish.

Kevin brought over a signed warrant and gestured for the rest of the team to get to work. The CSI photographer began with the victim and moved about the room like a cog in a well-oiled machine. From the coroner's office, the Chief Forensic Pathologist examined the body. Declan and Kevin did a sweep of the scene before stepping out to start interviews.

Ducking under the BRPD crime scene tape that established something of a perimeter around the library, Declan checked in with the uniform that had corralled the party guests. Here people huddled together in varying degrees of shock and annoyance. No one spoke above a whisper. "Do we have a name for the victim?"

"Lola Vasquez."

"Witnesses?"

"Five. The governor and his daughter, Inali—Lola's best friend—are waitin in there. Inali was the one to find Lola, she's understandably upset. We'll keep the other three out here, for now."

"Thanks." Declan followed Kevin into the governor's study, where they found the governor standing protectively next to his daughter. She sat in a chair, staring blankly at the floor.

Greeting the man with thick red hair and a waistline to match, Declan introduced himself. "Governor Grayson, I'm Declan Park. This is my partner, Kevin Wise. Would you mind speakin with us for a few minutes?"

"Of course. This is my daughter, Inali." The governor squeezed her shoulder. The young woman continued to stare vacantly, streaks of dried tears on her cheeks, seeming unmoved by the touch of her father or the presence of police.

Declan crouched in front of her and spoke softly. "Inali? Are you all right?"

The governor rested a hand gently against her back. "Darlin, there are some detectives here to speak with you."

Blinking up at Declan, Inali's startling blue eyes latched onto Declan with surprise. "Who are you?"

"My name is Detective Park. My partner and I would like to ask you some questions."

"Yes, of course." Inali's voice had a gravelly quality that came from unshed tears. "Daddy?"

"I'm right here, darlin."

She laid her hand over his on her shoulder and nodded to Declan. "What did you want to ask?"

Declan stood from his crouch and took the chair Kevin offered so he wouldn't be looming over Inali. "Did you know the deceased?"

"Lola," she said, pausing as a spasm of pain crossed her face. "Lola Vasquez. She is... she was my best friend."

"I'm so sorry," Declan said, giving her another moment to collect herself. "Officer Johnson mentioned you were the first to find her. Can you tell me what happened?"

"Lola wasn't much for parties. For people. She was only here because... because of me." Declan waited while Inali collapsed in on herself, allowed a few tears to fall. He'd seen so many in this position. Too many.

"Governor, would you mind tellin us what happened from your point of view?" Kevin asked, smoothly pulling the attention away from his daughter.

"I was in here, meetin with Judge Beaumont. It was about, oh, eleven o'clock or so."

"Jackson Beaumont?" Kevin clarified.

"That's right."

"Go ahead, what happened next?"

"Inali—she started screamin. Scared the livin daylights out of me. This door here connects to the library, you see, so I hurried to it with Judge Beaumont on my heels. When we went through, we saw Inali kneelin next to Lola, grabbin her shoulders. She'd stopped screamin and was cryin. Broke my heart."

"Do you always conduct business meetins at your parties, Governor?" Declan asked.

"A public servant's work never ends, I'm afraid."

"Did you see anyone else in the room?"

"No," the governor said.

Kevin looked up from his pad of paper. "Did you touch the victim in any way? Feel for a pulse?"

"I didn't. First, I pulled Inali away—she became hysterical, you see. Jackson checked for a pulse. There wasn't one. And then he called the police. Such a terrible tragedy."

"That it is," Declan replied. "Inali? Do you feel up to continue?"

She forced herself to straighten and accepted a tissue her father offered. "When I got to the library, Lola was on the floor. At first, I thought she'd fallen. Then I saw the man. He'd been crouchin over her, but he stood quickly and backed away."

"Can you tell me what he looked like?"

"He" —Inali cringed, pressed her palms against her temples. Governor Grayson looked alarmed and wrapped an arm around her, but she held up a hand to indicate she'd continue— "He was average height for a man—about my height, I'd guess. Five foot eight. Five nine at most. He had dark hair. Brown, maybe some gray. His eyes... he looked right at me. Blue. Shock blue. Hard gaze. I saw a tattoo on his hand, right here."

Declan watched her trace a line from wrist through thumb and forefinger. He took notes, even as his partner did. His own scribblings weren't always specific details but impressions he got as someone spoke. Thoughts and questions that he'd follow up on later. Kevin was the more detailed of them, taking down word for word. "Any scars, other visible markins?"

"No."

"Do you remember what he wore?"

"A suit, like most men here. Gray. He had a mask in his hand. We were givin them away at the door."

"What did he do after you saw him?"

"He ran," Inali said. "Pulled open a window and went through."

"Which window?"

"On the left. Beside the reading table."

"Thank you, Inali. You've done well. If you remember anythin else, please call me anytime." After giving her his card, Declan switched his attention to the governor. "I understand how shocking this night has been. If you both wouldn't mind, I'd like you to come down to the station tomorrow."

"What for exactly, Detective?"

"I'm hopin Inali can tell us more about Lola, and we'll take a more detailed statement. It would be much appreciated."

"Of course. I'm gonna take Inali upstairs now, make sure she settles in. I'll come back down if you need anythin else."

Declan nodded and waited for them to leave. When they were alone, Kevin waited before collecting the next witness. "Somethin's buggin you. What is it?"

"Inali is genuinely grievin, and in shock. I have a feelin she'll remember more later, but I'm pretty amazed at the detail she did give."

"Maybe she has a photographic memory."

"So, you noticed it, too."

"It's not entirely unusual for a traumatic moment to be burned into a witness's memory."

Declan paused, glanced down at his notepad. "What did you think of the governor?"

"Seemed concerned about his daughter."

"Is there a but?"

"There's always a but with a politician."

"He's hidin somethin." At Kevin's arched look, Declan simply shook his head. "I know, I know. Conspiracy nut. But you didn't feel that?"

"You're not gettin all hippy-dippy on me, are you?"

"Maybe I am," Declan shot back. "I'm just sayin, I won't take anythin he says at face value."

"We never do." Opening the door, Kevin waited for Declan before meeting the next witness. When they walked out, four other officers were conducting interviews before releasing the guests to go home. Declan and Kevin brought in Jackson Beaumont next.

Judge Beaumont towered over Declan and reminded him of a surly cowboy from an old western. With his suit, Jackson wore snakeskin boots and a large buckle on his belt proclaiming him the 1995 LRCA bronc riding champion.

Though his glory days in the saddle might be over, Jackson still had a lot of sway in Baton Rouge as a criminal court judge. Declan didn't know much more about him, but that would change. "Thanks for speakin with us, Judge Beaumont. We'd just like to ask you a few questions."

"Sure thing, son."

Declan bristled at being called son, but let it slide. "Did you know the deceased?"

"No. A terrible tragedy, it was."

"It always is. Can you tell us what happened?"

"The governor and I were meetin, I'd say it was right around eleven o'clock."

"What were you meetin about?" Kevin asked.

"Oh, well, we've been discussin a rollout of educational material on the opioid epidemic. Start in the schools, catch em young."

Kevin jotted down notes before asking his next question. "That's to do with your charity, doesn't it?"

"That's right, son. A topic close to my heart, after all."

"The news of your brother's death was a shock to all of Baton Rouge."

It took Declan a moment, but he realized why the name Beaumont had sounded familiar. Austin Beaumont had been famous in the rodeo circuit as well—more so than Jackson or their father, who had been killed during a bull ride. Being from Baton Rouge, the news of Austin's overdose had been covered for weeks.

"A terrible, terrible thing. A man in his prime reduced to drug use. I'll never understand what was goin through his mind at the end, but I'll always cherish the earlier memories of my little brother."

"It sounds like you honor him with your charity," Declan said. "How long would you say you and the governor spoke for?"

"Half an hour or so. Inali's screamin gave us both a fright. Cyrus jumped up and ran to the connectin door and that's when we saw Inali. She was hysterical, poor thing."

"Was she touchin the body?" Kevin asked.

"It was difficult to tell. I could only see her back, you see. Cyrus pulled her away and I checked for a pulse. There wasn't one." He paused, seemingly overcome by grief. "Poor, poor thing. I called 9-1-1 and asked for an ambulance, even knowin it was too late."

"You didn't see anyone else in the library?"

"Not until I was callin, then a couple came in. They must have heard the commotion."

Declan nodded, extended his hand to shake. "Thank you, Judge. If we have further questions, would you mind if we called?"

"Of course, I know how it goes."

"Appreciate it."

Kevin led the judge out. "We've got two more who heard the scream. Ready?"

"I'm ready." Raelynn Bailey walked in with Jaser Parrish; her eyes wide not with shock but curiosity. After Declan made introductions, he offered the two a place to sit. Raelynn wore a black leotard with a purple, green, and gold sequined skirt while Jaser wore a suit. Declan gestured toward Raelynn's outfit. He'd seen several other women in the main room wearing the same thing. "You're with the dance troupe?"

She bobbed her head. "That's right, Detective. This was my first performance with Statik Moves."

"And where do you work, Jaser?"

"I'm the governor's personal assistant." The dark man with unusual amber eyes shifted closer to Raelynn, his arm slipping around her back. "We were together when we heard Inali scream."

"Tell us about what happened."

"We just met tonight," Raelynn said, sneaking a glance up at Jaser. "Before my first dance performance."

"What time was that?" Kevin asked.

"The first performance was at eight o'clock. I—I basically put my foot in my mouth and then hid from Jaser until after the second performance. He found me to apologize even though he had nothin to apologize for. It was all me." Heat rose from Raelynn's neck to settle in her cheeks. Kevin stifled a grin while Jaser smiled indulgently at her.

"I brought her into a quiet corner so we could talk. I was in the middle of askin her out when we heard Inali start screamin."

"You were?" Raelynn asked in surprise.

"I was. I'd like to try again, hopefully with better results."

She smiled happily. "I'd like that."

Declan didn't do as good of a job at hiding his smirk as his partner did. "Where was this quiet corner?"

"Not far from the library," Jaser answered. "We ran there when we heard Inali; I opened the double doors and saw the governor pullin his daughter away from someone on the floor."

"That poor thing..." Raelynn whispered. "I wanted to help but another man was already there, makin a call to 9-1-1."

"Could you see if anyone was touchin the body?"

"No," Raelynn answered, shaking her head. "I could only see Inali's back until her dad pulled her away."

"Did you see anyone else in or around the library?"

"The hallway was empty," Jaser said. "And only Governor Grayson, Inali, and Judge Beaumont were in the library when we got there."

"Did either of you know the deceased?" Kevin asked.

Raelynn shook her head as Jaser spoke. "Only in passin. I know Inali from workin for the governor, and Lola was her best friend. Lola always seemed withdrawn. Almost always had a book with her. Never bothered anyone."

"Do you know of her other friends? Boyfriends?"

"I only ever saw Lola with Inali. Inali has other friends, but none as close to her as Lola was."

"Thanks for your time. If you would both stop by the station in the next few days for follow-up, we'd appreciate it."

Declan stood and led them out. Before she made it through the door, Declan held Raelynn back for a moment. "Hey Raelynn, there's a great little café near the police station, if one were inclined to grab lunch with a fellow witness after stoppin by."

"I'll keep that in mind. You're a good egg, Detective Park. And it's just Rae."

"I'll see you soon, Rae."

Leaving the rest of the interviews to the other officers, Kevin followed Declan back under the caution tape. "What do you think? Professor Plum, in the library with a candlestick?"

Declan's lips twitched as he approached the Chief Forensic Pathologist. "My bet is Mrs. Peacock. Never trust a politician," he murmured. Louder he asked, "What have you got?"

"Latina female, early twenties. Blunt force trauma to the back of the head. The coroner will confirm it but I'm guessin she's been gone an hour, two at most."

"I trust you more than the coroner, Sandra."

"You know I love it when you blow smoke up my skirt, Dec."

He offered her half a smile before squatting beside the body. Declan studied the once-beautiful face, used his gloved hands to check her nails for signs of defense. Kevin crouched opposite, examining the area around her neck. "No visible marks on front. Was she found face up or face down?"

"Face up."

Kevin looked to his wife. "Odd, for a back of the head blow."

She pursed her lips and nodded. There was more than one odd thing about the state of the victim, but she didn't want to speculate quite yet. "This is gonna be a top priority for all of us. You saw the media already outside. Damn bloodsuckers, if you ask me."

"Hey, my best friend was out there," Declan reminded her.

"I'll tell Seth the same thing to his face. Just because I love him like a brother doesn't mean I have to like his job."

"How soon can you get a report to us?"

"I'm sure the coroner will agree to movin the autopsy to the top of the list. A day, two at most."

"Thanks, Sandra. The kids all right?"

"Sleepin peacefully at your ma's. She really is a peach."

"I know it. We'll see you in a bit."

Chapter Six

Declan and Kevin took one last look through the library and the surrounding area before meeting the homicide supervisor near the front doors. Forensics had found footprints outside the window Inali had said she'd seen a man escaping; judging by the size and style the team presumed it was a male's prints. All other physical evidence needed to be taken back to the lab to be studied.

Uniformed officers managed to keep the media at bay, allowing the guests to leave without being accosted. When Declan and Kevin joined Sergeant Lewis and Detectives Wilson and Santiago, the sergeant asked for a briefing before heading outside.

Lewis stood on the steps with his detectives to his sides and addressed the waiting news crews. "My name is Sergeant Gordon Lewis and I'll be making a statement about the events tonight. I can confirm there was a murder at the governor's mansion, but we are withholdin the name of the victim until the family can be notified. This is an ongoin investigation and we'll be takin no further questions at this time."

It didn't stop the reporters from calling out, but the sergeant led the way down the steps, his detectives on his heels. The coroner van awaited the body; Declan glanced back to see Sandra leading the stretcher out of the doors. Lola had been covered with a black coroner's bag. He should have been numb to it by now, but the sight of a body bag never ceased to give him chills.

He looked over at the desperate crowd of reporters and spotted Seth behind a camera, giving him a brief nod of acknowledgement. Best friends or not, work had to be kept separate.

The sun had just begun to rise by the time Declan and Kevin made it back to the station. They went straight for the breakroom to pour two cups of the black sludge that passed for coffee. Together with Wilson and Santiago they took over a conference room, building the case on a whiteboard and spreading interview notes out on the table.

Declan read through each account before passing them along to Kevin. Santiago scanned the documents into a laptop to use as an electronic murder book, while Wilson transferred them to a binder for a hard copy version. Two officers had been dispatched to the home of Lola's parents; Declan knew it wouldn't be long after that her name would be plastered all over the news.

Gordon stopped in and took a good look at the four detectives that had been at it all night. "Take a few, get some rest. You're no good to me as zombies."

"What's your plan?" Declan asked Kevin as he stood and stretched.

"Thought I'd get the kiddos, bring them to my ma's. You?"

"I'll grab a cot, try to sleep. See you back here by" —he checked his watch, checked again when he didn't believe how late it had already gotten— "three o'clock?"

"Works for me. See you in a bit."

Wilson and Santiago went home for a nap while Declan headed back to an empty cell. He settled on the hard mattress and found himself staring up at the ceiling. They would have to go and speak with Lola's parents, find out more about her. From all accounts, she'd been a shy, sweet young woman who loved to read. Who could possibly want her dead?

With a blow to the back of the head, Declan couldn't believe it would have been an accidental death—though stranger things had happened. They'd have more to go on when the autopsy got completed.

He closed his eyes, willing himself to sleep even knowing it would be anything but restful.

Δ Δ Δ

Declan's eyes shot open and he sat up with a start. His brain had been attempting to make connections even as he slept, and something finally clicked.

Pulling his shoes back on, he hurried toward the conference room to find Kevin had just arrived back, looking refreshed from a quick shower and a bite to eat. He pushed a container of leftovers toward Declan. "Your ma sent this over. It was so nice of her to keep an eye on the kids."

Declan took the container, popping it open and eating a crawfish cold. "She's the best. Thanks for this. Come here, I thought of somethin." Curious, Kevin watched as Declan flipped through 8x10 photos of the crime scene and laid them out on the table. "See where Lola is here?"

"Sure. I remember the room pretty well."

Ignoring his partner's sarcasm, Declan picked out three statements; Governor Grayson's, Rae's, and Judge Beaumont's.

"Governor Grayson said he could see Inali grabbin Lola's shoulders when he entered the room from here. Rae said she could only see Inali's back when she entered from the main doors, here. Those both make sense. But Judge Beaumont? He said he couldn't see if Inali was touchin Lola or not. He said he could only see her back."

"Which would mean he would have come in from the main doors," Kevin concluded. "Or everythin happened so fast he didn't pay attention to Inali."

"You asked him specifically if he saw Inali touchin Lola, and he said no. 'It was difficult to tell. I could only see her back.' Those were his exact words."

"Let's assume he lied about that. *Why* would he lie about that?"

Declan opened his mouth and closed it again. "I don't know. Yet."

"Let's keep the conspiracy theories to a minimum for now, all right? Raelynn's here."

Looking through the doorway, Declan spotted the young woman gazing around the precinct with the same wide-eyed curiosity as she'd had the night before. "Let's find out more details about the party. I feel like we've only scratched the surface."

"Lead the way."

Declan waved to Rae and showed her to an empty conference room that was routinely used for interviews. When he offered coffee or water, she declined. Rae, barely nineteen and away from her hometown of Hammond for the first time ever, had her auburn hair cut into a short pixie style and a casual elegance that came across even when wearing jeans and a sweater. Her wide, soft brown eyes reminded Declan of a doe. Innocent eyes. Too innocent for what had happened the night before.

"Thanks for comin in so quickly, Rae. Did you manage any sleep last night?"

"Not really. Jumped at every little noise, you know? Course, I don't sleep much as is."

"I'm sorry for that. Can I ask you about a few things before you heard Inali scream?"

"Sure."

"What time did you arrive at the mansion?"

"Around seven o'clock. The dance troupe drove together in a van."

"Had you ever met Inali Grayson before last night?"

"No. Jaser pointed her out to me just before the first dance routine."

Declan noted the slight blush in her cheeks and grinned. "Did you get that date?"

She turned a deeper shade of pink and ducked her head. "Not yet. But he's got my number."

"I have no doubt he'll use it. So, you saw Inali a little before eight o'clock, is that right?"

"That's right."

"Did you happen to see her again, between eight o'clock and her scream?"

Rae's eyebrows creased as she thought this through. "I did. She sorta floated from group to group. Always had a smile on her face, but she looked kinda sad."

"What do you mean?" Kevin asked.

"Have you ever seen a girl who should have it all—beauty, brains, the perfect life? But if you look close, you see stress behind her eyes? Like there's no one who knows the real person behind the façade? Kind of like that."

Declan stared at Rae for several beats of time. Perhaps she wasn't so innocent after all. Or her innocence helped her cut through the bullshit. Either way, she'd surprised him. And he didn't surprise easy. "I do know what you mean. You think Inali had that look?"

"Oh, for sure. I mean, you met her, right? She's gorgeous. All tall and dark and sultry. What I wouldn't give for that kind of dancer's body, the exotic looks. I'm not exactly the typical body type for dancin. But it's my passion, so what do you do?"

"What indeed. When was the last time you remember seein Inali, before the scream?"

She thought it through for another minute. Declan could practically see the gears grinding in her head, could almost read each thought as it flitted across her expressive face. "Just before our second performance, which was at ten o'clock."

"Did you ever see her at the party?" Declan asked, showing a picture of Lola pulled from her social media page.

Rae shook her head. "I don't think so. Not before... you know, the library."

"I know this isn't easy to go through again. We appreciate you comin in," Kevin said.

Declan finished his notes and nodded. "You've been a big help. Thanks, Rae. I'll have you sign your original statement, but if you think of anythin else, please don't hesitate to call or come in."

"I've still got your card. Catch you later, Detectives." They all stood and Declan opened the door for Rae to exit. Governor Grayson and Inali stepped off the elevator with a man that could only be their lawyer; Declan watched as Rae marched straight up to Inali and wrapped her in a hug. "You poor thing. I know you don't know me, but my name is Rae and I'm just so sorry to hear about your friend. Even though we're strangers right now, I'm here for you."

Inali, understandably startled, just stared at Rae. When Declan approached and offered Rae a blank sheet of paper with a pen, she gave him a huge grin. "You're a mind reader, Detective

Park. Here's my number. Call me if you need anythin, or just need to talk."

Tossing the pen back to Declan, Rae waved and left the station. Declan turned to Governor Grayson. "Which of you would like to go first?"

"First? I thought we'd speak together, as we did yesterday."

"Apologies, Governor. For this, we'll need to speak to you separately."

"Ah, well..." Grayson looked at his lawyer, who nodded. "Inali, darlin, would you feel up to speakin with the detectives here?"

"Yes. That's fine."

"And you are?" Kevin asked the lawyer as they settled in the conference room.

"Stewart Lancaster. I understand my clients have already answered your questions, Detectives. What more are you lookin for here?"

Declan spoke to Inali directly instead of rising to the lawyer's subtle bait. "How are you feelin, Inali?"

She shrugged. "How should I be feelin?"

"However you want."

Her eyes flicked up for the first time, and something sparked in the sapphire depths. "You're the first person to say that."

"It's the truth. And I feel awful for havin to go over last night again, but I'd like to know more about the party and more about Lola."

"Go ahead, Detective."

He decided to get the party details out of the way first, knowing speaking about Lola would be more emotional for her. "Tell me about your evenin before you found Lola. Were you there before anyone else arrived?"

"Yes. Since my mother passed away, I've been the hostess for my father's events. I help make sure things run smoothly, and I'm there to greet the guests."

"Can you take me through the night? Everyone you remember speakin with?"

She took a deep breath and dived in. Kevin wrote down every detail, every name. As Rae had said, Inali seemed to flit group to group making small talk, the perfect hostess. When she got to the time period of the second dance performance, her eyebrows creased. "After that, I—well, I'm afraid I'm not sure."

Declan studied Kevin's notes, the details she'd rattled off until that moment. It seemed every second of her time was accounted for—until ten o'clock. "You remember watchin the performance?"

"I—hm. No, not really." Rubbing at her temples with her fingers, Inali shook her head and looked apologetically at Declan. He saw the pain of a headache in her gaze, much as she'd experienced the night before. "I apologize. Normally I have a better memory than this. I must have blocked it out after..."

"I think my client has answered more than enough questions," Stewart began, but Inali waved him off.

"No, this is important. You said you had some questions about Lola?"

Kevin took the lead. "Could you give us a list of her friends, apart from you? Boyfriends?"

"To be honest, Lola didn't have any other close friends. A few acquaintances, which I'd be happy to give you. No boyfriends. Not that I knew of."

"Did she ever mention a person that might have expressed interest in a relationship that she wasn't interested in?"

"No," Inali replied. "She would have told me if somethin like that happened. What you're really askin is if she had any enemies, right? She honestly didn't. She didn't have a mean bone in her body."

Exchanging a glance with his partner, Declan nodded. "Would you be willin to work with a sketch artist? To describe the man that you saw?"

"Of course."

"Thanks, Inali. And if you remember anythin else, just let me know. You have my number?"

"Yes, I still have your card."

"All right. Call me or Detective Wise, personally. Understand?"

"I understand." They stood, and she reached out to shake Declan's hand. When they clasped, she met his gaze and Declan found a steely determination in her eyes. "Find the bastard that did this. He needs to pay."

Chapter Seven

As Kevin settled Inali with the sketch artist, Declan watched the governor speaking with his lawyer. That strange feeling Declan had gotten the night before still made itself known. He knew the governor was hiding something. He knew it in his gut. In his bones.

The two men entered the room, escorted by Kevin. Declan gestured to the chairs across from him. "Please, have a seat, Governor."

"I'd like to make this quick, Detectives. I'm afraid I have some meetins to attend."

Kevin sat forward, his hands loosely clasped. "We're tryin to get a feel for the party. Inali was kind enough to list out everyone she spoke with; we'd like you to do the same."

"My client doesn't have time to give you a play by play."

Cyrus held up a hand, effectively silencing his lawyer. "I'm afraid he's correct. However, I will make sure my assistant gets a list to you by the end of the week."

"It's much appreciated."

"Did you watch the second dance performance, Governor? The one that began at ten o'clock?" Declan asked.

Cyrus smoothed a hand across his ginger hair. "Yes, of course. With my daughter."

"Inali was with you durin that time? For how long?"

"Yes. We spent some time together, just the two of us. Parties like that can get to be so hectic, we like to carve out a little father-daughter time."

"How long would you say?"

"Oh, an hour or so. Then I met with Judge Beaumont."

"Where was Inali while you met with the judge?"

The governor shifted in his seat. "She was feelin tired, so I left her to rest in the music room, just down the hall from my study. She must have felt better after a bit, because she went to find her friend in the library..." The governor trailed off, the perfect mask of grief flitting across his features. Kevin opened his mouth to ask a follow up, but the governor checked his watch and sighed, all vestiges of remorse gone. "I'm afraid I really must leave. If you have further questions, please feel free to submit them to my assistant."

Declan walked the governor out, feeling dissatisfied. Instead of voicing the theory that had begun to form, he checked in with Inali. "How's it comin?"

"This is harder than I thought," she said with a soft smile.

The artist shook his head. "You're doin wonderful, Ms. Grayson. We should be wrapped up in ten minutes or so."

"You have a ride home?"

Inali nodded. "Dad's sendin a towncar."

"All right. Let me know if you need anythin." Leaving them to their work, Declan joined Kevin again. "Let's go visit Lola's parents."

Kevin held up the car keys. "One step ahead of you."

△ △ △

Lola's childhood home reminded Declan of his own. Blue floral couch, white wicker chairs. Crosses on the walls and no less than five Virgin Mary statues in the living room alone.

Accepting the lemonade from Camila Vasquez, Declan sat and offered his condolences. Camila and her husband Renaldo nodded their thanks even as fresh tears welled in both their eyes. Camila used a balled-up tissue to dab at her lashes before speaking. "Please, have you found out anything? Who would have wanted to hurt my little girl?"

Her voice broke, but she managed to hold herself together. Declan never ceased to be amazed by the strength of women. "I'm afraid we have nothin concrete yet, Mrs. Vasquez. Would it be all right if we ask you a few questions?"

"That is fine. My husband, he doesn't speak English so well. I will translate for him."

"Who did Lola hang out with? Who were her friends?"

"Inali, bless her heart. She was always there for our Lola. She rarely hung out with anyone else."

"Did you know of any significant others?" Kevin asked.

"No. Our Lola, she was very... studious. It is not that she didn't like boys. I think she just didn't notice them." Renaldo asked a question, which Camila answered briskly. Declan watched the exchange, wishing not for the first time that he'd at least taken some Spanish in high school. "Apologies. My husband wanted you to know about a boy named James Walsh."

"Who is James Walsh?"

Renaldo spoke, his voice harsh and eyes tight. Camila placed a hand on his arm to calm him. "He come to the house a few times. He went to school with our Lola. University. They had a class together and he came to study. That is all."

Declan nodded, though he knew there was obviously more to the story. After asking a few more questions, he and Kevin excused themselves. Kevin waited until they were in the car to speak. "We need to find James Walsh."

"I was thinkin the same thing."

Kevin gave Declan a hard look. "Renaldo walked in on James makin a move on Lola. He called him a white devil. Sounded like Renaldo kicked him out."

"You speak Spanish?"

"Some."

"Aren't you full of surprises?" Declan entered James Walsh into their search system and came back with a hit. "Looks like he's still on campus. Nicholson Apartments."

Kevin maneuvered his way to the west side of LSU, where upperclassmen housing was located. They made their way to the third floor and knocked on James' door. Declan heard footsteps approaching the door and watched a shadow cross over the peephole. "Who is it?"

"Detective Park and Detective Wise," Declan answered, holding his badge up. "We'd like to speak with James Walsh."

The door opened and a young man with light brown hair and a pair of horn-rimmed glasses answered. "What'd he do?"

"We just have a few questions. Is James home?"

"Sure. Hey, James!" the young man walked through the kitchen and knocked on a bedroom door. "Police are here to talk to you."

James pulled the door open with wide eyes. "What?"

Declan waved from the doorway. "James Walsh?"

"Yes, that's me."

"We have a few questions. Mind if we come in?"

"S-sure," he answered, pulling his sweatshirt tighter around his body and hugging his arms to himself. "What's this about?"

Kevin looked at the roommate. "Mind if we speak privately?"

"Oh, yeah, sure. I'll just be in here." He pointed behind him with a thumb before slipping into his own room. Declan was certain he'd have his ear plastered to the door.

"James, do you know Lola Vasquez?"

"Sure, we were in a fictional writin course together last semester."

"When's the last time you saw Lola?"

"We passed by on campus a couple of times in the last few weeks. Why?"

"We spoke with Lola's parents. Her father insinuated that you made unwanted advances on her."

"What? No, that's not what happened. We studied together a few times. She was so shy, but really sweet too, you know? She didn't open up much unless we were talkin books. Then she'd get all animated and her face would light up—it was cute. I kind of liked her. So, I thought I'd make a move, see where it goes."

"What kind of move?" Declan asked darkly.

"Oh, no, nothin like that. I swear. I actually asked her if I could kiss her. I'm part of the Ask First campaign on campus. I only have the utmost respect for women." James' wide, earnest eyes would have seemed almost comical, had the conversation not been so serious.

"What happened after you asked permission?" Kevin asked.

"Lola said yes. She admitted she'd never been kissed before. Honestly, I'm not sure if she actually liked me or just wanted to try

60

it. Her dad burst in before we made contact, though. He yelled a lot and grabbed my arm, practically tossed me down the stairs. Lola and I didn't talk again after that."

"All right. That's all the questions we have today."

"What's goin on? Are her parents tryin to accuse me of somethin?"

"Thanks for your time," Declan reiterated, walking back to the door. Pausing at the elevator, Declan double-checked they were alone. "You believe him?"

"I do. Man, I kinda feel bad for the kid."

"Yeah. I don't think he was lyin."

The elevator dinged and the partners stepped inside. Kevin pushed the ground floor button and asked, "Where to now?"

Declan sighed. "Back to the station."

∆ ∆ ∆

Declan stared at the sketch of a man with hooded eyes and a scruffy chin. "Who are you? Why would you have hurt Lola?"

"He talk back?"

"Not yet," Declan answered Kevin, setting the sketch down and leaning back in the chair. Kevin set down two coffees and joined him. "Any luck on identifyin him?"

"Nothin yet. Lewis wants to have a meetin in twenty."

"Gives us time, then." Declan took out the notes he'd made thus far and spread them over the table. Things weren't adding up. They rarely did in a murder investigation, but Inali's missing chunk of time bothered him the most. The governor had vouched for that time, but it seemed just a bit too convenient. Declan didn't believe in convenience, not when it came to an alibi.

Inali seemed like a genuinely nice young woman, but he couldn't deny the strange things that had been happening. Besides her missing chunk of a party she'd been hosting, her odd and sudden onset of a headache whenever she spoke about finding Lola didn't mesh with her perfect, detailed recall of the man who had escaped through a window.

Forensics had found a footprint outside the window that didn't match any of the landscaping crew that kept the mansion in top horticulture shape, so that part of her story was at least supported. They still waited on a confirmed time of death and any other findings the autopsy would bring.

"Hear from Sandra yet?"

"Not yet. She'll let us know." Kevin watched Declan read through the same statements, over and over again. "What exactly are you lookin for?"

"Anythin that makes sense."

"Let's go have that meetin. See what the others have to say, let them know about our interviews today."

Declan nodded, gathering up all the papers again. They met with the other detectives and the officers that had been first on scene, each taking turns explaining what they'd found. It wasn't much.

Lewis listened to each before speaking. "What you're sayin is, it's been twenty-four hours and we don't have a murder weapon or any motive or evidence to back up Inali Grayson's suspect?"

"Yes, sir."

"Our victim's name has been released to the media. We have the tip line fully manned, as I'm sure the calls will be pourin in." Lewis sighed, rubbing his fingers along his forehead. "Go home, all of you. Get some sleep. I want you back here bright and early."

"Yes, sir," they all repeated back.

Declan and Kevin walked out together, stopping to gather their bags. "What's on your mind?"

"None of it matches."

"Stories never match."

"Not like this. Stories are consistent across the board, until about ten o'clock."

"The second dance performance. Inali can't remember anythin for two hours, even though the governor vouches for her time."

"Right. Which is a lovely coincidence on its own, and also makes no sense. Grayson and Inali disappear together for an hour at a party they're hostin? And then Inali stays incognito for another hour? Doesn't add up. Rae also said the last time she remembered seein Inali was just before the dance."

"Who else would have seen Inali?"

"Anyone at the party could have. Accordin to the governor, he and Inali watched the dance from the second-floor balcony. They should have been visible, had anyone looked up."

"Let's have the officers start callin the witnesses tomorrow. We'll come up with a few questions so it's not so obvious."

Declan looked at Kevin. "You think Inali could have done this?"

"She was first on scene. If the governor is lyin to us, she's the only one I can see him lyin for. But then her memory blank could easily be from the traumatic experience of findin her dead friend."

"But you don't think she could do it."

"No. But we're not here to judge character, we're here to gather facts. Sandra should have autopsy results tomorrow. She'll be able to tell us the strength it would take for a person to leave that kind of mark on the back of Lola's head. Let's not jump to any conclusions before then."

"You're right. We both need some sleep. I'll see you in the mornin."

Chapter Eight

Parking in the lot for an office supply store, Sadie gathered her remaining energy and stepped out. She shouldn't have stayed up so late the night before. She knew better. It had just been so long since she'd been to one of the Park's crawfish boils that she couldn't help herself.

No matter the reason, Sadie paid the price for her lack of sleep. Tonight, she would go to bed early. And sleep like the dead.

Picking out some basic items she'd need, Sadie walked out of the store and found herself the perpetrator of a hit and run. Her shoulder slammed into a larger, solid form and she stumbled and lost one bag in the process. "Oh! Goodness gracious, I'm so sorry."

"Quite all right," said an all-too-familiar voice.

Sadie looked up and blanched. "Declan?"

"Last I checked. I didn't expect to see you around these parts. Can't say I mind."

Sadie felt heat rise and settle into her cheeks. Declan scooped up her fallen items and held onto them. "Thanks. You're just gettin off work?"

"That I am." Declan glanced at the liquor store he'd been heading for, thought better of it. "You have time to grab a coffee?"

Hesitating more from surprise than indecision, Sadie nodded. "I'd like that."

Holding out his hand to indicate Sadie should lead the way, Declan fell into step beside her as they first loaded her bags into her car and then continued on toward the café. He pulled open the door to Coffee Call and ushered Sadie inside. "Haven't been here in years."

"Me either. Hasn't changed a bit."

"Coffee?"

"Actually, I'll do herbal tea."

"Tea it is." Declan stepped up to the counter and added an order of beignet fingers. They settled at a table in the vivid blue-and-white dining room, sharing an awkward smile as Declan sipped his café au lait and Sadie stirred her tea to help it cool. "Beignet?"

"No, thanks. They look amazin though."

"How's your store comin?"

"It's comin. Wasn't too productive today."

"How come?"

"Stayed up late partyin, of course. Speakin of, you look pretty worn out yourself."

"I grabbed a few hours this afternoon. Happens on a big case."

"There was a news story on the radio on my drive here. You're investigatin the murder at the governor's mansion?"

"I can't really talk about it."

"Oh, of course not."

Sadie went quiet and Declan wanted to kick himself. Clearing his throat, he took a bite of the pastry and went for an ice breaker. "What's your favorite food?"

"Easy. Tacos."

"What kind?"

"That's the beauty of tacos. You can use any kind of meat, different toppins. You could eat them every night for a week and each one could be completely different."

"You've put a lot of thought into this."

"You ever have to answer the desert island questions? You know, if you could only choose one kind of food to bring with you to a desert island? One movie, one person?"

"Can't say I have."

"I guess my friends are more interestin than yours."

"I'll tell Seth that."

"I'll tell him myself." Sadie grinned, took a drink of her tea. Even took a moment to congratulate herself on making a good decision with the tea instead of caffeine-filled coffee. "What about you?"

"Favorite food? Or desert island food?"

"Both."

"Favorite food is Skittles, hands down." Sadie laughed. "But desert island food? I'd say steak and potatoes."

"Very responsible answer."

"Even better if I could bring the whole cow. And a steer. Start a cattle farm. Then I could slice off the eyes of the potato and plant them for more later."

Sadie's eyes sparkled with humor. "What about vegetables?"

"I'm sure the island would have somethin growin on it."

"I do believe that's the best answer I've heard. If you're bringin sustainable food sources, I might just pick you as the person to bring with me." Sadie's mouth snapped shut and a blush crept up her neck. She could teach a class: How to Put Your Foot in Your Mouth 101.

"All right, but I'm bringin *The Princess Bride* as my movie. No arguments."

"Deal."

Sadie found herself relaxing after that. Conversation flowed easily, as if the years between high school and now had never happened. She laughed more than she could remember in recent history. They sat together much longer than either had anticipated.

After polishing off a refill on their drinks, Sadie finally capitulated to her exhausted body. "I should really go. I promised myself I'd get some decent sleep tonight."

"Yeah, I should, too." Declan stood, came around and pulled her chair out. As they walked out, he paused, waiting for Sadie to face him. "We should do this again."

"Have a drink?"

"Or dinner. We could get tacos."

Smiling, Sadie nodded. "I think I would like that."

Taking a chance, Declan scooped up her hand and placed a kiss against her knuckles. "I look forward to it."

As he walked away, Sadie held her hand against her heart and felt the first dizzying dive into an emotion she dare not name.

∆ ∆ ∆

Walking into the courthouse, Declan took a long draw on his coffee. He'd slept better the night before than he'd imagined he could, and he attributed that to Sadie's calming influence. She'd helped him forget about the job for a brief window of time. Had helped to separate him from the investigation, given his mind a break.

Of course, he'd then been a bit restless for other reasons.

Kevin led the way to Judge Beaumont's chambers, politely knocking on the doorframe and greeting the judge's assistant. They waited only a few minutes before being allowed access to his inner office.

"Detectives, how can I help you?"

"Thanks for seein us on such short notice. We'll try not to take up too much time," Kevin began.

"My pleasure."

Declan took lead. "You said you met with the governor before the second dance routine?"

"Er—no, son, *after* the second. Just after."

"My mistake. Did you watch the dance performance?"

"I did."

"Where were you standin?"

The judge shifted in his seat. "With the rest of the crowd. The troupe performed near the main entrance."

"Did you see the governor or Inali durin that time?"

"Now that you mention it, I believe I did. They were together, watchin from the balcony."

"Did you see Inali again before your meetin with the governor?"

"Can't say I did, son. She's usually not involved with her father's business."

Declan's eye twitched. "Detective."

"Pardon?"

"Detective or Detective Park. I'm not your son."

Judge Beaumont's jaw worked without sound. "Of course. *Detective.*"

Declan noted the derision in the word and smiled to himself. Getting under the judge's skin had been easier than he'd suspected. Kevin cleared his throat and continued the questioning. "My partner meant no disrespect, Judge. We're just tryin to piece together the night, you understand."

"Do you have children, Detective?"

"I do."

"Imagine what it must be like for Cyrus, after losin Inali's mother. He's protective of her, more so than ever. She takes too much on, overworks herself. He's told me he's had to force her to take a break. When we heard that poor child screamin, Cyrus was frantic. He'd do anythin for Inali."

Declan glanced over to Kevin. "I'd expect nothin less. Appreciate your time, Judge Beaumont." Declan stood and made to walk out, stopping in the doorway. "Oh, Judge? Mind sendin over that information for the rollout?"

"It's still in the works, son—Detective. Proprietary information, you understand."

"I'll only use it to verify your alibi. Scouts honor."

The judge pressed his lips into a thin line. "Fine. I'll have my secretary send it over."

"Much obliged."

The partners left without a backward glance. Kevin took the driver's seat on the way to the coroner's office. "You shouldn't have pissed him off."

"Partly I was tryin to trip him up, partly I was tired of bein called 'son.'"

"You still shouldn't have pissed him off. Not this early on. He has enough pull to put up roadblocks on the investigation."

Declan stayed quiet for a while. He didn't have Kevin's easy way. He spoke his mind, whether or not opening his mouth also inserted his foot. "This is why we'll make good partners."

"Good cop, bad cop?"

"I was thinkin more nice cop, tough cop."

"Sexy cop, ugly cop?" Kevin said with a grin and Declan knew he'd been forgiven. He delivered a two-knuckle punch to Kevin's arm. "Ouch. Hey, don't distract the driver."

"Whatever. Just get us to the coroner in one piece."

△ △ △

Kevin held the official autopsy report, flipping through the pages with Declan reading over his shoulder. Time of death: estimated between eleven and eleven-thirty. Cause of death: blunt force trauma to the back of the head. Sandra joined them and moved swiftly over to Lola's still form. "We have a few minutes; I gave all the assistants errands."

"What did you want to tell us that couldn't be said in front of anyone else?"

Sandra tucked a stray chunk of hair back behind her ear as she leaned forward. The rest of her auburn locks had been secured into a bun at the top of her head. It had the messy, hastily thrown together look that others spent hours perfecting; since Declan spotted a spare pen in the pile, he decided Sandra went for function over form and any fashion trend copycat was strictly incidental.

"My initial report said blunt force trauma to the back of the head." Sandra carefully turned the head and showed the laceration there. "That did happen, but I don't believe it caused her death."

"What do you mean?"

"Do you see any bruisin? There's not any. This happened post-mortem."

"So, how did she die?" Kevin asked.

71

"Best guess? Asphyxiation."

"She was choked?"

"Didn't say that."

"Sandra..."

She held her hands out to stave off arguments. "Bear with me here. The body had been deprived of oxygen, but there are no signs of struggle. No bruisin. No fibers inhaled, if they had used somethin like a pillow. No foreign substance whatsoever in her lungs to say that she'd inhaled a toxin, nothin in her stomach either. She wasn't drugged, poisoned, or forcefully knocked unconscious."

Declan's eyebrows slanted in. "I'm not followin. What could have caused asphyxiation without physically touchin her?"

Sandra smiled. "*That* is the right question."

"You have no idea," Declan murmured. "But you've put blunt force as the official reason?"

She looked between the two, sighed. "What am I supposed to say? Magic?"

Declan looked to Kevin. "Is it just me, or does this case make less and less sense the more facts we uncover?"

"You're right on that. Is there any way to tell how much force a laceration like the one on the back of her head would have taken?"

"Unfortunately, no. Any able-bodied adult could have done it. I can say it hit more on the right side and at a level swing." Sandra demonstrated by bring her right hand out and swinging forward. "It also could have been a left-handed cross hit. Had it been the actual cause of death, I might have had more to go on."

"Can you tell anythin about what kind of object could have possibly been used?" Declan asked.

"The shape would have been smooth. No bumps or ridges, no sharp edges. The governor missin any trinkets?"

"We're waitin on that. Thanks, Sandra. I owe you one."

"I didn't do it for you. I did it for all this sweet lovin." She poked at Kevin's flat belly and gave him a wink. The fact that they were within three feet of a corpse didn't seem to faze either of them.

"All right, enough of that. You're not careful, you'll be pushin out baby number four."

"You should give it a go sometime, Dec. You're home now, settlin in. Can't tell me there aren't any girls sniffin round." His thoughts flicked to Sadie, and must have been clear on his face because Sandra gave him one of her private smiles. "When your balls decide to drop and you work up the nerve to ask her out, we'll all do a double."

"There's no girl, Sandra."

"You know what they say about protestin too much."

"I used to like you."

"Nah, sweetie, you love me. That means it's all right that I drive you crazy, because you'll always forgive me."

"Say good-bye to your woman, Kev. We've got work to do."

While Kevin gave Sandra a kiss on the cheek, Declan took a last look at Lola. She'd liked to read, Inali had said. Hated parties. Had been smart, kind. Much like Sandra had been back in high school. Sandra had been in class with him and Seth and had always marched to her own beat. It had surprised them all when she came home from her second year of college and started dating Kevin. Yet, seeing them together now, Declan realized they were meant to be.

As they left, Declan put a call in to the governor. He reached Jaser Parrish instead. "Mr. Parrish, this is Detective Park. How's it goin today?"

"Just fine, Detective. But call me Jaser, my family's full of teachers named Mr. Parrish. I like my individuality."

"Understandable. We're still waitin on that list of people the governor spoke to, along with any possible missin items from the house. Any idea when we might be seein that?"

"I'll check with Maggie, the governor's secretary, and make sure it gets over to you by end of day."

"Thanks, Jaser. Will we be seein you at the station sometime soon?"

There was a pause. Declan waited. "I've got a busy schedule." Declan didn't respond, just kept waiting. "I'll stop by soon as I'm able."

"Sounds fair. I'll keep an eye out for that information this afternoon." As Declan hung up, his phone rang—Gordon Lewis. "This is Park."

"You and Wise get up here. We've identified the suspect."

Chapter Nine

Jackson Beaumont sat at his desk reviewing a case when a not quite unexpected visitor arrived. The governor made himself at home, pouring a glass of scotch from a carafe tucked away in a cupboard. "Bit early for that, isn't it, Cyrus?"

"Not this week." Cyrus settled in a chair and sipped the drink. "They've identified Levi Jones."

"I suppose a search warrant will be comin through here any minute."

"I need you to push it through."

"You know it won't come to me. Conflictin interest and all."

The governor speared him with a look. "You and I both know who has the most pull around here."

Jackson leaned back in his chair, clasping his hands over his stomach. "Haven't I done enough for you this week?"

"You really want to compare scorecards?" The subtle reminder wiped Jackson's hovering smirk from his face. Cyrus nodded, taking another sip. "Make sure it gets approved. No delays."

"That pissant detective and his kiss-ass partner were in here this mornin. Askin questions about you and Inali."

"I assume you handled it."

The judge shrugged. "Sure, but neither of them seemed satisfied. Just thought I'd warn you."

"If it comes down to it, the detectives will be handled." Downing the rest of the scotch, Grayson rose and made to leave. "Just worry about your end of it."

Jackson watched the governor leave. Picking up the phone, he muttered to himself. "What the Quad wants, the Quad gets."

Δ Δ Δ

Well, that was useless," Declan said as he slipped into the passenger side of the car. "None of the tenants knew who Levi Jones was, and the landlord was just lookin for his fifteen minutes."

"Lewis approved the final draft of the affidavit and sent it to the courthouse about twenty minutes ago. If all goes well, we should have the search warrant in another hour."

"We've got two uniforms to keep an eye on the buildin. I could use a coffee."

"Beer would be better, but coffee'll do." Kevin headed to the nearest drive-thru, ordering four coffees and some pastries to bring back for the officers stuck on lookout.

They'd barely taken a sip when Declan's phone rang. "This is Park."

"We've got the warrant," Lewis said. "Wilson and Santiago are on their way back, and I'll meet you there."

Hanging up the phone, Declan stared at it for a moment before speaking. "We're good to go."

"That was fast."

"Yeah. It was."

Declan and Kevin waited for Wilson and Santiago before approaching the landlord and showing him a copy of the search warrant. The helpful man opened the door to Levi Jones' apartment and peered inside like a giddy schoolgirl.

Kevin paused on his way by. "We'll need to keep this area clear. If anyone comes by, can you redirect them for us?"

"Oh yes, of course. My pleasure."

Declan chuckled to himself as he slipped on a pair of gloves and took a look around. The main room seemed to function as living, dining, and kitchen. One door led to a small bedroom with a neatly made bed. A second door revealed a surprisingly clean bathroom with a pedestal sink and standup shower. A few coats hung in a closet beside the front door, along with a spattering of shoes which were bagged for evidence.

Wilson and Santiago began in the main room while Kevin moved to the bedroom. Declan joined him, searching the closet. It seemed clothes were missing—empty hangers and an empty laundry basket—while a few drawers of the dresser had been left askew.

None of them found any cash or anything else of value. No safe. By all accounts, it seemed Levi Jones had left in a hurry and not been back.

"Anythin useful?" Lewis asked when he arrived.

"Not really," Kevin answered, going over what they'd found. "Nothin screams murderer."

"Let's take one last sweep. Double check anythin that could be a hidin place."

The four detectives nodded and got to work. While Declan checked out the living room shelving for a hollow book or hidey-hole, Santiago called out from the bathroom. "Got somethin in here."

Declan hurried to the tiny room and watched as she pried a loose tile from the wall. Santiago stuck her hand inside and retrieved an object about six inches long and three inches in diameter. Moving in to get a closer look, Declan's eyes widened as she turned the figurine back and forth. "Is that blood?"

"Bag it. Let's get it to forensics," Lewis said from the doorway. "I think we're done here."

They left, thanking the landlord on the way out. "If you see any sign of Levi, call us immediately," Kevin reminded him.

Lewis issued orders as they left. "Park, put out a BOLO for Levi Jones and release the photo to the media. Wise, file for an arrest warrant and a UFAP. Let's get a red notice in case this bastard tries to run, or has already. Santiago, Wilson, get the evidence straight to forensics." The two uniformed officers still waited outside. "You two, stay here until end of your shift. You'll be relieved then."

"Yes, sir."

Declan got on the phone as Kevin drove back to the station. After speaking to the dispatcher, he ran his thumb and forefinger across his forehead. "Any of that feel right to you?"

"Which part? The neat and tidy home of a bachelor suspected of murder, findin what appears to be the murder weapon in a loose tile in the shower, or the fact that Lewis joined us?"

Kevin managed to hit every nail on the head. "All of it. His exit scene looked staged, especially compared to the tidiness of the rest of the place. And tell me this—why would a person murder a girl, bring the murder weapon home to hide it without even botherin to wipe off the blood first, and then pack a bag to leave? This is either the dumbest criminal..."

"Or he's bein made to look like the dumbest criminal."

"How well you know Lewis?"

"He's been the homicide supervisor since I came on. Well enough, I suppose."

"You trust him?"

Kevin shook his head. "No, Dec, don't even go there."

"I'm not goin anywhere. Just askin a question."

"You start suspectin our own, you'll be in a world of trouble. He's under as much pressure, or more than, as we are to solve this. Cut him some slack."

Declan didn't argue but he didn't let it go, either. Leaving Baton Rouge when he did had given him some perspective that Kevin didn't have. He'd seen more corruption than he'd ever thought possible.

It was one of the reasons he'd decided to make the move back—but, it seemed, there were some things he wasn't able to escape.

The partners had barely walked into the station when Jaser arrived and waved them down. "Detectives, fancy meetin you here."

"Mr. Parrish, nice to see you," Declan said, surprised at seeing him there so soon.

"Just Jaser, remember?"

"Right. You brought the information from the governor?"

"I did," Jaser said, tapping the edge of a briefcase against his palm. "And I figured I'd answer any other questions you had at the same time."

Kevin gestured him toward a chair by the desks, accepting an envelope that Jaser pulled from the briefcase. Kevin slid two pieces of paper out, along with a few photos. Glancing at the first photo, Kevin silently held it out to Declan. It was a shot of the library, where a figurine about six inches long and three inches in diameter sat prominently against the shelf.

Without reacting, Declan accepted one of the lists and glanced over it. "Thanks for bringin this in. When are the pictures from?"

"Just a couple of weeks ago. The mayor was bein interviewed about his proposed budget and these were taken to check for light. The governor asked the paper to send them over."

"Durin the party, do you remember the last time you saw Inali?"

If Jaser was taken back by the question, he didn't show it. "I think around nine o'clock, maybe a little after. She was headin toward the library."

Both Kevin and Declan looked up. "Did you see her go in the library?"

"No, just headin that direction. I was on the opposite side of the main room."

Kevin opened his mouth to ask a follow up when all their attention got diverted to a television hanging on the wall. The sketch of Levi Jones had been plastered over the news in a matter of minutes. Though the volume was down, a ticker tape across the bottom asked the public to call the tip hotline if they had any information on his whereabouts.

Declan glanced at Jaser and noticed the surprise on his face. "What is it?"

"What's that about?" Jaser asked in return.

"He's wanted for questionin. You know him?"

Jaser's eyes shifted toward Kevin and back again. "I like my job, Detective Park."

"Sure."

"But I want to help Inali get closure."

"This can be off the record, Jaser." Declan and Kevin waited patiently. Jaser finally gave in.

"Levi Jones. He wouldn't have been at the party."

"Why's that?" Kevin asked.

"He wasn't welcome."

The partners exchanged a look; finally, some insider information on their suspect. "It's all right, Jaser. Go on."

"Do you know much about the governor's wife?"

"Catori Grayson, née Verdin. Married Cyrus Grayson seven months before Inali was born. Catori was killed in a car crash six years ago." Kevin saw Declan's raised eyebrow and shrugged. "What? I did my research."

"Well," Jaser said, "Levi was her college sweetheart."

"Interestin, but I'm not sure how that matters."

"From what I gather, Levi was still in love with Catori. The governor actively banned him from the premises. I was there once, when Levi showed up on the governor's doorstep. It was just after the accident, and I'd just started workin as an intern. I overheard the whole thing. Levi was a wreck, accusin the governor of killin Catori. Threatened to find Inali and tell her the truth. Cops came and escorted him off the property."

"Did you ever see him on the property again?" Kevin asked.

Jaser shook his head. "Not when I was around, anyway."

"Thanks for comin in," Declan said. "And for the information."

"You're welcome, long as that last part stays between us."

Jaser leaned down to retrieve his briefcase from the floor. Doing so shifted his shirt just enough to reveal a small drawstring bag secured around his neck by a leather cord. Declan's eyes narrowed in recognition. "Do you practice?"

Jaser straightened slowly, met Declan's gaze head on. Carefully lifting the bag into full view, he answered, "I don't exactly advertise it, but I do. Is that gonna be a problem between us?"

"That depends."

"On what?"

"Light or dark?"

"Light," Jaser said with half a smile. "Always light."

Declan gave him a brief nod. "Then there's no problem."

After shaking both detective's hands, Jaser left. Declan took the newly vacated chair and leaned back. "Was that a voodoo bag?" Kevin asked.

"It's called a gris-gris," Declan answered absently. "Anythin come up on Levi bein escorted from the governor's house six years ago?"

"No. Only thing was the DUI some twenty-five years back."

"Think the governor's seen the sketch by now?" Declan asked, gesturing toward the television.

"I'd imagine so. Might be time to pay him a call."

Chapter Ten

Jaser left the police station with something niggling the back of his mind. For a moment he placed a palm over his gris-gris, took a few deep breaths to center himself. He couldn't believe he'd forgotten about what Rae had found the night of Lola's murder. It had to still be in his pocket from that night. With everything that had happened, he'd forgotten all about it.

Deciding he had time to stop home, he went straight to his closet and dug out the suit he'd been wearing the night of the party. Feeling the slight bulge in the pocket, he took a plastic bag and used it to extract the drawstring bag. His stomach in knots, he studied the symbols painted around the outside of the bag. He didn't know much about the dark side of his practice, but he knew enough to stay away.

One person could give him some insight. The only person he would trust with something like this.

His maw-maw.

Mhina Abara grew up in third-world Mali. At the age of fifteen she married a man three times her age in order to escape poverty. The man had money and a penchant for abuse. After their first night together Mhina was with child, and she took any punishment her husband could dish out, knowing she was creating a better life for her children.

Within three years Mhina had two small children, a girl and a baby boy. Her husband was killed in rebel crossfire, leaving a seventeen-year-old girl, single mother of two, the sole recipient of his small fortune.

Using it all to escape her war-torn country, Mhina eventually found her way to America, where she worked her fingers to the bone in any job she could find. She never married again— refused to ever allow a man to have any control over her life again.

Mhina's daughter grew up to be an English teacher, eventually marrying a fellow teacher. They had two boys, Fallon and Jaser. Mhina lived with her daughter and helped raise her grandbabies, teaching them about where she came from and her beliefs. While Fallon shied away from the practice, Jaser thrived in it.

He walked into his parents' house now, knowing they would both still be at work. His father had worked his way to principal, while his mother still happily taught high school English. Jaser found his maw-maw in her sunroom, tending her plants. Her face brightened and she embraced him with a warmth that rivaled the very sun beating through the windows.

Holding his face between her hands, Mhina studied her grandson with concern. "Let me take a good look at ya, boy. What is this shadow I see?"

Jaser took a step back and let out a long breath. Carefully extracting the small black bag from his pocket, he held it out for his grandmother to inspect. She did so from a healthy distance. "What can you tell me about this?"

"Where did you get that?" she said with a hiss, physically retreating from the object. "You've not been messin with the dark arts, have you boy?"

"No, maw-maw, I promise." Jaser steeled himself to tell her the whole story. "On Mardi Gras, I was workin at the governor's house. He had that big party."

"That girl was murdered."

"That's right. Her name was Lola. She was Inali's best friend."

Mhina murmured a blessing under her breath. "That poor, sweet girl."

"Just before Inali found Lola's body, I was in the hallway outside the room it happened in. I found this on the ground. I was gonna expose of it, I swear, but then I heard Inali start screamin so I shoved it in my pocket and forgot all about it... until now."

Taking the bag from her grandson, Mhina inspected it, making the occasional sound of displeasure. "You remember what I told you about the Petro Loa?"

"Sure. Originated in Haiti. Spirits darker and more aggressive than anythin from Africa, or what we believe in. Evil."

"Not fully evil, my boy. Nothin in this world or the next is fully good or fully evil. But those lookin for the darker forces tend to turn to the Petro Loa. They feed the darkness and use it for their own perverted purposes." Mhina brought the bag to her alter, laid out a pile of sea salt and set the bag atop. Lighting incense, she cleansed the area and set a protective circle around the space. "Whatever happens, stay back."

Jaser swallowed hard but obeyed. He watched as his grandmother carefully extracted the drawstring bag from the plastic one. Opening the strings, she dumped the contents into a copper bowl. Some of the items were easily recognizable—salt to represent the earth, incense cone for air, tea light candle for fire, and a small vial of water—but the black substance that poured out had his eyes narrowing. "What is that?"

Leaning close and taking a sniff, Mhina reared back with a snarl. "Gunpowder. Black pepper. And blood." She looked at her grandson and clarified. "Animal blood."

He didn't question how she knew that. She knew many things that defied logic. "Those along with the symbols..."

"He was summonin death."

Chills raced down Jaser's back and settled as nausea in his stomach. His throat was dry as he spoke. "Who, maw-maw?"

"Only one would risk his soul this way. The ghost." A name no one who knew it dared to repeat. Kofi. Something close to terror crawled along Jaser's skin. He watched as Mhina cleansed the spell items and secured them in a metal lockbox. She nodded in satisfaction as she closed her protection circle. "I will dispose of that properly."

"Maw-maw, I need you to think back. Every whisper, every rumor you've ever heard about the ghost. Tell me everythin you remember."

"You know I don't like talkin bout such things, my boy."

"Please. It's important."

She watched him again. Saw more than he intended. "Fine. On one condition."

"Sure. Anythin."

"You tell me about this girl. The one that's already made an impression on your heart."

Nothing about his grandmother should have surprised him anymore, but every once in a while she could still sneak one by him. "Not much to tell. Her name is Rae, we met the other night... at the party."

"Oh, I see. Well, don't wait. I can see she's special—don't let her get away."

"Yes, ma'am," Jaser answered automatically.

Nodding with satisfaction, she turned her attention to the matter at hand. "No one knows where he came from. Who his people are. Anyone who's had the unfortunate opportunity to see his face doesn't remember its characteristics. It's been said he has sigils tattooed all over his body."

Jaser's eyes widened. Pulling out his cell phone, he did a quick search and pulled up the sketch of Levi Jones. Turning it toward Mhina, he pointed at the tattoo Inali had described to the sketch artist. "Sigils like this?"

Murmuring another blessing, Mhina nodded. "Where did this come from?"

"They've got the wrong guy," Jaser said, more to himself. "Oh, Inali, what did you see?"

"What's goin on? Jaser?"

"Sorry, maw-maw, I've gotta go. Thanks for your help, I'll see you soon." He kissed her forehead and ran out the door.

He needed to do two things. One, he would have a look at the governor's library, searching for things the police wouldn't have known to look for. Two, he would speak with Inali. Something was very, very wrong.

When he arrived at the governor's, Jaser was surprised to see the detective's car parked in front of the doors. He entered the mansion and made his way to the governor's study, stopping just outside the opened door.

He recognized the voices of both Detective Park and Detective Wise, staying quiet so he could eavesdrop.

"Do you recognize the man in the sketch?" Detective Park asked.

"I'm afraid not," the governor answered. "Who is it?"

"Levi Jones."

"Is it really?"

"You do know him?"

"Why, yes, but not well. It's been several years since I've seen him, even. He's not aged well."

Jaser knew if he wanted to roll his eyes, the detectives must be struggling, too. Detective Wise asked the next question. "How do you know him?"

"He dated my wife when they were in college. We had a few chance meetins over the years, that's all."

"Would he have been on the guest list for your party?"

The chair creaked; Jaser imagined the governor leaning back. "Can't imagine he would have been, but then I don't have much to do with the guest list. My staff plans these things."

"When was the last time you saw Levi Jones?" Detective Park asked.

"I honestly can't say I remember."

"You're sure about that?"

From the speakerphone, the governor's lawyer spoke up. "I believe my client has answered sufficiently, detectives."

"If you happen to remember any more details, let us know," Detective Wise said.

Jaser stepped away from the study and slipped into the library. It had seen little use this week; even the governor avoided the area. When Jaser turned to survey the room, he was startled to see Inali sitting in a reading chair in the near-dark. "Inali? Are you all right?"

Flipping on a light, Jaser moved closer to examine his friend. Sad eyes looked up at him and it tore at his heart. "Jase. What are you doin here?"

"Lookin for you," he said, feeling better that it wasn't a complete lie. "Wanted to see how you were feelin."

She shrugged. "I'm sad. Angry. And feelin a little useless."

"That's not true." He sat across from Inali and leaned his elbows against his knees. "You gave the police their only suspect. That's not useless."

"I suppose," she said, her gaze wandering to the floor, sliding over the window and back to Jaser. "It just doesn't make any sense."

"Death rarely does." Jaser sat quiet for a moment before pushing the boundaries. "Can I ask you somethin about that man?"

"Sure."

"The tattoo you described—you said you saw it on his hand, right? Did he have any others?"

She looked up as she tried to recall. Wincing in pain, she brought her hand to her forehead and rubbed at the throbbing there. "No, not that I remember."

Jaser noted the sudden onset of a headache and frowned. "And you don't remember ever seein that man before? He didn't look familiar to you?"

"No," she answered, her eyebrows creased. "Why? Should he look familiar?"

"No reason he should. I just thought, if he hurt Lola for a reason, he must have known her. Been around her someway, somehow."

"If he knew Lola, I didn't know about it. I feel like I don't know anythin. Oh, Jase, why? Why did she die?" Inali burst into tears. Jaser pulled her into a hug and let her cry it out.

His search of the room could wait.

Chapter Eleven

With a deep breath, Sadie pushed the door wide and flipped her handmade sign to OPEN. She'd spent the last few weeks working—on opening her store, closing on her house, and fighting for Eva. Now, with displays set and coffee brewing, one piece of the puzzle clicked satisfyingly into place.

Her online orders had kept her flush during the transition time, and she had plans to expand that end of it as well. Even if she didn't sell much in the store itself, she knew her bread and butter would keep her rent paid.

When her first customer entered, Sadie grinned and welcomed her mom, accepting the happy bouquet of daisies even as they hugged. "Sadie, it's wonderful! I'm so proud of you."

"Thanks, Mama. Who knew this is what would happen when I did that project for school?"

"The success and ingenuity of my children never ceases to amaze me."

Two women entered the store cautiously. "You open, darlin?"

"Why, yes, I am. Come on in, take a look around. Let me know if you need anythin." Sadie found a vase, placed the cheerful flowers inside.

"I won't keep you, honey," Diana said. "But I will take that beautiful rockin chair for Virginia."

"She'll love it. Her shower's this weekend, right?"

"Sunday afternoon. Will you be able to make it?"

"I believe so," Sadie answered, ringing up the sale and giving her mom a family discount. It had been three weeks since Virginia's high blood pressure scare and she'd had to quit her job. Sadie had visited her once, but made a mental note to make sure she went to the shower. "You've got the truck with you today?"

"Grabbed the keys before your father could."

Sadie let her customers know she'd be back, helped her mom secure the rocker in the pickup. "Thanks for comin in today. It means a lot."

"I wanted to be your first official sale. Have a wonderful rest of your day. Love you, sweetie."

"Love you, too, Mama," Sadie replied, hugging her again. "Make sure Daddy helps you with that chair."

"You bet your bottom I will."

Sadie waved her off before heading back into the store. She asked her two customers if they had any questions, told them where she'd found a hutch that had had a broken shelf and missing glass that she'd painstakingly fixed and painted a brilliant teal. They continued to wander, exclaiming over throw pillows and candle scents, finally deciding on a few smaller items each.

"This is just a wonderful place. Will you be doin a grand openin?"

"That I will! We'll be havin a big party in three weeks, April thirteenth. Here's a flyer, I hope you can make it."

"We surely will," one of the women answered. "Thanks, darlin."

"See you next time."

While she waited for more customers, Sadie sat at her worktable and pieced together some jewelry. Adding a worktable to the main store had been a stroke of genius on her part. She also had her laptop set up, so she'd see any alerts of on-line orders right away.

Madeline came in midmorning—also buying a gift for Virginia's baby shower—as did several of her friends from high school throughout the day. Many family members stopped by, all buying at least a small item. It meant the world to Sadie to have such support.

Her brother even made an appearance on the way to the news station. What she didn't expect was for Declan to walk through the door.

"Why, Declan Park, as I live and breathe," Sadie said with a wide grin, punching up her accent a few notches for dramatic effect. "What brings you by?"

"I wasn't gonna miss your first day," he replied with a matching smile. For a few moments, nerves took over and made them both feel awkward. The fact that they still hadn't grabbed that dinner didn't slip either of their notice.

Sadie broke the tension by picking up the closest item and holding it up, game-show style. "Can I interest you in a candle?"

"I thought I'd pick somethin out for Ma. Any suggestions?"

Eyes lighting up, Sadie came around the counter and showed him a vase painted in swirls of blues. "As it happens, Madeline was in here earlier eye-ballin this. Stick some pretty flowers in there and you'll be her favorite son."

"I'm her only son," Declan said, taking the vase. Sadie waited without a word. "Oh, right, she likes Seth better. I'll take it."

As they walked toward the register, Sadie pulled out paper and began wrapping the vase for protection. She snuck a glance at

Declan, saw the bruising under his eyes that told her he hadn't been sleeping well. "How's that case goin?"

"At a bit of a standstill. Been workin on some other things."

Reaching over the counter, Sadie selected a bottle and handed it to Declan. "Here, have this on the house. Rub a few drops into your sinuses and along your chest before bed."

"What is it?"

"A mixture of oils. Lavender, chamomile. Some others. It'll help you sleep."

"I sleep fine."

"But you're not gettin rested. Just trust me and try it, all right?"

"I know better than to argue. I'll give it a try." He reached for his phone as it rang, bit off a curse when he saw who it was. "This is Park."

Sadie watched him as he paced away, muttering a handful of words before hanging up. "Work?"

"Yeah. Sorry, but I've gotta run. Will you hold these for me?"

"Sure thing. Take that bottle, though. Promise me you'll use it."

"Promise. The store looks wonderful. I know you'll do well here." He hesitated, then leaned over and kissed her cheek. "I still intend to take you up on that dinner."

With that, he left. For a moment Sadie held her palm to her cheek, enjoying the tang of warmth and nerves swirling through her system. Shaking her head, she snapped herself out of it and went back to work.

By the end of the day, she'd been worn plum out. But instead of dragging herself up the stairs and rolling into bed, Sadie straightened displays and restocked. Wiped down windows and cleaned the bathroom. Counted out her till, secured the money in a safe.

Satisfied with a successful first day, Sadie gave in, trudged up the stairs, and fell into bed, turning on the television just in time for the news. Seth always supported her; she liked to do the same for him. Exhausted as she felt, Sadie sat straight up when she spotted Declan leading a man in hand cuffs to the back of a police cruiser. Scrambling for the remote to turn up the volume, Sadie watched the full story with rapt attention.

"A manhunt has ended as an arrest was made in relation to the murder of Lola Vasquez. Accordin to Homicide Supervisor Sergeant Gordon Lewis, Levi Jones was spotted at a Greyhound bus stop on the corner of Highland and Roosevelt earlier this afternoon. The attendant who sold Jones a bus ticket immediately notified the police. Jones, whose sketch was released two weeks ago, took off on foot when he spotted police cars.

"Jones got three blocks away before he was detained. No word yet on what he'll be charged with."

Sadie sat back and turned the television off. Suddenly she didn't feel so tired anymore.

Δ Δ Δ

Grant Currie had been researching for two hours straight when the first name on the letterhead walked into his cramped office. Blinking up at the imposing man who had the reputation of being a shark in the courtroom, Grant straightened and flipped the heavy book closed. "Mr. Carter, how can I help you?"

"How long have you been here, Grant? You can call me Winston."

"Thank you, Winston. What can I do for you?"

"A case came in. Murder accusation. Frank and I thought you should take point."

Excitement reared up. Grant had been assisting on cases for more experienced lawyers, but had yet to take on his own. And a murder at that! He swallowed once and kept a straight face as he answered, "Thank you kindly. I'll give it my all."

"You'll have a team to assist you. There's gonna be some media on this, more than your average murder."

"The girl from the governor's mansion?"

"That's right. You've got our trust on this, Grant. The firm is behind you. Anythin you need, just ask."

Grant stood, packed his briefcase. "What's the client's name?"

"Levi Jones."

"He's in custody right now?"

"That he is."

"I'll head down and meet him, make sure he's not talkin."

Winston stopped him before he could get out the door. "Good luck, son. Keep me updated, all right?"

Grant nodded and hurried away. With a heavy sigh, Winston Carter walked back to his office to make the call.

Chapter Twelve

When Kevin found his partner, Declan had been staring through the glass at Levi Jones for a good twenty minutes. The man suspected of murdering Lola Vasquez hadn't spoken since they'd placed him in the back of a cruiser. Before that, Levi had been adamant in his innocence.

"Ready to go in?"

Declan glanced at his partner and nodded. "Lawyer's on his way?"

"That he is."

"Let's see if he'll talk to us." Following Kevin through the door, Declan took one last look at Levi alone in the room. "He doesn't have a tattoo."

Kevin stopped outside interrogation's door. "Inali was in shock. Maybe she saw a shadow, or just get mixed up."

Declan grunted in response and stepped into interrogation. He sat across from Levi, with Kevin at his side. "Where were you the night of March fifth?"

Levi remained quiet, shaking his head as if under compulsion.

"Levi, if you answer our questions, this will all go easier on you."

"I didn't do this."

"Didn't do what, Levi?"

"I didn't kill that girl. I didn't do it."

"Where were you the night of March fifth?"

He shook his head again, refusing to make eye contact. Kevin pushed a glass of water across the table. "Cooperate with us. If you didn't do it, we'll find who did. But we need to know the whole story."

Both detectives waited. Sweat pooled along Levi's forehead. He fought an inner battle, one Declan hoped swayed in the investigation's favor. Finally, Levi opened his mouth to speak. "That night..."

The door opened and Grant walked in. Setting his briefcase down, he crossed his arms and gave the detectives a disapproving look. "I'd like a word with my client. Privately."

Levi's mouth had snapped shut. He refused to make eye contact with anyone in the room. Withholding his frustration, Declan stood and marched out of the room. When Kevin followed, he spun with a fire in his eyes. "He was about to talk! Son of a bitch."

"Dec, calm down, man."

Sucking in several deep breaths, Declan turned, hands on hips, when Grant walked back out. "Who the hell are you?"

Grant adjusted his glasses but didn't let the tone change his demeanor. "Grant Currie. And you are?"

"Declan Park. Wait—Grant Currie? Didn't you date Savannah White?"

"That was several years ago, but yes."

"Huh." Declan had already been off in New Orleans when those two had gotten together, but he'd heard all about it from Seth. Seth, who had a misguided notion that he would woo Savannah when she made that leap from girl to woman. Seth, who had been deeply disappointed when she'd fallen hard for nerdy little Grant.

Sizing up the man now, Declan acknowledged the fact that nerdy had become proficient and little had become lean. "If that's all the questions concernin my personal life, may I ask what my client is bein charged with?"

"We've got enough for first degree, involuntary."

"All right, well, Levi will not be speakin to you without me or someone from my team present."

"Then he'll be moved to holdin."

"Fine. He'll stay there while I work on his bail. Good day, gentlemen."

Though Declan felt a grudging respect for the man, he didn't have to admit that out loud. "Let's get the DA's office over here. We'll also have to call Inali, have her identify Levi in a line-up."

Kevin nodded. "I'll call the DA's. You call Inali."

△ △ △

Sipping on his fourth or fifth—he'd lost count—cup of coffee that afternoon, Declan studied their facts while he waited to meet with the Chief of Litigations from the District Attorney's office.

Kevin lounged in the chair beside him nursing his own mug. They'd been putting in long hours on this one. Hopefully, they'd both get a much-deserved break with the suspect in jail.

When the woman with chestnut hair and the deepest green eyes Declan had ever seen walked in, both men straightened in greeting. Declan held out his hand. "I don't believe we've met. Declan Park."

"Autumn Hoyt," she said, accepting his hand to shake. "Nice to meet you, Detective."

"You as well."

"Kevin, good to see you. How're Sandra and the kids?"

"Spunky as always."

Autumn smiled, having a genuine fondness for the forensic pathologist. "They'll keep you on your toes."

"And how's Arabella?"

"Six goin on thirty."

"Her little girl's a genius," Kevin said to Declan. "Smart as a whip and sweet to boot."

"I look forward to meetin her."

"For now, down to business." Autumn popped open the file in her hands and spread it out on the table. "We have enough to charge Mr. Jones with voluntary manslaughter. He's lawyered up, correct?"

"That's right. Carter and Munger." Autumn's lips pursed. Declan grinned. "Not a fan?"

"You know that stereotypical lawyer that everyone hates? Winston Carter was the poster boy for the campaign."

Kevin crossed his arms over his chest. "They sent over the lead on Saturday. Young, for a case like this. Grant Currie."

"I recognized him, friend of a friend kind of thing," Declan said, giving Grant his due now that he was out of earshot. "Good head on his shoulders."

"I'll be speakin with him soon. He's requested bail, but with Levi already a proven flight risk, he'll be denied. We've got his first hearin on Monday and my office will be formally chargin him on Friday."

"Thanks, Mrs. Hoyt."

"Just Autumn. No need to be so formal."

"Same goes. We'll see you on Monday—go salvage some of your weekend with your daughter."

"I plan on doin just that. Give my love to Sandra and the kids," she said to Kevin and, with a wave, left.

"She seems easy to work with. You know her well?" Declan asked once the room was clear.

"Well enough. Knew her husband."

"Knew him?"

"Yeah," Kevin said with a sigh. "Passed on some years back. Autumn was in law school when it happened, Arabella just a couple of years old. She's been through the ringer."

"That's awful."

"Jefferson was a good man. Worked with halfway houses for teens, that's how we met. My first call as a beat cop led me right to him."

"She still wears a ring."

"She's still committed where it matters. In her heart."

For a moment, Declan studied his partner. Kevin had always been something of a romantic. Maybe that's why he'd met the love of his life so early, why they were already well on their way to a brood large enough for their own basketball team. And for just a moment, Declan wondered if the same was in the cards for him.

Δ Δ Δ

All right, let's run it down," Sergeant Lewis said. "We've got a witness placin Levi Jones standin over Lola Vasquez's body. On inspection of Levi's apartment, we found a muddy pair of shoes that matched the print outside the window our witness saw him escape from. Hidden in Levi's bathroom was a figurine with blood and hair matchin Lola Vasquez, presumably the murder weapon. Am I missin anythin?"

Declan and Kevin both shook their heads. Levi Jones would be officially charged in the morning, and Lewis wanted to be sure it went off without a hitch. The look on Declan's face must have been a dead giveaway, for he set his sight on him. "What is it, Park?"

"Sir, while we found the figurine and shoes in Levi Jones' apartment, we found no physical evidence linkin it to him. No fingerprints or any other DNA on the weapon, apart from Lola's. There wasn't even any DNA in the shoes. There should have been at least some skin cells, some leg hair."

Lewis sighed and leaned back in his chair. He didn't disagree with the younger man, but he had his orders from the top. "They were found in his residence. We have the witness. We're goin forward."

"Might I have a word alone, Sergeant?"

Lewis nodded at the rest of the group in dismissal. Once they were alone, he said, "What's on your mind, Park?"

"I don't feel comfortable movin forward with this case."

"To be frank, I don't give a shit. You'll let the prosecution press charges, and when the time comes, you'll testify."

"Sir, with all due respect, I don't think I can do that."

"Look, Park, this comes from the top. Chief Blackwood wants this wrapped up, yesterday. Do you have any idea what this department has been through in the last few years? Over half the cases have gone unsolved. We're understaffed and homicides are on the rise. We're on level with Chicago, for Christ's sake. The citizens are losin faith." He paused, reined in his temper. "Don't get me wrong here, Park. I like you. You've done good work so far, and you had outstandin commendations from your last department.

But when the Chief of Police tells you to do somethin, you do it. At least, you do if you value your job."

Declan pressed his lips together to prevent himself from letting loose with a snarky comment. It would get him nowhere, no matter how satisfying it sounded in theory. Right now, his best choice was to toe the line. "I understand. Sir."

Chapter Thirteen

Armed with a bow-topped gift, Sadie marched up the walk at Loretta May's house and circled around to find the rest of the party gathered in the backyard. She spotted Virginia relaxing in a comfortable chair and headed over to say hello. Kissing her on the cheek, Sadie said, "Are you sure you're six months along? My goodness, lady, you look fantastic!"

"Thanks, Sadie. The truth is, I'm goin stir-crazy. I've never had more than a few days off in my life. Even as kids I went to camp durin the summer just for somethin to do. I don't know what to do with myself. Any-who, how are you? How did your first week fare?"

"Amazin. Stayed busy every day." Sadie studied her friend's face, an idea springing to mind. "You know, I could really use some part-time help at the shop. You could pretty much sit all day. If you don't think it would be too stressful, I'd love to have you."

"Really?" Virginia's whole face lit up. "I'd love to! When can I start?"

Laughing, Sadie said, "Why don't you stop by Monday? I'll show you round, see what's what."

"It would only be until the baby's born."

"No problem. Gives me time to find someone more permanent."

"Welcome, Sadie!" Loretta May called out, pushing a glass of lemonade into her hand. "Glad you could make it, darlin."

"Thanks for havin me. You did an amazin job decoratin."

"Well, it's not every day I become a grandma. Come on, I'll show you where to put your gift."

Squeezing Virginia's hand on the way past, Sadie followed Loretta May to a table already overflowing with packages and added hers to the pile. She'd decided on making a sweet pink blanket with *Clarabelle* embroidered along the edge, as well as a few necessities like diapers and onesies that Sadie'd designed fun prints for.

"Hey, sweetie," her mom said, joining her at the table.

Loretta May had already spun away to greet more guests, so Sadie handed over the glass of lemonade in favor of a bottled water. "Drink this for me, would you?"

"Sure, darlin. Come on, I'm sittin with Madeline and the girls."

Sadie followed her mom, found 'the girls' included Carolyn, along with Sarah Jane and Betty Sue—both Madeline's sisters-in-law, and Loretta May's younger siblings. Joe was the only boy in the family, and the eldest of the bunch.

Madeline and Joe had been married so long, Sadie'd always seen his three sisters as Madeline's sisters, as well. They certainly got along well enough.

"Now what has Joe David been keepin himself busy with since retirement?" Betty Sue asked. Sadie had known Joe all her life, and the only people she'd ever seen get away with calling him Joe David were his sisters.

"Fishin, mostly," Madeline answered. "And gettin in my hair. That man needs new hobbies."

"He's welcome to come help on my remodel," Sadie offered, only half joking.

"That's right! Tell us all about your new place," said Sarah Jane.

Carolyn grinned and gave Sadie a wink. "Sadie's found herself a real diamond in the rough."

"We're hopin to get the keys next week, right Aunt Carol?"

"That's right, darlin. It'll be all yours."

"And what about that precious girl? How's that comin?" Betty Sue asked.

Sadie took a breath and let it out. "It's comin. It's a slow process, but I'm dottin all my I's and crossin all my T's."

"I'll be prayin for ya both," Betty Sue promised.

"Second that, and Hallelujah!"

Madeline smiled at Sadie. "I'll let Joe know about your offer. I'm sure he'll jump at the chance to hang out with James and the boys."

"It'd be much appreciated."

"And how's my sweet little Declan?" Betty Sue asked. "He hasn't come round to see his favorite aunt lately."

"You're right, he hasn't come to see me in quite some time," Sarah Jane said with a smirk.

Sadie felt her ears heat for no particular reason.

"Oh, you know Dec. Busy as a bee in pollinatin season. Been workin on that murder case at the governor's place from Mardi Gras."

"No, he nabbed that? Atta boy!"

"I heard he arrested that man yesterday," Betty Sue said. "That one in the sketch."

"I hope they fry em," Sarah Jane said.

"What happened to innocent til proven guilty?" Carolyn asked.

Sarah Jane brushed away her concern. "They've got an eyewitness, the news said. What more do you need?"

"Enough about work." Betty Sue leaned forward, wiggled her eyebrows. "He meet a girl yet?"

The heat spread from Sadie's ears down her neck and chest. Sinking into her chair, she took a swig from her bottle and hoped no one noticed. A smile hovered over Madeline's lips. She glanced surreptitiously at Sadie before answering, "None I know of."

"Well, then, who can we set him up with? Charlotte? Donna Jo? Riley?"

"Isn't Riley his cousin?" Carolyn asked.

Betty Sue waved this off as inconsequential. "Second cousin once removed. At least we know she comes from good family."

Sadie choked out a laugh, but quickly covered her mouth. "Coughin fit. Excuse me."

As she ran off to the bathroom, Diana and Madeline exchanged a knowing look. "That girl's got it bad," Diana said, just loud enough for her closest friend to hear.

△ △ △

Pulling up in front of the run down, shabby house, Sadie sat at idle and stared. She could officially claim the title of homeowner. The idea thrilled her down to her toes.

Construction would begin the next day. Along with her dad's help, she'd hired one of his friends, who happened to run a roofing company, to assist. Another one of his buddies had been a plumber for more than thirty years, and he'd agreed to update the pipes for a reasonable fee.

One of the benefits of living in Baton Rouge—while not a conventional small town, it sure felt that way as far as connections were concerned. Sadie also had her brother to help with painting and weeding, and other smaller chores. As long as he remained willing, she would use him.

Once everything else had been completed, all the floors would need to be refinished. While she knew she could do that by herself, she sincerely hoped her volunteers would still be willing to help at that point.

Hauling herself out of the SUV, she began to unload a mower and weed whacker to start the long process of getting the yard into shape. Just as she grabbed the cord to start the mower, a car pulled up and parked along the curb.

"Hey, Seth!" she called out, overjoyed to see her brother wearing ratty jeans and an old t-shirt. That meant he'd come to work.

"Reinforcements are here," he announced, holding his arms out to encompass himself. "Where can I start?"

"If you'll mow, I'll weed-whack."

Seth frowned at the push mower, then looked at her yard. "You should really invest in a ridin mower."

"Eventually. But for today, you can skip the gym."

After a little more grumbling on Seth's part, they both got to work. She spent most of her days working with her hands in the creative sphere, but sometimes it felt nice to do some old-fashioned hard labor. A couple of hours later, sweaty and happily exhausted, they sank onto the bottom stair—still in good enough condition to support their weight—and Sadie cracked open two bottles of water from a cooler in her trunk. "Look at what a difference this has made already. I'd like to work on the porch today, too. You up for it?"

"Feed me, and you got it."

"Chinese? Or pizza?"

"Chinese," he decided. "Had pizza for breakfast."

For a moment, she stared at her brother with consternation. "Of course you did."

Shaking her head, she grabbed out her cell phone and brought up the number for their favorite place, luckily in delivery range. While they waited for the food to arrive, they began hauling out tools from her SUV. Once they figured out how much new stuff they would need, she would make a trip to the hardware store.

Not one to sit around, Sadie immediately began tearing up rotted boards. She wore gloves, while Seth opted to use his bare hands. They had a pretty decent pile on the freshly mowed lawn when the delivery car pulled up.

While Sadie dealt with the food, Seth grabbed two more bottles of water, along with a coke for himself, and did his best to wash his hands. They settled back on the bottom step and tore into containers of fried rice.

Sadie had chicken and steamed broccoli—Seth never quite understood her healthy eating obsession—while he dug into the spiciest General Tso's he'd ever found. She'd even ordered him egg rolls and fried dumplings. He'd earned them after the work he'd put in so far, and would continue to do.

"How is Declan settlin in?" Sadie asked nonchalantly after they'd both inhaled enough food to settle that hunger ache.

"Why don't you ask him yourself?"

Sadie pursed her lips. "I don't have his number."

"I'll give it to you. I'm sure he won't mind."

"You're so annoyin," she muttered. Brothers could be so dense. After the night they'd had coffee and Declan had mentioned dinner, he'd never called. Then he'd stopped in to the store, even brought up the promised dinner, but that had been it. She couldn't very well call *him*, whether she had his number or not.

"What else are brothers for?"

Seth wasn't an idiot. He'd known Sadie had harbored a crush on his best friend through most of their childhood. He might not have recognized it until his later years, but especially now, looking back, he knew she'd had it bad for a long time. He knew Declan would never act on it—at least not when she'd been a kid.

But the way Seth had seen Declan look at Sadie the few times they'd run into each other since he'd moved back—well, things may have changed. The tension between them was thicker than a hog on its way to slaughter. To change the subject, he asked, "How's the business goin?"

"Great so far. Virginia has been a really big help, it's just too bad she won't be long-term."

"One day at a time, right?"

"That's the way it goes. I've got a lot on my plate, but I'm hopin that'll ease up once the house is done and I work out the kinks of runnin a brick-and-mortar."

"But then you'll have Eva," Seth reminded her. "And a whole new definition of busy."

"It'll all work out. I know it." Seth had also learned long ago not to argue with sister. Or his mom. Any woman, really. Such endeavors always turned into a losing battle. More so with Sadie, when she got one of her feelings about something. If she said it would all work out, he felt inclined to believe her. "Enough about me. How's your fancy cameraman job goin?"

"Real good. You know that brunette weather girl?"

"Let me guess. You asked her out for drinks to discuss climate change."

"You take all the fun out of it."

"Is there anyone at that place you haven't slept with?"

He shrugged. "They all know what they're gettin into. I don't pretend to be anythin I'm not."

"You're gonna run out of dates soon. You'll have to move just to find someone to ask out who hasn't already been treated to the Seth special."

"Funny you should mention that."

Sadie stared at her brother in shock. "What? Don't tell me you're actually thinkin of movin."

"Not exactly, but there's an openin for an international cameraman position. I was thinkin bout applyin."

"That would be amazin and awesome, but wow."

"It's highly competitive, Sade. It's not like I'd get it."

"You hush your mouth. You're the best cameraman and if you want that job, you'll get it."

"Thanks. That means a lot. Keep it between us for now, all right?"

"Of course. Just keep me in the loop."

He nodded and that was that. They finished their meal and went back to work. By the time the sun dipped behind the horizon and shot bright orange and pink streaks across the sky, the porch no longer had rotted or missing boards. Seth stretched his aching back. "Well, I'm worn slap out."

"Worth it. Now I won't have to worry about Dad or any of his friends fallin through a rotted board," Sadie said, standing back to inspect their work. "Thank you so, so much."

"Don't worry, I'm just rackin up all the favors you owe me."

"How about I start payin it off with dinner?"

"I've actually got a date," he said, grinning at Sadie's knowing look. "Yes, the weather girl. But I'll take a raincheck on that, and I'll swing by tomorrow, just... not too early."

Sadie rolled her eyes, loaded up the last of her tools. "Only if all of your climate change knowledge impresses her enough she feels the need to discuss it again in the mornin. If not, I expect you here bright and early."

The sun had barely made its appearance and Sadie had her hands full directing crews and making decisions. She helped where she could, sometimes just handing tools to someone on a ladder or in the crawlspace, along with keeping everyone supplied with water—and when the time came, lunch.

Seth showed up just in time for food, as if he'd planned it that way. He got some good-natured ribbings from their dad's friends as they gathered in camp chairs in the backyard. Early that morning, Sadie had pulled a picnic table out of her storage and brought it over on one of her trailers, so the food at least had somewhere to go.

All the men had brought their own seats—this wasn't their first rodeo. Her dad had gotten through all his preliminary work on the kitchen, and planned to begin tearing down the wall after lunch. Both Sadie and Seth would help with that.

Just as they were gathering to go back at it, a beat-up, rusty red truck found a spot along the street and its owner got out, wearing faded jeans and a thick work shirt. Sadie's heart skipped a full beat before taking off across her newly mowed lawn.

"Hey, Dec," Seth called out. "You're just in time for some grub."

"Says the guy who just rolled out of bed," James said before greeting the man he considered a second son. "How are you, Declan?"

"Good, sir. Finally got some time off, could use a good demo session." Declan gave Seth a manly half-high-five, half-shake before lifting a hand in Sadie's direction. "Hey, Sadie. Hope you don't mind some extra help."

"Always," she replied through her suddenly dry throat at picturing Declan wearing a tool belt. "If you're lookin for demolition, you're just in time."

"I'm all for it," he said with a grin.

They trooped back inside to their respective projects. Sadie pulled on a pair of work gloves, offered some to the boys. This time, they all took a pair, along with goggles her dad insisted on. "Safety first, ladies and gentlemen."

"No hard hat?" Seth asked. "Orange vest?"

"You act as if gettin hit in the head would do you any damage," Declan said with a laugh.

"Hey, some of us rely on our good looks. You've got the brains, you don't have to worry about your ugly mug."

"It's fine, chicks dig scars," Sadie said to settle it. "Now let's tear this mother down."

Equipped with a sledge hammer, Sadie took the first satisfying swing. She could feel every sore muscle from the day before and knew she'd be paying the price that night, but still managed to power through.

They stripped it down to the studs, taking trips out to the dumpster that had arrived that morning to throw in the discarded pieces of sheet rock. When they uncovered the wood frame, they began the tedious task of unscrewing each screw to save the long pieces for use somewhere else. If they couldn't use it in the house, Sadie could find some purpose for them in her shop.

Taking a water break, Sadie stepped outside and leaned against the railing overlooking the backyard. She still had a lot of work to do out there, but at least she could see it now. She'd uncovered quite a few neglected plants that she felt confident she could bring back to life.

The back door opened and closed, and when she inhaled the scent of musk and sawdust, she knew Declan had joined her. "This is quite the project you've got goin."

Smiling up at him, she said, "I know it. Thank you, again, for helpin."

"I would say anytime, but..."

"You've got a job and a life? I understand."

He leaned sideways against the rail so he could really look at the smart, beautiful girl who'd blossomed into a smart, beautiful woman. "You look good, Sadie. Happy."

Her damn, traitorous heart stuttered in her chest. "Thanks, I think."

"I definitely meant that as a compliment. Seth mentioned you don't have my number."

She glared back toward the kitchen. "Did he?"

"I'm sorry I haven't called. It's been so busy at work I haven't had time to breathe."

"It's fine. I feel the same way."

"I will call. I swear it." Taking out his phone, Declan asked for Sadie's number, sent her a message. "There. Now you can reach me, too, in case you need anythin."

He pushed back, held open the screen door for her to enter. Found inexplicable satisfaction that he'd thrown her off guard. Sadie squared her shoulders and thanked him as she approached the door.

"Back to work. I hear the boss is a real pain in the ass."

"You ain't seen nothin yet," she shot back before sauntering into the house.

Chapter Fourteen

It took nearly two months for the construction to wrap up. Every day Sadie fell into bed, plum exhausted yet giddy. She put as much time as she could toward the house, but still had a business to run. Most days she greeted the crew in the morning, made sure there were no issues, then would stop by during the hour she closed for lunch.

Most of the work involved things that couldn't be seen. She knew, once those were complete, painting and buffing floors would be quick. The kitchen took the longest by far, but as her new stove, fridge, and other appliances were delivered, she knew the wait would be worth every second. And then the day her stunning copper counter—which would make up the island and separate the space between kitchen and dining room—finally arrived, Sadie knew they were on the home stretch.

On top of construction and a new business, Sadie had taken all the foster parent courses that Clara had recommended. And whenever Eva stayed with Maybelle, she went to visit. The young woman seemed to withdraw further and further into her shell. Sadie knew she had to have patience, but it wore exceptionally thin as Eva continued to retreat.

She asked Virginia to handle the store for three days, so she could finish up the cosmetic portions of the house before moving in on Saturday. On Thursday, she entered her blissfully silent home and just stared in wonder.

With all the work, a layer of dust and grime covered every available surface, but she was so close to moving in she could almost taste it. Starting on the top level, Sadie cleaned each room top to bottom. The larger of the two rooms on the top floor would be for Eva—it boasted a low window that just begged for a window seat, along with a walk-in closet.

The smaller of the two rooms would be Sadie's home office. It took most of the morning to finish the top floor and as she wound her way down to the main level, she heard a knock on the door.

"Hey, Seth," she said with a bright grin on opening. Her brother never let her down.

"I'm here. Gotta see it through to the end."

"Thank you so much. I've cleaned the top floor," Sadie told him. "It's ready for a new coat of paint."

They collected painting supplies from the truck, hauled them upstairs. "Which color where?"

Sadie had chosen a light lavender for Eva's room, as purple was her favorite color. "This will go in here. The white will be in the office and bathroom."

"White? Seems a little borin for you," Seth said with a wink.

"Savannah offered to do a mural on one of the walls," she said with a laugh. Her brother knew her so well. "And I have some ideas for the bath, but white will be a good backdrop for that."

"Called it. I'll get started in here, you go do your thing."

Nodding, Sadie headed back down the stairs as her brother plugged his phone into a small set of speakers to blast his music. To start, Sadie focused on the master bedroom. She cleaned top to bottom before gathering the items for painting. Instead of setting up, she decided to check in on her brother.

He had already applied the first coat in Eva's room, and had gotten partway through the office.

"Looks great," she complimented him. "Needin lunch yet?"

"Always. I'll finish up here and meet you downstairs."

After ordering, Sadie set to work laying out tarps and had just started taping her bedroom walls when the food arrived. Seth joined her in the living room, where she flipped a crate upside down to use as a table. "It looks amazin in here. When I first saw this place, I thought you were nuts."

"I'm sure you're not the only one. It just felt right, you know?"

"Not really. But that's so you."

"Have I thanked you again for your help?"

"Don't worry, I'm still bankin all the favors you owe me," he said with a grin. "So far, I think I've earned your first born."

Rolling her eyes, Sadie took the last scoop of fried rice. They'd started on Chinese food, might as well end on it, too. "I have no doubt. But, seriously, thank you. For more than your hard work—for your support, too."

"What are brothers for?" he asked, not for the first time.

When Seth left that day, the second coat of paint had been applied to the whole upstairs and master bedroom, and Sadie had managed to clean the rest of the lower level. She stayed and applied the first coat to the main floor. Tomorrow, she'd finish painting the living room and dining room, then polish the floors.

Seth couldn't help the next day but he'd promised to be there for moving day, along with any help he could finagle. He'd already done so much for her, Sadie knew she'd be unable to say no to any favor he asked for the next few years.

Once the paint dried and the floors settled, Sadie lit a candle in each empty room and walked around with a bundle of sage to cleanse the space. She wanted a new, fresh energy to start her life there. Not just for herself, but for Eva, too. This would be a new beginning for the both of them.

As when she did this for her shop, Sadie added the weight of her words to the cleansing incense. "Into this smoke, I release all energies that do not serve me or mine. Be gone, all negativity, so that I may shine. Only positivity and light may enter here. Banished are any evil spirits that linger near. This I ask, one by three. As I will, so mote it be."

Once done, Sadie drove to her shop to spend the final night in her little loft. Tomorrow, she'd finally get to live in her home.

△ △ △

Too excited to sleep in, Sadie drove to her storage unit and began loading boxes into one of her trailers before dawn. Seth and her parents would be by to help later, but she figured she could get the bulk of it done by the time they arrived.

She saved the large furniture for when she had help, too. If she hadn't been so sore from the last couple days of cleaning and painting, she felt like she could have managed more on her own, but she also had plenty to do without adding impossibly awkward furniture to the list.

When the first trailer had just a little bit of space left, Sadie spotted her dad's truck backing toward her unit. Her mom jumped out to help direct him back without hitting anything, then gave Sadie a warm hug.

"I can't wait to see the finished product," Diana said, then spotted the loaded trailer. "My goodness, how long have you been out here this mornin?"

"About an hour. Couldn't sleep."

"Hey, sweetheart," her dad greeted her. "We brought a thermos of coffee."

"Sounds perfect. I'll take some of that now, move my SUV out of the way. I was thinkin we could load some into the truck, then fill up the second trailer with furniture."

"Sounds like a plan," he replied, rubbing his hands together. "Any idea when Seth will get here?"

"It's Seth. If we see him before nine, I'll be impressed."

They got to work without much more conversation. Seth showed half an hour later—early for him—and helped Sadie and their dad wrangle the couch into the trailer. Once the storage unit sat empty, Sadie led the parade to her home. They pulled up along the curb, just before a welcome addition to the party.

Declan got out of his truck, stretched his arms back. When he spotted the giant thermos of coffee Diana held, he pledged his undying love for her.

"Oh, you're such a sweet talker," Sadie's mom laughed, pouring him a healthy amount into a to-go container. "Good to see you, sweetheart."

"Conned into movin heavy boxes for your best friend's little sister?" Sadie quirked a smile, playing off her racing heart.

"Didn't take much connin. I was told there would be pizza and beer."

"Guaranteed," Sadie told him, lifting the door to the trailer. Grabbing a light box, she made her way to the front door and flipped on lights as she went. Her mom followed, eager to see the rooms now that they'd been painted.

"Oh, honey, it's beautiful," Diana said with a hitch in her voice. "No one truly saw the gem that was hidin in this house, but you did. It's just wonderful."

"Thanks, Mom," Sadie answered, feeling a little emotional herself. "I hope Eva loves it, too."

"Oh, she will," Diana said, wrapping an arm around her daughter's shoulders. "Of course she will."

The men entered then with the couch between them. Sadie hurried to direct them, then headed back out the door herself. They brought in the rest of the furniture, then started on the boxes. With five people, unloading went fairly quickly.

Setting down a box in the office, Sadie stopped in the doorway of Eva's room. In the space sat a brand-new mattress, a dresser, and a desk. She had a canopy bed on order that would be there in a few weeks. She'd decided to use the little nook at the top of the stairs as a reading or work room, so Eva had options on where to do her homework.

Later, once Eva moved in, they would have a shopping day for the two of them to pick out some new furnishings together, but Sadie wanted Eva to have something to be welcomed home to. Heading back downstairs, Sadie called in a food order. After the months of construction, she now knew the owners—and delivery drivers—of all the closest restaurants on a first-name basis.

She had no dining table yet, but cleared off the coffee table in the living room to use for food. The couch itself would seat six, plus she had a couple of smaller chairs they could use for eating. As promised, she set out a six-pack of beer while waiting on the food to arrive. Seth and Declan each grabbed one and lounged in a chair, while she sat on the floor leaning against her mom's leg. Her parents sat beside each other on the couch, her dad accepting a beer while Sadie and her mom opted for water.

"Thanks for all your help, guys," she said.

"I would say anytime, but I really don't mean that. Stick around for a little bit, okay?" Seth grinned and nudged his sister with the toe of his boot.

"Plannin to," she said with a happy sigh. "How's your new place, Dec?"

"It's a small apartment in Spanish Town. Meets my needs."

"Doesn't say much," she said, standing to open the door. The car with the blue and red pizza sign stuck to the roof had stopped at the curb. Trading a fist full of cash for two large pizzas and a hefty salad, Sadie popped open both on the makeshift table and piled most of the salad on one of the plates the pizza place provided. Diana took the rest of the salad and a single piece of pizza, while the guys divvied up the rest between them.

"Nothin like pizza and beer after a hard day's work," Seth managed around his last bite.

"Agreed," Declan piped in. "Thanks for lunch, Sadie."

"It's the least I could do," she said, waving off his gratitude. "I couldn't have done all this without you. All of you."

Realizing how close to an awkward moment that had almost been, she began grabbing garbage to bring into the kitchen where she felt fairly certain she could find a trash bag. Declan followed her in with the rest of the trash. While she piled the spoils onto the only clear piece of counter, she heard Seth's phone going off. From over the island she saw him look at it and grin. "Sorry to eat and run, but I got a better offer."

Raising her eyebrows, Sadie became the nosy sister. "Hot date? Who this time, the sports girl?"

"Somethin like that. See you later," he added, rising to give Diana and Sadie a quick hug. "Dec, thanks for helpin out today."

"Sure, enjoy... whatever her name is."

"Plan on it." With a wide grin, he waved and left.

"We'd better get goin, too. Unless you want help unpackin?" her mom offered.

"No, no, you've done too much already. This is the fun part for me. Thank you so much, again." Sadie hugged both her parents, let them see themselves out. She dug through a box and came out victoriously with garbage bags in hand.

"Impressive," Declan said, helping her hold it open to dump garbage in. "Seth hasn't changed at all, has he?"

"Tell me about it. He's gettin old, he'd better find someone he likes well enough to stick around pretty soon."

Declan laughed. "I would be terrified to meet the woman that can hold him down."

Done with the garbage, Sadie left the bag by the back door and grabbed two bottles of water she'd stocked earlier in the fridge, offering one to Declan. He took it and leaned against the counter, watching her.

"What?" Sadie asked, suddenly self-conscious.

"Nothin. Just tryin to see the little girl who used to annoy the crap out of me in there."

Rolling her eyes, she told him, "I'm sure I could still annoy you."

"I'm sure you could. I guess I'm just tryin to say, I'm impressed. Not many people would do what you're doin."

Shifting to hide the warmth she felt at his words, Sadie responded, "I think a lot of people would."

"No, they wouldn't. But then, you were always one to go your own way." Draining the bottle of water, he asked, "Sure you don't want any help unpackin?"

Sadie's thoughts were a little uneven. Declan's total one-eighty when it came to dealing with her had completely thrown her off. "No, but thanks. It's somethin I'd like to do on my own."

"All right. I'm gonna take off, then. Let me know if you need someone for the heavy liftin."

Smiling appreciatively, Sadie answered, "Thanks. And again, thanks for helpin today."

"Sure," he responded, opening the front door and stepping out.

Sadie leaned against the jam, watching him. Before she could talk herself out of it, she called out. "Hey, why don't we finally have that dinner? You could over next week. That'll give me incentive to get done unpackin, and I can cook you a proper thank-you meal."

"I'd like that," he said. "Wednesday?"

"Sounds perfect." He lingered just a moment more, his eyes searching hers. They were a light brown, honeyed in the setting sun. Their gaze held just long enough that Sadie's heart began to pick up its rhythm.

"See you then," he said with a bright smile before turning to leave.

Sadie continued to stand in the doorway as he got in his truck and pulled away. When she closed the door, she placed one hand over her now rapidly beating heart as if holding it in place.

That might have been the dumbest thing she'd ever done.

Chapter Fifteen

Sadie spent the first week in her new home feverishly unpacking, using every spare minute away from her store making her house livable. It felt so good to be able to go grocery shopping again, and use her pots and pans to make a meal.

She'd spent the first afternoon of the move washing off all her kitchen items and putting them away, followed by making her bed and putting her clothes away. If she had at least those two rooms in decent order, she knew she wouldn't feel quite so frayed.

In her spare time, she'd finished her dining table at the shop- made of reclaimed wood that had a bench on one side and four chairs for the other side and the ends- which she painted a soft white and used a beautiful French-style stencil on.

On Wednesday morning, nerves were jittering around her stomach so bad she could barely think straight. Before opening the shop, she shopped for dinner that night, splurging on a bouquet of bright yellow flowers that would complete the homey feel she'd been going for. Splitting up the flowers to be able to enjoy some in each room, she left three rose buds in a glass jar for the table to keep it simple.

Then, she spent the day completely and utterly distracted. Declan had always been the ultimate boy next door, like a brother to her. One she shot hoops with, one who punched Danny Larko when he'd made her cry, one who walked in the Nichols' family home without a knock because it was his second home.

For years, her unrequited love had lived inside her, miserable and festering, knowing it would never be returned. But now?

Declan would be at her home, in what could be unequivocally classified as a *date*. Her mind, as it had so many times in the last week, shot back to the lingering look they shared as he'd left. The kiss on the hand at the coffee shop, the kiss on the cheek at her store opening. Then, her thoughts drifted to the way his muscles flexed as he helped Seth and her dad wrestle her sofa through the doorframe. The way his body felt when he wrapped his arms around her.

No, this was no longer simply the boy next door. Somewhere in the six years since she'd seen him last, he'd turned into a man—and she hoped he saw her as a woman.

She rushed home from the shop, leaving Virginia to close up. There were still three weeks left before Virginia's due date, and this week would be the last Virginia worked at Sadie's Things. Though Sadie would miss her terribly, she couldn't begrudge the woman wanting to be a stay-at-home mom. She'd do the same, given the chance.

First things first, Sadie took a quick shower to not only freshen up but also to help appease her nerves. She planned on making stuffed peppers for dinner, and had already made dessert, so she knew she had time to make herself presentable before Declan arrived.

Choosing a dress the same blue as her eyes, Sadie dabbed on makeup and ran a straightener through her hair before throwing all the ingredients together for dinner. Slicing the peppers down the middle, she scooped in the hamburger mixture and poured some extra homemade tomato sauce on top.

Placing the dish in the oven, Sadie stood and took a last look around. She'd managed to unpack all boxes, even if some items were not quite where she'd like them to be in the long run. For the final touch, she added a single candle beside the flowers on the dining table. Satisfied with what she'd accomplished in the last week, she smoothed her dress and shoved her hair out of her face. She even felt sort of calm.

Until Declan knocked, and all the nerves that had subsided came rushing back. Taking the deepest breath possible, Sadie opened the door, enjoying the little clang of bells from the cluster on the doorknob. He wore a black button down and jeans, snug in exactly the right places. Their eyes met and the longer they stayed locked the wilder her butterflies flew.

Suddenly, a huge smile grew on his face and she felt her pulse stutter. He offered a bottle and said, "You look great. This is in case we get thirsty."

"Thank you," Sadie whispered. Personally, she felt parched, but had a feeling wine wouldn't be the thing to quench her thirst.

Turning, she headed for the kitchen to open the bottle and let it breathe. He'd stuck with Shiraz, knowing she preferred red. "Smells delicious."

Sadie started and immediately felt ridiculous. His voice was close, much closer than she'd expected and he'd been so quiet entering the kitchen. Or she'd been distracted. "Thanks, again. I made you stuffed peppers, with a cashew cheesecake for dessert."

"Sounds great, even if I'm not sure what cashew cheesecake is. Anythin I can help with?"

"Nope, just a few more minutes and it should be done. How about a glass of wine first?"

"Where are your glasses?" She pointed to the cupboard and made herself busy tossing the salad. Once poured, Declan handed her a glass. "Here. How'd the unpackin go?"

"Pretty good. Would you like another tour?"

"Sure."

Skipping the master bedroom, she led him back through the dining and living rooms. She'd picked up most of the furniture at flea markets or garage sales, seeing something in them that needed to be brought out. Even the couch had been a discarded mess when she first found it, but she'd torn off the shredded material and replaced the stuffing, then re-upholstered the L-shaped piece in a dark blue with white trim. She'd used a mixture of happy yellow and lighter blue pillows to offset the dark.

"You have a very eclectic taste," Declan commented, standing in front of a bookcase that Sadie had added molding to and painted a bright turquoise. At her glare, he held his hands up. "In a good way, I promise. I'm just not very creative, and everythin in here doesn't seem like it should work, but it does. I could never pull it off, that's all."

"Well, thanks. Someone told me once that if you like it, no matter what it is, it'll match. So, when I'm out shoppin, I keep that in mind. If I fall in love with a piece I take it, whether or not I know what I'm gonna do with it."

"Good philosophy." Their eyes met again, and though she wanted to move she felt frozen in place.

The timer shrieked from the kitchen, snapping Sadie out of her state. "Um, the food's ready. I'll go grab it, you can look upstairs if you'd like."

Leaving him there, she went back to the kitchen to take out the pan of peppers and put in a small loaf of bread. Setting the timer again, Sadie headed upstairs. She found him in her office, flipping through a sketchbook she'd left on the drafting table that she used as her main work space. Pausing in the doorway, she watched him as he looked at her innermost thoughts.

He looked up after just a few moments with a sheepish grin. "Hope you don't mind."

She gave a deceptively casual shrug. "Of course not. What do you think?"

"These are wonderful. How many of these have you brought to reality?"

"Most," Sadie said. She'd never been good at sharing her work until completed, and somehow, his opinion meant everything. Sadie looked down at the open page. There were several rough drawings of a four-poster bed, a dress design opposite that. Fashion, furniture, artwork—it was all in there. She tapped the page. "This is actually very similar to the one I ordered for Eva. I would have built it myself, but wasn't sure I'd have the time. I ordered it from a contact in California instead."

"It's gorgeous. I think any teenage girl would feel like a princess sleepin in a bed like that," he said. "If you need help puttin it together when it gets here, I'd be willin."

"Thank you. I'll keep that in mind. The bread should be about finished, if you're hungry."

"Starved."

Sadie brought the food to the table while Declan set out mismatched dishes. Somehow, they still managed to go perfectly together. They sat, Sadie serving peppers while Declan cut into the loaf. When he offered her a piece, she shook her head. "I don't eat bread."

"I thought so, but wasn't sure," he said. "What all *do* you eat?"

"Well, meat and vegetables, mainly. Some grains. I stay away from bread and sugar, most dairy..." She trailed off at the look on his face. She got that look a lot. "It's not as bad as it sounds."

"I'm sure," he answered, then poked at his dinner with a fork. "So, I take it this isn't rice?"

"Cauliflower rice. Though I will eat rice occasionally. Those couple months without a real kitchen was horrible. It's been nice to get back into a somewhat normal routine."

"What made you choose to eat that way?" Declan asked, taking his first bite and deciding he didn't miss the rice.

"Just wanted to be healthy, mostly. Savannah was the one that got me started on it. I think because she hates to cook, and I love to, so she knew I'd cook for her. We both managed to stick with it. Whenever I eat somethin else, I feel gross and sick. It's crazy."

"You miss her." He said this not as a question, but a statement. The melancholy in her voice when she spoke about her best friend shone bright as day.

"I do. Sometimes I feel bad for her movin to Lafayette to be around me, just for me to up and leave again. But, she met Branson—that's her boyfriend—so I don't feel too guilty."

"What's she doin for work?"

"She's at a local museum, gets to teach classes occasionally. You know how talented she's always been with her art, and she's expanded into pottery, too."

"That's awesome," Declan replied. "I've always been impressed by the two of you, how creative you can be. I don't think I have that gene."

"But you do somethin I never could. How is it, bein a cop? Really?"

"It's both the best and worst job I could imagine. I'm not sure how else to describe it." Bringing out dessert, Sadie refilled the wine and watched as Declan tried a small, testing piece. Felt pleased when his face cleared and he smiled. "That's really good. Do I want to know what it's made of?"

"Probably not," she said with a chuckle. "No sugar, no cream cheese."

"And yet it tastes like cheesecake. Amazin."

They finished their dessert and another glass of wine. Since she didn't drink much, the alcohol hit Sadie a bit harder than she'd expected. Feeling bolstered by it, she leaned forward and grinned. "You know, I used to have the biggest crush on you."

"Really?" Declan answered, also leaning forward. His eyes darkened as he said, "I *was* rather charmin, wasn't I?"

"Ha!" Sadie burst out with a snort. "Not even close. I think I just liked that you always paid attention to me. You taught me how to play basketball, remember?"

"I do," he said quietly. They were so close, he could smell the flowery scent he would forever associate with her.

"Of course, you tormented me almost as much as my brother, and the crush went away."

Declan's lips quirked at the corner, his eyes refusing to leave hers. "And now?"

"Now, what?" Sadie asked, a little breathless. Somewhere in her brain she screamed at herself for revealing so much. Her gaze dropped to his lips.

"What do you think of me now?"

Her eyes shot back to his, her mouth parting to intake a breath. They were suspended in the moment; Sadie's brain kept trying to shout at her, but her heart refused to listen. She leaned closer, as did Declan. His tempting mouth hovered just inches away from her own. She could smell his intoxicating scent. Feel his heat. Almost taste him.

A cell phone rang, causing Sadie to lurch backward with a start. Frustration mounting, Declan smiled apologetically. "That's my work phone, give me a minute?"

Sadie nodded, unable to form speech. Declan moved into the next room, and she heard snippets of his conversation. Not wanting to eavesdrop, Sadie picked up empty dishes and moved them into the kitchen.

She'd rinsed off all the plates when he spoke from behind. "Sorry about that."

Spinning to find him closer than she'd expected, Sadie leaned against the counter to give herself as much space as possible and waved off his apology. "That's all right, I understand how important your work is."

"Yes, it is," Declan said, then took a step closer. There was hardly room to breathe. "But it also prevented me from hearin a very important answer."

"What answer is that?" Sadie asked, her brain in a haze as her hormones went into overdrive.

Instead of asking again, Declan reached out and cupped her cheek. His hooded eyes remained on hers, his thumb brushing just under her eye. He moved slowly yet unerringly toward her. Sadie froze to the spot, not moving toward him but not moving away, either.

His lips brushed against hers, just the lightest of touches. It ignited a spark that traveled along every nerve ending. For the first time ever, Sadie felt truly alive.

Declan pulled back to meet her eyes; they stared at each other in shock. Whatever had been awoken in Sadie, Declan felt it, too.

Sadie reached up, gripped his shirt in her fists, and dragged his mouth back to hers. They met with a frenzied passion. Sadie's mouth opened, and Declan took advantage—deepening the kiss, their tongues dueling in a perfect dance.

One of his hands gripped her hair while the other slid around her waist. The spark that had ignited with the briefest touch now burst into a raging inferno, engulfing them both. She pressed against him, her grip changing from demanding to hanging on for dear life.

With a gasp she pushed away, raising a shaking hand to hold the taste of him against her mouth. They stared at each other in a daze. Sadie took a deep, steadying breath before attempting to speak. "Whoa... Declan, I..."

"I didn't expect that to..." Declan began, only to trail off as he stared at her in shock.

With a shaky laugh, Sadie lowered her hand to lean against the counter. "I wasn't expectin that."

"Neither was I."

Sadie took several deep breaths, forcing oxygen back to her brain. "Look, Dec, I can't deny how great that was, but..."

"Uh-oh," he murmured, his eyebrows drawing into a crease. "There's a but."

Throwing up her hands in frustration, Sadie gestured around them. "This—all of this—it's for Eva. My focus right now has to be on her. As much as I'd like to explore what exactly *this* is..."

Declan's heart dropped. To be offered heaven only to have it ripped away- he took a deep breath before saying something he would regret. "I understand."

"You do?" Sadie couldn't hide the surprise in her tone.

Declan let out a sigh, ran a hand through his hair. "Of course. Not that I don't want to drag you into that bedroom right now" —he paused, enjoying the swift intake of breath Sadie couldn't disguise— "but I do understand."

She nodded, her eyes searching wildly around her for something to latch onto that didn't involve thoughts of Declan and her bedroom. Staring down at the counter, she finally spoke quietly. "Thank you."

Declan approached slowly, stepping close once again. He fought against his baser instincts, but had to treat the situation delicately. He'd only just found Sadie again—he wouldn't lose her over a poor reaction. Lifting her chin gently until her eyes to met his, he said, "I'm here for you. I don't want there to be awkwardness between us."

She nodded, unable to speak. After a moment's hesitation, Declan wrapped his arms around her back, pulling her against his hard frame. His head dipped down toward her neck, breathing in her unique scent and filling his lungs with it. They held each other for several long moments before Declan released her. "Let me help you clean up."

"No, you don't need to..." Sadie tried to decline, but he'd already started gathering the remnants of their dinner.

Giving in, Sadie turned on the water and began to wash. They moved seamlessly together, a fact that didn't go unnoticed by her. Wiping his hands on a towel, Declan leaned casually against the counter. "Can I help with anythin before Eva arrives?"

"The only thing I really have left is the bed."

"When is it set to arrive?"

"Two weeks."

"I can come by that Friday, if you'd like," Declan said.

Though her initial reaction told her to decline, Sadie realized he offered more than his help. He'd extended an olive branch to help ease over the awkwardness of her rejection. "That'd be great. I'll provide dinner."

"Even better. I should take off." Nodding, she walked him to the door. They stood uncomfortably a moment before he leaned in to kiss her cheek. She fought against the need to take it further. "I'll see you in a couple weeks."

Chapter Sixteen

Patting the earth around the last of the flowering plants Sadie had picked for her garden, she sank back on her heels and wiped the sweat from her forehead. Summer was in full swing and even her straw hat couldn't beat back the bright rays. She tilted her head back and closed her eyes, first feeling grateful for the vitamin D before asking the sun to nourish the vegetation.

She'd put her heart and soul into this little backyard retreat. Not only had she chosen mainly edibles to use in her cooking, but she'd also woven protection and harmony into her plantings. It would be a perfect place for her to get in touch with nature and meditate, and she also hoped that Eva would get a semblance of peace in this beautiful space.

Standing and brushing off the larger chunks of dirt from her pants, Sadie went inside to get ready for work. It would be Virginia's last day, and she wanted to send her off with a celebration. The cupcakes she'd baked the night before—made from coconut flour and real cocoa, along with avocado frosting—sat on the counter, next to a parting gift Sadie had been working on in secret.

Virginia came in an hour after opening. When she saw the cupcakes and presents, she got teary eyed. "You didn't have to do this."

"I wanted to. It's been so much fun havin you here, I'm really gonna miss you."

Virginia wrapped her arms around Sadie and let the tears fall. She couldn't control them, anyway. "Maybe I can help out once the baby comes."

"Absolutely not. You spend every second with that precious angel. Only once you start goin stir crazy will we talk about you comin back."

"Deal," Virginia said. When Sadie handed her the wrapped box covered in ribbons, she opened it with more tears on the way. A *baby's first year* scrapbook with pages already designed, ready for a photo or two to be inserted. "Oh, Sadie, you shouldn't have."

"It was my pleasure. Now, let's have a great last day together, shall we?"

Δ Δ Δ

Two weeks had gone by awful quick. Without Virginia's help at the store, Sadie had managed to keep herself busy enough to forget about Declan's promise to help put together Eva's bed. At least, she'd forgotten until she'd arrived home and realized he'd be there any minute. When the knock came, she wiped her sweaty hands against her pant legs and said to herself, "Don't be nervous. Don't be nervous."

Her mantra only heightened the tension. Declan Park was on the other side of that door. The man she'd been half in love with her whole life. The man she'd kissed, then rejected, just two weeks before.

Opening the door, Sadie stared for a moment. He hadn't shaved in a few days, leaving a sexy stubble along his jaw. His eyes were on the lighter side of brown, brought out by the clean white shirt he wore with a snug pair of jeans. He made her heart go pitter-patter. Regret settled like a knot in her stomach.

Since she hadn't moved, Declan took it upon himself to step inside. Kissing her cheek in greeting, he slipped off his shoes and raised his eyebrows. "Is it already upstairs, or do you need help carryin it?"

"No," Sadie said, then realized he'd asked two different questions there. She needed to snap out of it. "I mean, yes, it's already upstairs. I managed to get the box open and lugged the pieces up one by one."

"You know I would have helped with that."

"I know, but I didn't want to keep you too late. In case you had a hot date or somethin." She tossed him a grin over her shoulder, even when the thought of him with someone else broke her heart.

"No hot dates, unless you include the pizza that I'd be heatin up if you don't feed me."

"Now I really have to take pity on you. Luckily, I prepared for the worst."

"Whatever's cookin smells wonderful. All right, you have all the tools needed?"

Sadie lifted one of several tool bags. "Right here."

They organized the pieces and decided on the best course of action. Once they began tightening the screws, Declan took charge while Sadie leveled out the parts. "Tell me the truth. If I hadn't been here, would you have done this by yourself?"

"I'd have tried, but I'm not so stubborn that I'd risk injury. Probably would have cajoled Seth into helpin."

"Be better for him than whatever he's actually doin on a Friday night."

They shared a smile before lapsing into an easy silence. Neither felt the need to fill it. Once they'd completed the base, Sadie said, "It seems you've got a knack for this."

"I've always enjoyed workin with my hands," Declan admitted. "But my job hasn't really given me the opportunity to delve into it."

"That's too bad. I couldn't imagine livin without my creative outlets. Of course, my job is creative—maybe my hobby should be doin math equations?"

Chuckling, Declan tightened a bolt before pointing toward the pile of pieces on the floor. "Hand me a few more screws, would you?"

Sadie complied, while holding her piece in place. This was definitely a two-person job, and she was grateful to Declan for volunteering. "Speakin of work, how are you handlin the transfer?"

"It's different. Smaller city than New Orleans, which means smaller staff to handle whatever comes up."

"Murders have been high the last couple years, accordin to the news."

"That's true."

"How do you handle it, day to day?"

Declan met her gaze. Such warmth flowed from her eyes, concern for him fueling her line of questioning. It filled his chest and made him ache. "I focus on the positives. Bringin justice for the ones that are gone, bringin closure to the families that are still here."

He did his best to hide it, but Sadie saw the anger and sorrow he felt. She wanted to comfort him, but feared it would be taken the wrong way. She'd already pushed the limits in their relationship—no need to shove him over the thin line they walked.

Declan tightened the last screw on the canopy and stood. "Ready to lift it into place?"

"Ready." On three, they lifted and secured. Once done, Sadie took a step back and brought both hands to her mouth. "Oh, it's perfect."

"Come on, let's get the mattress." Together they positioned the mattress and slid on the lavender sheets. As Sadie smoothed the white comforter into place, she felt a wash of sadness overcome her. "What's wrong?"

"I just wish Eva was here already. She gets worse and worse every time I see her, and it's already been several weeks since that. I just worry."

"Get used to that," Declan said. When she didn't smile, he crossed the barrier between them and wrapped her in a hug. "Hey, it's all right. Everythin will work out, you'll see. Eva will be here in no time."

Feeling ridiculous, Sadie sniffed and nodded, pulling away when she wanted to hold tight. "Thanks, Dec. You've been a good friend to me."

"I promised you I'd be here."

"You did." To hide her breaking heart, Sadie pasted on a smile and asked, "Hungry?"

"Sure thing. I'll clean up the tools and join you in a minute."

Taking the opening to regain her composure, Sadie walked down the stairs while sucking in deep breaths. By the time Declan joined her, she'd brought most of the food to the living room. After pouring herself a glass of wine and offering one of the stragglers of beer to Declan, they settled in on the couch.

"It all looks delicious," Declan said, loading a plate with a little bit of everything. Sadie had created a smorgasbord of healthy food. "When did you get to be such a good cook?"

"Just picked it up here and there," Sadie said, shrugging. "I still have a lot I'd like to learn."

He took several bites before answering. The silence between them was easy, comfortable. "I make a mean steak. And baked potato. That's about the extent of my culinary skills."

"Good for your desert island, bad for you. Your mom must be beside herself," she said with a grin. Sadie had learned more in the kitchen from Madeline than she had her own mom. Nothing against Diane—Madeline just had more patience when it came to Sadie's particular learning style.

"She did always want a girl. I think that's why she first took you under her wing."

"Your mom probably wanted to kick me out, but she doesn't have a mean bone in her body."

"Oh please. She loves you. Why wouldn't she?" His eyes met hers, and Sadie felt those damned butterflies winging across her chest. Her mouth went dry, and she fought against the desire screaming through her body.

A loud knock sounded on the door, startling Sadie and Declan both. Shaking her head at her own ridiculousness, she stood to answer it.

"Girl, what's goin on?" Savannah charged in, dropping bags and shoes and sweatshirts randomly. It wasn't even chilly. When Savannah rounded the corner, she stopped abruptly on spotting Declan on the couch, a stuffed mushroom halfway to his mouth.

Sadie picked up the discarded items—including no less than three sweatshirts—and dumped them in a basket by the door before speaking into the silence. "Declan, you remember Savannah."

"How could I not?" Declan said with a grin, standing to give the airy blonde a hug. "Good to see you again, Savannah."

"Declan Park? Damn, the years have been good to you!" Savannah answered, making an obvious show of checking him out.

Sadie hid a grin when Declan's bland look switched from Savannah to her. "I'll let you ladies catch up. Thank you for dinner, Sadie."

"You don't have to go," Sadie began, but he waved her off.

"I'm sure the two of you have some catchin up to do. I'll see you soon—Fourth of July, right?"

"Plannin on it. Thanks for your help."

Savannah plopped herself on the couch, fixing herself a plate of leftovers while Sadie walked Declan to the door. As they stepped into the night, Declan turned to Sadie. "She hasn't changed a bit."

"And I wouldn't want her to," Sadie said before turning serious. "Please don't feel like you have to go."

"No, it's all right. Do let me know if you need any more help."

"I will."

Leaning in, he kissed her cheek and it sent the butterflies winging once again. "Good night."

"Night, Dec," Sadie said softly. She watched him make his way to his truck before turning with a little sigh. Savannah had already plowed halfway through a plate and offered a cheesy grin when Sadie returned.

"Now I see why you weren't pickin up your phone," Savannah said, wagging her eyebrows suggestively.

"It's not like that," Sadie said, then looked around the room. "Where *is* my phone?"

"Men make you forgetful."

"I guess." Sadie sank into the sofa before studying her best friend. "What brings you to town?"

"Oh, no." Savannah shook her head, sitting up straight. "You don't get to change the subject yet. Declan? You two were just, what? Hangin out on a Friday night, gettin all cozy on your couch?"

"Well... yeah," Sadie answered. Dropping her head in her hands, she let out a groan. "Oh, Savannah, I think I screwed up."

"Tell me about it. I'm here, and he's not."

"No, before tonight. He came over for dinner a couple weeks ago, as a thank you for helpin me move in. He—he kissed me." Savannah's jaw dropped, losing a piece of food along with it. Sadie let out a bubble of laughter before handing over a napkin. "Can't take you anywhere."

"Wait, back up—he *kissed* you? Tell me everythin. I want details. Was it amazin?"

Sadie slouched back. "I guess, technically, I kissed him. And it was incredible. But I stopped it, told him I couldn't do a relationship right now."

"Hold on." Savannah set her plate down, raising up a palm. "You mean to tell me, Declan—the boy you pined after for years— *finally* showed interest, and you *turned him down?*"

"Yes."

There were several beats of silence. "You *go* girl! Playin hard to get. I love it."

Sadie shook her head, amused by her oldest friend. "Not really playin. My focus has to be on Eva right now. He said he understood."

Sobering, Savannah nodded. "I'm proud of you for what you're doin, but don't wait too long. Before you know it, he'll meet someone else and you'll be kickin yourself."

Narrowing her eyes, Sadie studied Savannah's face. "What's happened?"

Sliding one hand in her pocket, Savannah pulled out a delicate gold ring topped with a sparkling diamond. "Branson proposed."

"That's great!" Sadie exclaimed, grasping the ring to study it closer. Then, her eyes flicked back to Savannah's face and saw what she'd been trying to hide. "What's wrong?"

"Nothin," Savannah answered, taking the ring back and shaking her head. "It's just... Grant."

Understanding instantly colored Sadie's tone. "You're wonderin what if."

Sinking back into the couch, Savannah let out a sigh. "It's ridiculous, right? Branson is amazin, and I love him."

"But you're also in love with Grant. As you have been since you met."

"It's just... the way things ended... I've never had closure."

Scooting closer, Sadie wrapped an arm around Savannah's shoulders. "You know what you need?"

Savannah looked up with her large emerald eyes. "White hot chocolate?"

"Lucky for you, the ingredients are a staple in my house."

"Have I told you recently that you're my favorite?"

"Come on," Sadie said, standing and pulling Savannah up with her. "You haven't even gotten the tour."

Savannah made herself comfortable on one of the barstools at the kitchen island, watching Sadie as she set to work on her treat. White hot chocolate had been a long-time favorite of Savannah's, and she'd been over the moon when Sadie had come up with a recipe to fit their paleo-based eating style.

Sadie filled a saucepan with almond milk, cacao butter, and coconut cream, adding in a few drops of stevia and heating it all on the stove. She slowly stirred the concoction while asking for more details on what had been going on with Savannah. "When did Branson pop the question?"

"Last night," Savannah answered.

Raising an eyebrow, Sadie turned to fully face her friend. "Last night? And you took off today? What did you tell him you were doin?"

"I said I wanted to tell my family in person."

Shaking her head, Sadie turned back to her task. "You're playin with fire, Savannah, you know that."

"I know," she said with a groan, dropping her head atop her arms on the counter. "I'm a horrible person."

Taking out an immersion blender, Sadie frothed the drink before pouring it into two mugs. Carrying them over to the island, she slid one in front of Savannah before speaking. "You're not a horrible person, but you need to figure out what you're gonna do. Branson is a good man—even if he's not the man for you. He doesn't deserve to be jerked around."

Cupping the hot chocolate between her palms, Savannah nodded and took a delicate sip. "I know. I'll figure it out soon."

Chapter Seventeen

S adie woke to the sun streaming through her window and it made her smile. She loved nature and took every opportunity to appreciate it. For just a moment she let the rays warm her face, and she gave thanks for the life-giving heat.

Rolling out of bed, Sadie wrapped herself up in a robe and slid on a pair of slippers before heading to the kitchen. She wanted a cup of coffee and to see how Savannah was feeling.

To her surprise, she found a pot of coffee already warming. Pouring herself a cup and fixing it with her homemade creamer, Sadie followed the thrumming beat of 80's rock to find Savannah upstairs in her office. The smell of paint hit her first and as she rounded the corner, she found her best friend had been hard at work for at least a few hours. "Savannah, it's beautiful!"

Savannah startled and spun around so quickly paint splattered from her brush onto the floor covering. Streaks covered her face and hands, along with the overalls she'd pulled on. "You scared me, lady. Good mornin."

"Good mornin to you. How long have you been up?"

"A couple of hours. Couldn't sleep," she said with a shrug.

Sadie stood beside her and studied the wall. Savannah had created a secret garden, exploding with flowers, a stream teeming with life, and the light of hidden fairies among the trees. "I love it."

"I'm glad. I've got a little more to do, but you get the idea. Think Eva will want one?"

"I bet she will, but we'll have to wait and ask her. Thank you so much for doin this."

Savannah wrapped an arm around Sadie's back. "You're welcome, sweetheart. Did you bring me a refill?"

Laughing, Sadie offered her own cup. Savannah took a sip and handed it back. "Why don't I make you breakfast? Come down whenever you're ready."

Sadie left her coffee for Savannah and went down to fix herself another. She pulled out some vegetables she'd diced, eggs, and chicken sausage, throwing it all in a pan to heat. As she scooped the scramble onto plates, Savannah appeared. "Smells wonderful. Just needs—"

"Hot sauce?" Sadie finished for her, plopping the bottle on the counter before joining her on the stools. "So, come to any epiphanies last night?"

"No," Savannah answered, stabbing at a chunk of egg with her fork. "Seein Grant yesterday completely threw me off. I thought it'd be easier—all this time that's passed, me havin Branson. But Grant is just... Grant."

Sadie opened her mouth to answer but snatched up her phone when it began to ring. When she saw the number, her voice came out breathless. "Hello?"

"Sadie, it's Clara. I have some news."

Sadie's eyes shot to Savannah. She knew it was silly to feel guilt for talking to Grant's fiancé, even though Clara was also her lawyer. Savannah shot her a questioning look back, which Sadie ignored for the moment. "What is it?"

"Justine Wentworth got arrested last night. Eva's been placed in protective custody."

"What does that mean? Can I go get her?"

"It means we can set an emergency hearin. Since it's a Saturday, I'll push for a Monday court date. I know the judge who's been assigned to the case—old family friend. It shouldn't be a problem."

Wide eyes latched onto Savannah as Sadie answered, "Goodness. That's amazin news, thank you. What do I need to do?"

"Hang tight for now. I'll call you back as soon as I have a time set."

When they hung up, Sadie stared in disbelief. "That was Clara. Grant's... my lawyer. Eva's mom got arrested. I might get to bring her home this week."

"Horrible circumstances, but that's awesome news! What can I do to help?"

Looking around in a daze, Sadie shook her head. "I don't know."

Laughing, Savannah grabbed Sadie and pulled her into a hug. "We'll figure it out."

△ △ △

The next few days were a complete blur. Savannah helped with last minute details, and made sure Sadie ate. For Sadie, nothing else mattered but the phone call from Clara telling her to be at court.

She'd managed to set a hearing for Monday, as promised. Sadie showed up, surprised to see her parents there as support. Though they couldn't go in with her, it boosted her spirit to know they waited in the hall. Clara ushered her into the courtroom, showed her where to sit. She'd submitted medical records from both Eva and Justine, asked the person from child protective services to testify. The woman had come to Sadie's home on Sunday afternoon to inspect, and see that Eva had a space to live in. That part, at least, Sadie had passed with flying colors.

With Justine moving from jail to rehab, again, the judge made a quick decision.

"In light of the evidence presented by the council of the plaintiff, I'm orderin temporary custody of one Evaline Lee Wentworth to Sadie Lynn Nichols, pendin trial. Sadie Nichols, do you hereby swear to look after Evaline's health and welfare? Take care of Evaline's basic needs, enroll her in school, and ensure she attends?"

"I do, your honor."

"With the holiday this week, I recommend Evaline be released to Ms. Nichols immediately. Court is adjourned."

Tears filled Sadie's eyes as she turned to Clara and threw her arms around her neck. "Thank you, thank you so much!"

"You're so very welcome, honey. Let's go get that paperwork so you can pick Eva up."

When Sadie exited the hall, she found her parents and ran to them, enveloping them both in a hug. "I got her. She's comin home with me."

"That's so wonderful, sweetheart," her mom responded, tears in her own eyes. "What now? Where do you go?"

"She'll have to come with me," Clara interrupted, having followed Sadie from the courtroom. "Pleased to meet you, I'm Clara Clark."

"Oh, you're Grant's new girlfriend."

"Fiancé, actually," the woman replied. "But that part's new."

"You got a good one there. Grant's a sweetheart."

"I think so, too. It was lovely to speak with you, but we better head on."

Sadie looked to her parents and smiled. "I'll call you after I get Eva settled. Thank you so much for comin today."

"Of course, sweetheart. We're here for you. For you both."

Nodding, her emotions still hovering too close to the surface, Sadie turned to follow Clara. They picked up the necessary paperwork, then drove separately to where Eva had been staying. While Clara dealt with releasing Eva, Sadie got ushered to where the girl sat despondently in a chair in what could be considered a game room.

Heart breaking at the sight, Sadie knelt before her and spoke softly. "Eva? Honey? It's me, Sadie." No response. No eye contact. "I'm gonna take you home with me, Eva. I've got a nice room all set up for you. Would you like that?"

Her tiny shoulders lifted and dropped. Sadie reach out to place a palm against her arm but pulled back quickly when Eva flinched.

"It's all right. Everythin will be all right now." Sadie turned at the sound of Clara's heels against the tile floor and looked up with concern. "She won't respond."

Clara bent forward. "It's ultimately your choice, honey. You can stay here, or you can go home with Sadie. Personally, I'd go with Sadie. You'll have a room there, and I hear she's a great cook. What do you say?"

Eva shrugged, stood. Her dark hair fell in limp lines across her forehead. Whoever had butchered her hair obviously hadn't been a professional. Anger bubbled up inside Sadie, but she ruthlessly pushed it down. "Do you have anythin with you?"

Eva shook her head. Clara explained, "She only has what she's wearin."

Nodding, Sadie took in the stained shirt, the tattered jeans a size too small. The torn shoes. "Not to worry. We can remedy that."

Guiding her from the place, being careful not to make any physical contact, Sadie opened the passenger door and waited for Eva to settle inside. Closing the door, she faced Clara.

"Thank you so much. I know the war isn't over, but we've won this battle. I don't know if I can ever repay you."

"It's my job, honey. Not just that, it's been my pleasure. I'll give you a call tomorrow, see how she's settlin in. Let me know if you need anythin at all."

"I will. Thank you."

Sadie got into the driver's side, put the car in gear. At first, she attempted to keep up a stream of one-sided conversation, but quickly gave up and let them settle into silence. When they reached the house, Sadie brought her inside, led her up the stairs.

"This'll be your room," Sadie said. "I've picked out a few things for you, but I thought we could go shoppin together. You can also come look at the store, see if there's anythin you like there."

Eva nodded, stepped into the room and sank onto the edge of the bed. Her eyes had seen too much in her young years, and it made Sadie's heart ache.

"Why don't you get comfortable, I'll make us some lunch," Sadie said before heading back down the stairs. Blowing out a breath, Sadie turned instrumental music on low before getting to work on comfort food—she'd even bought bread for Eva. Sliding two slices into a pan sizzling with butter, Sadie topped each with a slice of cheese before heating tomato soup beside it. Classics were classics for a reason—she just hoped Eva would have an appetite.

Making herself a salad to go with her soup instead of the sandwich, Sadie brought it all to the table before calling up for Eva. She came down the steps slowly, still not making eye contact or speaking.

"Hope you like grilled cheese," Sadie said with a smile. "And if there's any other food you do like, just let me know. There's a lot I don't really eat but I'm happy to get it for you."

Eva nodded again, staring glumly into her bowl of soup. To Sadie's relief, she brought a spoonful to her mouth.

Sadie joined her at the table, digging into her salad to let her soup cool. She watched as Eva tore off a chunk of the sandwich to dip into the hot liquid.

"You'll start your new school in about a month," Sadie continued the one-sided conversation. "I was thinkin for the Fourth we could visit my parents, they can't wait to see you. Their neighbors usually throw a barbecue, and you can see fireworks from their backyard."

No response this time. It didn't deter Sadie. "We can stop by the shop this afternoon, so I can show you around. You could even help out once in a while, earn some extra money if you'd like."

Another nod. Her eyes had yet to meet Sadie's.

"What do you like to do for fun?" Sadie asked, going for the direct route to get a response. Eva shrugged. "That's all right. I'm sure we'll find somethin."

Still nothing.

"Me, I've got too many hobbies. Paintin, sewin, refurbishin furniture, any other craft, basically, and I love to read. I've left some of my favorites in your room, if you'd like to check them out.

There're also some sketchbooks, and a diary. Or, if you're more into science, we could always get some experiment kits."

Tearing off another chunk of sandwich, Eva continued to eat slowly. Sadie let the silence fall over them, the soothing strains of Tchaikovsky the only respite.

When Eva stopped eating, about half the meal remained, but Sadie knew they'd have to slowly work up her appetite. She needed to feel comfortable and safe, first. "Why don't we head to the store? Then we'll pick out some clothes."

Eva nodded and put on her shoes. Seeing the ragged, too-small pair reminded Sadie to make a shoe stop after clothes. They drove quietly; Sadie pointed out a few things along the way, but mostly left Eva to her thoughts.

After parking near Sadie's Things, they walked to the small clothing store where Sadie had become friendly with the owner, a woman named Carly Jo. Sadie found her to be the epitome of southern charm and felt comfortable handing Eva over to her very capable hands.

Carly Jo moved like a whirlwind, measuring up Eva by sight and gathering armfuls of clothes for her to try on. After hanging all the selections in one of the dressing rooms, Carly Jo left Eva and joined Sadie near the front of the store.

"She's just a doll," Carly Jo said. "Shy little thing, but we'll get her out of that shell."

"She just needs some time."

Eva eventually emerged, with a small pile over her arm. There were mostly jeans and t-shirts in the stack, which Sadie figured were the most comfortable for her. Sadie was glad she'd chosen *something*.

"Lovely choices!" Carly Jo boomed, rushing over to take the pile from her. "What else do you need? Belts, shoes, socks, scarves, jewelry?"

Eva looked over to Sadie, the first full eye contact she'd made. Smiling gently, Sadie answered for her. "Maybe a couple of belts, and why don't you look through the jewelry to see if you like anythin?" Carly Jo only carried flip flops and heels, neither of which they were looking for that day. "We'll get some new sneakers at our next stop."

Eva nodded and wandered over to the displays of necklaces. Carly Jo picked out a few belts and had Eva decide which ones she liked. As she rang up the purchases, Carly Jo asked, "Would you like to wear anythin home, darlin?" Eva hesitated again, but finally nodded. She selected a pair of jeans and a shirt with a butterfly across the front, heading back to the changing room. Carly Jo winked at Sadie. "She'll feel like a whole new woman."

Nodding, Sadie helped bag up the rest of the purchases and thanked Carly Jo profusely for her help. When Eva emerged, they added her old clothes to one of the bags before heading back to the car.

Sadie stopped at a large shoe store and helped Eva pick out two pairs of sneakers, along with a sandal appropriate for school. Even once they headed into fall, they still lived in the south and the days would remain hot for quite some time. Eva put on one of her new pairs of shoes, and Sadie held her old ones in one hand.

"Would you like to keep them?" Sadie offered, worried she might have some kind of attachment to the beat-up pair. When Eva shook her head adamantly, Sadie happily dumped them in the garbage on the way out.

Their last stop was Sadie's Things. Sadie unlocked the door and allowed Eva to go inside first.

"Come on back, I'll show you my work areas first," Sadie said. In the first room, she showed Eva a few things that were in progress before heading into the larger space. Then she gestured toward a table she'd set up the week before. "This is my newest obsession. I've been playin with stained glass. Truth be told, I'm not very good at it, but it sure is fun."

For the first time that day, Sadie saw something spark in Eva's eyes. She was interested in the stained glass, and Sadie felt her heart swell at how that tiny bit of light brought life to her eyes.

"Want to try?" Sadie offered casually. Eva reached out, though she still stood a good distance from the table. Drawing her hand back, she quickly shook her head. Swallowing back her disappointment, Sadie smiled instead. "Anytime you change your mind, I'd be happy to show you."

So fast she wasn't sure if she made it up, Sadie saw Eva's eyes dart up to meet hers before shooting down again.

It was a start. Sadie led Eva back to the main room, allowing her to wander on her own. She settled behind the register to tidy while Eva browsed. "If there's anythin you see that you like, it's yours."

As she worked, Sadie surreptitiously watched Eva as she moved around, seeming almost afraid to touch anything. She felt anger swell at Justine, not for the first time, but quickly squelched that. Anger wouldn't help anyone—no, if anything, it would do more harm.

When she saw Eva hesitating by a comfortable, overstuffed chair that Sadie had reupholstered with a fun lavender flower print, Sadie approached slowly. "That would be a great readin chair."

Eva nodded, but didn't move or speak. Using the marker in her hand, Sadie marked the tag *SOLD*. "I'm not sure we can wrangle that into my car so we'll have to wait for some help, but it's yours."

The smallest smile graced Eva's lips.

"Anythin else?" Sadie asked, to which Eva shrugged. "All right, we can come back another day. Let's go home."

Chapter Eighteen

When Sadie and Eva arrived for the barbecue, there were cars parked as far as the eye could see. Luckily, Sadie found an open spot in her parents' driveway and pulled in. Halfway down the street she spotted the beat-up, rusty red truck that annoyingly made her heart skip a beat. Pushing that aside, she looked over at the crowd that had already gathered in the Park's backyard.

She hadn't had much luck the last day and a half on getting Eva to open up. She just hoped if she kept up her steady patience and gentle tones, eventually the young girl would feel comfortable enough to speak. "Joe and Madeline are havin one of their famous barbecues. They're my parents' neighbors and longtime friends."

Eva looked at the crowd of people with wide eyes, and for a moment Sadie worried she wouldn't get out of the car. Maybe this hadn't been the best idea. Maybe she needed more time.

"Sadie, Eva!" Their names were called out, making escape nearly impossible. Sadie glanced over to see her mom hurrying over, and she got out to try and intercept. Eva followed hesitantly, clearly uncomfortable with the situation. Diana wrapped her arms around the girl, ignoring her rigidness. "Oh, honey, it's so good to see you. How are you, how are you settlin in?"

Eva froze and stared at the ground. Sadie had been too slow but made up for it now, pulling her mom away and into an embrace of her own. "Just fine, Mama, how are you?"

"Um, good," her mom replied, clearly uncertain. "Madeline already has a ton of food out, are you two hungry?"

"Sounds amazin," Sadie said, steering her mom in the direction of the neighboring yard. She didn't make it far. When she turned and found Declan standing several feet away, Sadie stopped dead in her tracks. He slipped into an easy smile, which only served to annoy her more than the truck.

"Hey, Sadie," he said, swooping in to kiss her cheek. He immediately turned to Eva and—keeping his distance—spoke to her. "You must be Eva. I bet you like lemonade." Eva nodded, still staring at the ground. "I know where to find the best in town. Come with me."

Before Sadie could argue, Declan sent her a reassuring smile and led Eva inside the house. Diana waited until they disappeared inside before speaking her mind. "What's wrong? Why isn't she talkin?"

"She's been through somethin traumatic. She needs to know she can trust us before she'll open up."

"That's ridiculous, of course she can trust us!"

"I know that." Sadie let out a sigh and tried to gentle her words. "But she doesn't yet. I'm sorry, I should have warned you. She doesn't like physical touch—I'm worried she was abused physically, as well as mentally. Just... be patient and give her time, all right?"

After a moment Diana nodded, her eyes glittering with tears. Sadie hadn't meant to make her mom cry and felt instant guilt. "Mama—"

Diana waved a hand, shaking her head at whatever Sadie had been about to say. "No, honey, it's not you. You were right, we should have done somethin sooner. That poor girl."

"She's with us now. Regret does nothin, we can only move forward and make better choices."

With a watery smile, Diana said, "Now why does that sound familiar?"

"Someone really smart used to tell me that as a child," Sadie said with a grin, wrapping an arm around her mom's waist. "She never thought I was listenin, but a few things made it through my thick head."

They walked to the backyard together and were immediately overwhelmed by greetings. Seth came over and made a show of looking around. "Where's Eva?"

"Declan took her inside. Actually, I was just about to go find them." As she spoke, she heard the screen door slam shut and glanced that direction. Declan headed toward them, alone. Sadie marched to meet him, anger in her eyes. "Where's Eva?"

"Relax, she's in good hands." Declan held out his palms in defense when he realized Sadie was about to blow. Deciding it was easier to show than tell, he grabbed one of her hands and practically dragged her inside the house. "Come on, see for yourself."

He found perverse enjoyment in the little bit of steam escaping from Sadie's ears. She'd always had a temper as a child but had really mellowed in the last few years. Declan realized he missed her little rants and knew he would continue to push her buttons just to see her riled up.

They stepped into the small mudroom just inside the backdoor, which opened into the kitchen. Declan paused there, bringing Sadie to a halt beside him. She fit perfectly in the niche of his shoulder.

In the kitchen, Madeline stood at the counter making mashed potatoes with Eva at her side. She had a bowl full of potatoes under an old mixer that had probably been a wedding gift thirty-five years earlier.

"Now, the *southern* way. Heavy cream and more butter than a single cow can make in a day," Madeline said with her heavy accent. She plopped the ingredients in with the potatoes and pointed at the *ON* button of the mixer. "Go on now, turn it on."

Eva flipped the switch—not realizing it had been set to *HIGH*—and chunks of potatoes flew, covering her from head to toe. She let out a squeal followed by a giggle, which caused Sadie to stare in shock as both Madeline and Eva dissolved into fits of laughter. Madeline managed to reach over and turn the machine off, but the damage had already been done.

"Was that the *southern* way?" Eva asked between giggles, mimicking Madeline's accent.

Declan tightened his hold against Sadie, and she tilted her face to look up at him. In less than five minutes, they'd managed to do what she'd been unable to do in the last two days—gotten Eva to talk. Something shifted in her chest when he looked down at her, delight clear in his honeyed eyes.

"Are you two okay?" Sadie asked, breaking away from Declan's gaze and stepping into the room, grabbing the paper towels on the way.

Madeline and Eva both turned, chunks splattered over both their faces with a heavy concentration on their shirts, laughter in their eyes. "Oh, honey, it's just a little spilt potato. Why don't ya'll finish this while I take Eva to wash up?"

As Madeline took Eva upstairs, Sadie faced Declan with a raised eyebrow. "If you wipe up the chunks, I'll grab the mop."

"Deal." They cleaned up quickly before Sadie set to work on what remained of the bowl of potatoes. Making sure the mixer started on low, she slowly upped the speed until they were properly whipped. Declan leaned over her shoulder to peer into the bowl. "Looks good."

On a whim, Sadie dipped one finger into the mixture and swiped it across his nose. She met his gaze with a twinkle of laughter. His eyes darkened; she took a step back. Too late, she realized she was pressed up against the counter with nowhere to go.

His lean form crowded her personal space, and she couldn't work up the ability to care. He smelled like barbecue smoke with an underlying scent of fresh-cut grass and it brought her back to the summers of her childhood. Hanging out at parties his parents threw where she hoped and prayed that he would look at her like this, just once.

He never had then, but he looked now. His hooded eyes dropped to her lips, and she sucked in a breath.

"Did ya'll get the potatoes done?" Madeline asked, coming down the stairs and pausing at the bottom to take in the scene.

Using the opportunity to slide away, Sadie smiled vaguely in Madeline's direction. "Yes ma'am, all done. I'll take them out."

Grabbing the bowl, Sadie escaped the kitchen and allowed herself to be swallowed up by the crowd in the backyard.

△ △ △

She managed to avoid Declan for the majority of the evening. Instead, she stuck close to Eva and her parents—Seth tended to be near Declan—and even though Eva didn't really speak, she seemed infinitely more comfortable. She even smiled once or twice.

As the sun sank toward the horizon, Declan and Seth uncovered the stash of fireworks they'd been hording. Legal ones, of course—Declan might have started off as a troublemaker, but he now took his profession seriously.

The younger kids waited excitedly for sparklers, rushing off toward the darkest part of the lawn just to see how far they could get. One of the adults inevitably had to follow in order to lead them back. Sadie watched as Eva accepted a sparkler and twirled it slowly before her eyes. A small smile lit her face, and Sadie pressed a hand over her heart at the pure bliss that settled over the younger girl's expression.

When Eva joined her again, Sadie asked, "Want to see the treehouse? It's the best place to watch the town's fireworks."

Eva nodded and followed Sadie to her parents' backyard, where she nimbly climbed the ladder still in place. She'd spent a lot of time up there as a kid, reading or painting. The boys used it as a clubhouse of sorts, though she'd almost always been invited to join.

They'd done sleepovers out there during the summer, when the air hung heavy with humidity and the nets they hung barely kept out the mosquitoes. Sadie and Savannah had shared many secrets in that place, too. She'd finally admitted her crush on Declan; Savannah'd spilled the news about her first time with Grant.

They'd dreamed and loved and cried up there. Now, she wanted to share that special place with Eva.

They sat on the floor, arms resting against the frame of the window. Below them, the kids still ran with sparklers, the adult boys still set off the more dangerous fireworks. Soon, the bigger show would begin.

"Are you havin fun?" Sadie asked after a few quiet moments.

"Yes," Eva answered, her voice barely above a whisper. "Thank you."

"Madeline is like a second mom to me. I spent so much time over there as a kid, she probably forgot I wasn't her kid."

"She's nice."

Looking over at Eva, Sadie nodded. "Yes, she is. Anytime you want to come visit, I'll bring you. She'd be happy to have you."

Eva didn't respond, but she did smile. That was good enough for Sadie.

The first town firework lit the sky, glowing red and white and causing a hush to fall over the barbecue crowd. They watched together for several minutes when Sadie caught Eva looking across the yard, toward kids her own age.

"You want to go join them?" she asked. Eva bit her lip, then nodded. With a little chuckle, Sadie said, "Go, have fun. I'll find you after the show."

With another small smile Eva climbed down, ran over the grass and sat near the group. Sadie turned her gaze back to the sky, enjoying every minute of the show. This had always been her favorite holiday as a kid, after Halloween. Not much had changed.

After a few more minutes, she heard someone climbing up the ladder. As soon as she saw the brown hair, Sadie knew Declan had found her. While her pulse quickened, she lectured herself on staying calm. They were friends. They'd always been friends. Just because they'd shared one explosive kiss and an awkward moment in his mom's kitchen meant nothing.

"Hey," he said with a grin, stepping into the small space before settling beside her. "Thought you might be up here."

"Best spot in town," she answered.

"Eva seems to be doin better."

"Yeah," Sadie said, looking over to the group Eva had joined. "Thanks to you, and your mom."

"You did that. She feels comfortable with you. We just nudged her along."

His words filled her chest with warmth, which she tried very hard to squash. This setting felt way too romantic already—the dark, secluded spot, the way the light burst and scattered over his features. Sadie sucked in a breath, forced her gaze away from him and back to the show.

Declan heard the gasp and soft sigh, turned his head to study Sadie for a moment. She looked so beautiful, so innocent with her wide eyes staring up at the sky. For a moment he felt sixteen again, the last time he remembered sitting up here with her. Seth had been there, too, and they'd watched fireworks just like this. She'd been young then, and he'd loved her like a sister. Their age difference had been too great to contemplate anything further.

But now—well, six years didn't seem so far apart. Before he could stop to think about what he was doing, his hand reached out to tuck a lock of hair behind her ear. Startled, she turned those wide, stormy eyes to him. Her mouth parted and his eyes dropped to her lips.

"Declan," she breathed. Her brain refused to work. She felt overloaded by his scent, his intense gaze. Sadie felt herself drawn to him, moving inexorably closer. Wanting to close that gap. Knowing she shouldn't. Placing a palm against his chest, she shook her head. "Please."

"I'm sorry," he whispered huskily. Need tore through him, battled hard. He reminded himself that Eva was more important than his own need. "You need time. Eva. Yup." Scooting away, he climbed onto the ladder, looked back as Sadie opened her mouth to speak. "Don't. It's okay. We're good. I'll see you later."

He ducked down, and Sadie felt her heart go with.

Chapter Nineteen

Bright bursts of flame exploded overhead and rained down against the dark sky. Declan, angry with himself and frustrated with the entire situation, kicked at a rock as he veered away from the crowd gathered in his parents' yard. He just needed a minute alone.

The thing was, there was something between him and Sadie. Neither of them could deny it, but he'd been too late. Or too early. Either way, he found himself walking off a need that couldn't be assuaged.

Declan walked the neighborhood like he hadn't done since he was a kid. Well past fireworks, well past everyone driving home. Still, his frustration hadn't subsided.

His phone rang and he answered without thinking. "What?"

No one answered. He could hear sounds, heavy breath. Muffled words. Glancing down at the screen, his eyes widened in surprise. Jackson Beaumont had butt-dialed him.

Curious, Declan put the phone to his ear again. The faint words became clearer. A smooth voice that sounded like death itself. "We're disappointed in you, Jackson."

"I kept to the story. I lied for the governor, gave us all an alibi. What more do you want from me?"

"Such insubordination. You forget what we did for you. For your brother."

"Always back to that, is it? You've got no proof. It was ruled as a drug overdose. The autopsy confirmed. You can't hold that over my head anymore."

Declan stood in mute shock; he didn't fully understand the situation, but he knew he was overhearing extremely important information. He fumbled to record the call, the phone slipping from his hands in his haste. When he lifted it back to his ear, he heard the final words before the call ended.

"Goodbye, Beaumont."

A strangled gasp; a dead line.

Phone still in hand, Declan took off for his car at a run. He had no idea if the judge had called him purposely or not, but one thing was clear: he now had somewhere to funnel his frustration.

$$\triangle \triangle \triangle$$

The Fourth of July gala Jackson Beaumont's wife liked to throw each year used to be enjoyable for him. He liked the food. He liked showing off his mansion. He loved schmoozing with other rich, powerful men.

Yet this year, he moved through the crowd as if on autopilot. He had a difficult time mustering up a fake laugh for the raunchy jokes. Couldn't care less what size fish one man caught or how low another's score had been at the golf course last week.

This holiday always made him think of his brother. Miss him, even. They'd been close, when they'd been young. Their dad had been hard on them, pushed them to do their best. Doing their best eventually created an air of competition that couldn't be overcome. Each always attempted to outdo the other, strived to be on Daddy's good side.

Tennessee Beaumont had been a tough man. A man's man. Raised in the saddle and the only way he knew to judge a man's character was by the saddle. Even when Jackson had won Bronc riding competitions, it still wasn't enough.

Austin had inherited the brawn, the athleticism. Jackson had always been the smart one. The smarter one.

The one who was left craving his father's approval long into adulthood.

Slipping into his home office, Jackson closed the door and poured himself a glass of his personal bourbon. Letting the thick liquid slide over his tongue, he moved to his desk to sit down. He had ten minutes, tops, before his wife came looking. He intended to enjoy every second of peace.

As he leaned back in his chair and brought the glass to his lips for another sip, a shadow stepped from the wall and into plain sight.

Jackson's first impression of the man was simply; darkness. Evil clung to him like a second skin. For a moment, Jackson wished he'd been more of a God-fearing man. Perhaps then he'd be wearing a cross. Have something in which to cling.

"Who the hell are you?"

"Who doesn't matter," the man said in a smooth, honeyed voice. The kind the devil would use to cajole an innocent soul. "What you can do for me, does."

"Did they send you?"

"They, who?" he asked, conversationally. Jackson squinted in looking at the man, felt as if he were peering through cloudy water. Like he was looking at a ghost. He thought he caught a glimpse of silver eyes. That couldn't be right. They must be blue, but the strange light was playing tricks on his eyes.

"You know who. *The Quad*." The latter had been said in a whisper, as if the judge feared speaking any louder would summon the very entity of which he spoke.

The ghost lifted a hand. In it rested a small drawstring bag. Jackson recognized it for what it was. Under the desk he slipped his phone from his pocket and dialed. "It's you. You were there that night."

"Which night is that, Jackson?"

"You know damn well which night." Jackson jumped up, his face bright red with anger. "You're the one who murdered that girl."

The ghost tsk'd in disapproval. "Such accusations. You think you have proof of this?"

"If I did?"

"We're disappointed in you, Jackson."

"I kept to the story. I lied for the governor, gave us all an alibi. What more do you want from me?"

"Such insubordination. You forget what we did for you. For your brother."

"Always back to that, is it? You've got no proof. It was ruled as a drug overdose. The autopsy confirmed. You can't hold that over my head anymore."

The ghost's gaze snapped to Jackson's. With the flick of his wrist, the judge's breath knocked from his lungs. Jackson stood helpless, unable to move, unable to breathe. His hands came up to his throat and pawed uselessly against the skin of his neck. The ghost watched without a change in breath or the flicker of lashes. He walked closer, impassive to the life-struggle happening before him. When he was close enough to whisper in Jackson's ear, the ghost said, "We know about the little file you've kept on your computer. You think you'll leave evidence for the police to find? You're sadly mistaken. You're as terrible a liar as you are a public official."

Darkness crept over Jackson's vision. The ghost watched without expression. "Goodbye, Beaumont."

The last thing Jackson would ever see was the shape of a tattoo, wrapping from wrist through thumb and forefinger.

△ △ △

At midnight Sadie's eyes popped open, her pulse racing. Unsure what had woken her, she lay quietly for several seconds willing her heart to slow.

A piercing scream had her shooting out of bed and running up the stairs. Pushing open Eva's door all the way, Sadie prepared to fight off an intruder tooth and nail when she found Eva asleep, her hands in fists.

Realizing the younger girl was having a nightmare, Sadie walked to the bed and laid a gentle hand on her shoulder. "Eva. Eva, sweetie, it's all right. It's just a nightmare."

Eva's eyes shot open and a sob escaped from her chest as she automatically sat up and scooted away from Sadie, huddling against the headboard. Sadie knew her reaction was automatic and nothing personal, but she still felt an ache in her chest.

"It's all right, sweetie. You were havin a nightmare. You're home, you're safe." Wrapping her arms around her knees, Eva latched onto Sadie with her too-large eyes. Encouraged, Sadie continued to talk, to soothe. "I used to have really vivid dreams when I was younger, too. I learned a trick to know when I was dreamin, then I could control what happened. Would you like me to teach you?"

Eva nodded, too frightened still to speak. Sadie understood the look and went for distraction instead. "The trick is: ice cream. Whenever I was frightened, I would hold out my hand and imagine ice cream. If it appeared, I was dreamin. If it didn't, I was awake. My favorite flavor was chocolate chip cookie dough. Do you have a favorite?"

Eva stared so long Sadie didn't think she'd answer. "Chocolate. With raspberries."

"That sounds mighty delicious right now. What do you say? Should we go get some?"

"It's the middle of the night."

"Who cares? This is an emergency."

Eva bit her lip as she thought about it. "Do we have to get dressed?"

"Absolutely not. What's a middle of the night ice cream run if you get dressed first?" Sadie opened the closet and pulled out a sweatshirt, tossing it toward Eva. "We can each wear a sweatshirt, but the plaid pants and slippers stay."

A smile finally lit her face. "Okay."

They went downstairs. Sadie pulled on her own sweatshirt and grabbed her wallet and keys. She checked the time; not much would be open at half past midnight, but Sadie knew the perfect place.

They settled at a small table in Louie's Café. The waitress headed over and introduced herself as Marla. "We've got an ice cream emergency, Marla. The lady will have the chocolate brownie dessert, and do you have any raspberries? Think you could throw a few on top?"

"I just bet we do. And for you?"

"I'll have a hot tea. Thanks."

Eva picked at her napkin and stared openly at Sadie. "I can't believe we're gettin ice cream in our pajamas."

Sadie shrugged. "Like I told Marla, it was an emergency. Good thing Louie's is open until two o'clock. Otherwise we'd be eatin gas station ice cream. Yuck."

Louie's was a small diner and a local treasure. Greasy food, late hours. Several other tables were full of twenty-somethings wolfing down breakfast after a night of partying. For a moment Sadie felt a tug of melancholy, but then she looked at Eva and felt the strange twinge of envy settle. She didn't want to be out drinking and partying all night. She was perfectly happy doing snack runs in her pajamas with her daughter.

Daughter. What a strange thing. Sadie hadn't thought of Eva in that way, even through all the preparations to adopt her. She didn't expect Eva to ever call her mom, but she felt as protective of her as she ever could be of her own flesh and blood.

"What are you thinkin about?" Eva asked.

"About you, about me."

Her face fell. "You don't want me around anymore."

"Goodness, no! Not at all. Quite the opposite. See, I was lookin around at these other people my age, and I was thinkin that I'd much rather be right here with you."

"Oh. That's nice."

"Do you like livin with me? Because I hope you know if you ever feel uncomfortable, you just tell me and I'll do my best to fix it. Or if you didn't want to talk to me, there are lots of other people that would listen and help you. My parents, Seth. Madeline."

"Declan?"

Sadie's heart jumped. Marla returned with the raspberry-topped dessert and tea. After taking a calming sip, Sadie said, "And Declan."

"You like him, don't you?" Eva asked, spooning up her first bite.

"Of course. We've been friends since I can remember."

"I mean, you *like* him like him."

"You don't miss much, do you?" Sadie murmured, studying Eva over the rim of her cup. Though Eva was young in years, she had a wisdom well beyond. Sadie decided to treat her as such. "I had a huge crush on Declan most of my life. He always saw me as his little sister. I still care about him, and I think he cares about me too, but it's not the right time for us."

"Because of me?"

"No," Sadie said firmly. "Because of me."

Eva took another bite, thought over that answer. "He's nice. Maybe you should change your mind."

Sadie almost choked on her tea. "I'll think about it."

Eva looked up, met Sadie's gaze head on. "I do. Feel safe, I mean."

"I'm glad." They sat in silence for a few moments before Sadie spoke again. "Sweetie? Do you want to talk about your nightmare?"

Looking to the table, Eva shook her head. "No. It was just a nightmare, right? Wasn't real."

Sadie nodded, and they finished their treats in silence. They made it home before two, and Sadie walked Eva to her room. Once she'd snuggled under the covers, Sadie started to turn out the light.

"Wait," Eva said. "Would you—could you stay in here?"

Her heart stilled in her chest, a strange, unfamiliar emotion swamping her. With a soft smile, she turned out the light and settled into the chair. Pulling a blanket over her lap, she sat and watched Eva's small shoulders rise and fall with her breathing. Eventually it evened out and Sadie allowed her own lashes to drift closed.

Chapter Twenty

Sadie woke early, temporarily confused as to her sleeping conditions. Then the night came rushing back and she rose to check on the still resting Eva.

She seemed peaceful, so Sadie folded the blanket on the chair and headed down the stairs. Starting the coffee maker, she took her first mug outside to breathe in the fresh, early morning breeze. Already the heat felt stifling, humidity heavy on the air. The sun had barely risen over the horizon, and butterflies fluttered happily from flower to flower in the garden.

The store would be open that day, and Sadie thought she would bring Eva with. Maybe now that she'd come out of her shell a little, she'd like to work on some of the projects Sadie had going. And maybe having a little money in her pocket would make her feel independent, feel like she had a little more control over her own life. Earning her own way had always worked for Sadie.

She gave Eva another hour to sleep before starting breakfast. Hoping the smells would wake her, Sadie fried up bacon, slid eggs into a pan. Once the eggs settled, she tossed in the veggies she'd already diced and sautéed.

Just as she slid the second omelet onto a plate, Eva made her way down the stairs with a fluffy pink robe cinched around her waist.

"Good mornin," Sadie called out cheerfully. "Hope the ice cream didn't ruin your appetite."

"I think I can force myself to eat," Eva replied, taking a seat at the counter. Sadie set down her plate, along with a mug of the healthy white hot chocolate Savannah favored.

"I was thinkin you could join me at the store today."

"All right," Eva answered, staring at the counter while poking at her meal with a fork. Sadie had figured Eva would be embarrassed about asking her to stay the night before, which was part of the reason she'd left the room before Eva'd woken up. Now she had to somehow address it, without further humiliating Eva.

"I have somethin for you," Sadie began, walking to her own room to grab the item she'd worked on that morning. The dream catcher had white leather wrapped around the outside, with lavender string and feathers. In the center, Sadie had attached a moonstone imbued with protection. "This is a dreamcatcher, you know what that's for?"

"To catch all the bad dreams," Eva murmured, reaching out with a hesitant finger to brush across a feather. "It's beautiful."

"We'll hang it in your room tonight, to help keep any more nightmares away. Sound good?"

Eva nodded. "Does that mean no more ice cream runs?"

"Never say never," Sadie said with a wink.

Holding up the dreamcatcher with both hands, Eva said, "Thank you."

Sadie understood the double meaning to her words. Not just for the dreamcatcher itself, but for being there when Eva needed her. "You're very welcome."

After breakfast, they drove to the store together while Sadie explained a typical day at Sadie's Things. Eva listened and nodded along, occasionally asking a question but mainly remaining quiet. They arrived at the store an hour before it opened, giving Sadie time for a proper tour.

"The smaller items near the register tend to go fast," she said, pointing out the stand of candles and loose tea mixtures. "I usually have to restock at least once a day. The jewelry, too. I try to keep the displays full. Once we get some customers, I'll show you how to run the register."

Eva nodded along, taking in everything Sadie told her. She filled a pitcher with cucumber water, set coffee to brew. Lit a few candles near the door, to further entice customers to buy.

They went into the back, where Sadie had a sanded table ready for paint, along with several other projects in varying stages of completion. Eva worked on the base coat of paint for the table while Sadie finished some pillow covers in the sewing area. Just before the doors opened, Sadie heard pounding on the door.

Getting up to see who was in such a hurry to get in, Sadie grinned and let in her best friend. "Savannah, what are you doin here?"

"I wanted to see the store," she said with a pout. "Why else would I be here?"

"Come on in, I'll give you the tour."

Savannah oohed and aahed appropriately. Eva joined them after finishing the first coat, paint splatters along her hands and arms. "Hey, Eva. How are you, sweetheart?"

Knowing well enough not to touch the younger woman, Savannah stayed put but smiled large. Her genuine attitude seemed to put Eva at ease. "I'm fine. Sadie showed me how to paint a table."

"Oh, fun! I love paintin, though I normally do canvas."

"You did the wall in Sadie's office?"

"I did. Do you like it?" Eva nodded. It looked as if she wanted to ask a question, but her eyes studied the ground instead. After sharing a look with Sadie, Savannah stepped closer, careful to maintain some distance. "Would you like a mural in your room?"

Eva's eyes shot up, first to Savannah and then to Sadie. Testing their reaction. Wondering if she would get in trouble for asking. "That would be nice."

"I asked Savannah if she would," Sadie cut in. "But I wanted you to be able to pick out the theme."

"Really?" Eva's whole face brightened, the smallest of smiles playing at her lips. "I'd like that."

"Why don't you look through some of my art books, see if anythin strikes your fancy?" While Eva bounced to the back room, Sadie propped open the front door. They'd be able to stand the heat for a couple of hours, hopefully. "When are you plannin on headin back?"

"Oh, I don't know," Savannah shrugged. "I'll stay through the weekend, at least."

"Your job's okay with that?"

"Yeah, I don't have a class scheduled until Tuesday evenin. As long as I'm back for that. This is a beautiful space, Sade. You've done well."

"Thank you. And, you know, if you ever decide to move back, I'd be happy to have you."

Savannah looked over the store, then glanced at the wall shared by a large, currently empty space. "That's a nice spot next door. Would make a wonderful art studio."

Sadie paused, looked up at Savannah. She'd said it lightly, but Sadie knew when Savannah meant something deeper than words. "It would."

With a fake, bright smile, Savannah headed to the door. "Well, let me know if Eva has an idea for a mural. I can work on it this weekend, if you want."

"Sure thing. See you later." Sadie waved and wondered, but didn't have long to think before customers arrived.

Eva turned out to be a big help, and the pride in her eyes when Sadie handed her compensation for the day filled Sadie with joy of her own. "Can I help again tomorrow?"

"You sure can. Let's close up now and get some dinner. I don't know bout you, but I'm starved."

"I could eat a whole gator," Eva said with a giggle. Music to Sadie's ears.

"I know a place. You even get a t-shirt for finishin."

"Maybe some other time."

By the time they'd closed up shop on Saturday, Savannah had completed Eva's mural. Sadie and Eva raced up the stairs together, eager to see the finished product. Savannah spun at the sound of their charging feet, a smile lighting up her face. "Welcome home, ladies. What do you think?"

Eva skittered to a stop and stared. A forest of trees had been painted in front of a purple night sky, the outline of the moon dead center. Sadie recognized runes of protection woven into the shape of the branches, of Savannah's own design. Tears filled Eva's eyes as she stared in wonder. "It's beautiful."

"So glad you like it. It just needs a few finishin touches— want to help?"

Managing to tear her gaze away long enough to look at Savannah, Eva nodded. "Yes. That would be amazin."

"I'll start dinner," Sadie said and left them to work.

After setting music to play, Sadie began pulling out vegetables and thinly sliced beef to make a stir-fry. Not only was it a quick meal after a long day at work, it was a favorite among the three of them.   As Eva's timid laugh trickled down the stairs intermingled with Savannah's boisterous one, Sadie took a moment to feel grateful for her life.   She'd never felt so full of love and happiness. It felt so fragile, yet unbreakable.

As she stirred in the sauce, Savannah and Eva came skipping down the stairs. For the moment, the shadows in both their eyes had disappeared. They'd both needed this. Maybe they all did. Then and there, Sadie decided they would have a girl's night.

They ate and talked about anything and everything but their troubles.   Savannah never mentioned Grant or Branson or her impending nuptials. Eva didn't once think about her mom or her life before that night.

"Remember when your brother and Declan kicked us out of the tree house when we were twelve?"

"Oh my goodness, yes! The one and only time they ever tried."

"Why? What happened?"

Savannah leaned close and grinned. "Well, I was sleepin over, and we snuck up there in the middle of the night and painted the whole thing bright pink. We left pink pillows and makeup and anythin girly we could find."

"The boys went out there the next day and were spittin mad," Sadie said with a laugh. "I'll never forget the way Seth yelled my name. We hid in the laundry room until Madeline set them straight. *They* had to apologize to *us*."

"Madeline was and is the best," Savannah said.

"Speakin of all things girly," Sadie said, clearing the dishes. "Put on your shoes, ladies. We're havin a girl's night."

Chapter Twenty-One

It took three attempts for Sadie to open her eyes. Her lashes felt stuck together. With a groan, she lifted her hand and felt around, then realized why they felt that way.

They were, in fact, stuck together. The fake lashes had seemed like a good idea when they'd done makeovers; sleeping in them was a whole other matter. She worked them loose as a faint noise had her sitting up, and Sadie realized what had woken her in the first place. Her phone.

She'd been lying on one end of the couch. Beside her were Savannah's feet, but her friend's head was buried under three pillows and a pile of blankets. Eva lay draped over an overstuffed chair, one blanket covering a leg and part of her stomach. Nothing about the position looked comfortable, but then again, Sadie'd been able to sleep anywhere when she'd been thirteen, too.

Her phone rang again, so Sadie carefully extracted herself from the couch and went in search of the offending device. She stepped over open candy boxes, scarves in an array of colors, and a mostly empty bowl of popcorn. Grabbing the phone, she saw it was her mom calling.

"Good mornin, sunshine."

"Mom? Is everythin okay?" Sadie adjusted Eva's blanket to fully cover and snuck off toward the kitchen.

"Of course, darlin. I was just callin to let you know Ginny had her baby this mornin. Nearly eight pounds. Mama and Clarabelle are both doin fine."

"That's so great to hear! Can we see her?"

"They'll have visitors startin at ten. Stop on by."

Since they still had a couple of hours, Sadie let Savannah and Eva sleep while she took a shower and dressed. She managed to loosen the lashes enough to remove them, though they still hurt. Never again.

The smells of breakfast woke both sleeping beauties and she shared the good news. Once they all ate and were cleaned up, they headed toward the hospital with one quick stop for flowers. Eva carried them inside, nervous to see a baby and to be around so many people at once.

Loretta May held her granddaughter while a crowd cooed and gawked. Virginia lay in her bed, the bags under her eyes the only testament to the hell she'd been through for sixteen hours. Sadie went there first, gave her an easy hug. "You get any rest, honey?"

"A bit. I'm fine, Sadie. Thanks for comin." Eva held out the flowers, which Virginia accepted with a soft smile. "Thank you. They're lovely."

"I'm gonna steal that baby away from your mama," Savannah said, adding her own hug. "You look real good for just givin birth. What's the secret?"

"Makeup. It's caked on."

Laughing, Savannah edged her way to the center of the crowd while Sadie greeted Diana and Madeline. Seeming to understand how overwhelmed Eva felt, Madeline gestured her over to a chair and sat with her. Following her friend's lead, Sadie snuck through to get her first glimpse of Clarabelle. "Oh, Ginny, she's perfect."

"I'll share, just give me a minute," Savannah said with a grin. But before she could hand her over to Sadie, a nurse arrived and shooed everyone out.

"Mama's gotta feed the baby. Come back in twenty."

Savannah grudgingly shifted Clarabelle to the nurse's arms and followed the rest out of the room. Sadie waited for Eva and sent Madeline a grateful smile.

"There's a waitin room just down the hall. We can gather there," Loretta May told the group.

"Would you like some water, or juice?" Sadie asked Eva.

"Apple if they have it. Or water."

"Savannah?"

"Coffee, hon. Thanks."

"Anyone else?" Sadie asked, and realized she'd need a tray to bring back all the orders. She made her way to the cafeteria. When she passed the bank of elevators they'd rode up on, Declan stepped out. Her heart tripped and stuttered, but she managed a smile. "Hey, Dec. Comin to see Ginny?"

"I'm sort of the uncle, so yes. Where are you headed?" Without any siblings of his own, and Virginia in the same boat, Sadie understood why he'd lay claim to Clarabelle.

"Cafeteria. Ginny's feedin the baby, so we got kicked out."

"I'll walk with you, then," he said, shifting his own bouquet of flowers so they didn't bump her while they moved. "How are you? How's Eva?"

"She'd doin real good. She's here, Savannah too."

"Let me guess. Savannah had somethin to do with this," he said, reaching out to run a bright pink patch of hair through his fingers.

He hadn't touched her directly, but she still forgot how to breathe. "Good guess. We had a girl's night."

178

"Say no more. I remember the tree house incident perfectly well."

"We were just tellin Eva about that last night. How funny."

"Seth and I were bein jerks. We deserved it."

Sadie looked up at him, saw the dark circles under his eyes, too. "You okay? You look a bit tired."

"Caught another big case."

"The judge. I heard about that. Any idea what happened?"

"Not yet," Declan said with a sigh. A fact that had given him the sleepless nights. "Let's not talk about such things on a happy day as this."

"No room for darkness when there's a baby in the world."

"True enough." He watched as she loaded up coffee, water, and juice. "How exactly were you plannin on carryin this by yourself?"

"Now, Declan, you know I always rely on the kindness of strangers."

"That makes me doubly glad I happened by when I did."

Their banter was light, but Sadie snuck another look at his expression. The thought of her getting help from another man bothered him. Interesting.

When they brought the drinks back to the waiting group, Declan's aunts pounced as soon as they set sights on him. "Betty Sue and I were just talkin about you, my handsome nephew."

"Why does that worry me?"

"Oh, pish-posh," Sarah Jane said, slapping him lightly on the shoulder. "You remember Donna Jo Stinton, don't you?"

Declan didn't like where this was going. "Pastor Stinton's daughter?"

"That's right! We ran into her just this mornin after service, isn't that right, Betty Sue?"

"That's right. Such a sweet girl. Single. We told her you were back in town and she said she'd love to get coffee with you."

Sneaking a quick look at Sadie, who was studiously ignoring the entire conversation, Declan tried an easy smile with an iron-clad excuse. "Sorry, I've got a big case right now. Wouldn't be fair to Donna Jo."

"She knows all about your work, Declan. It'll be no trouble."

Both aunts were grinning widely and nodding their heads. He'd fallen into this trap before, one too many times. Moving away had helped, though not entirely. The only way out now was to stall. "Once this case is solved, maybe."

"I'll give you her number. Make sure you call her."

The nurse appeared, coming to the rescue. "Ya'll can see her now."

"Go ahead, kids. We'll wait out here for a bit, enjoy our coffee," Loretta May said, giving her sisters a meaningful look.

"Dibs on first hold!" Savannah called out, rushing past Sadie, Eva, and Declan.

The other three walked at a more sedate pace. Declan greeted Virginia and handed off his flowers, shaking Travis' hand before getting his first view of the baby. "Wow, she's tiny."

"Most babies are," Savannah answered with an eye roll. With one more squeeze, she shifted the bundle to Sadie's arms.

"Oh, hello there," Sadie said, bouncing softly. Declan reached out with a hesitant finger to stroke her cheek. Clarabelle managed to free a hand and latched onto his finger with a death grip. Sadie smiled up at Declan as his shocked gaze met hers. Something passed between them, fierce and elemental. For a moment, Sadie forget anyone else was in the room. Forgot that anyone else existed.

Then she blinked and forced herself to look away. Eva watched from a few feet away, afraid to get any closer.

"Why don't you sit down, Eva? You can hold her for a while."

"Really? I won't hurt her?"

"Tell you what," Declan said, smoothly transferring the baby to his own arms. "Why don't we both sit, and when you're ready, you can hold her on your own?"

Eva swallowed and nodded, pulling the two chairs close together. Declan eased himself down, leaning close but still careful not to make unnecessary contact with the teen. As they both cooed at Clarabelle, Sadie's heart was completely lost.

△ △ △

Declan walked back into the station feeling infinitely lighter than when he'd left that morning. Spending time with new life, with love and happiness, had been exactly what he needed. Seeing Sadie had merely been a bonus.

He met Kevin and they made their way to the coroner's office. Declan still couldn't fully wrap his mind around the events of the last three days. After receiving the call from Judge Beaumont, Declan had called dispatch to send any available officer to the judge's home. By the time the first officers arrived, the judge's wife had found him in his office, dead. She'd called the ambulance after finding an empty bottle of pills beside the body. There were no signs of foul play.

Though not the lead on the case, Declan had asked to be a part of it, as he had reason to believe Jackson's death had to do with Lola Vasquez's murder.

When he explained to Sergeant Lewis about the phone call he'd received, Lewis simply brushed it off as a coincidence. The homicide supervisor hadn't seemed concerned that the judge admitted he'd lied to cover for the governor.

There had been so many people at the party taking pictures and videos that Beaumont had been caught sneaking into his office, but not one showed someone else following him in.

Declan didn't push the issue. He'd told Kevin and Sandra about the call, knowing Sandra would examine the body herself. He trusted Kevin, but Declan was having a hard time trusting anyone else at the department.

Especially Sergeant Lewis.

Declan had no proof of foul play. But that didn't mean he'd stop investigating.

"How's Ginny?" Kevin asked as they made their way through the halls to the morgue.

"Wonderful. Happy. Clarabelle's perfect."

"This'll make Sandra start thinkin about another."

"You okay with that?"

"Of course, man. I want a baseball team."

"Jesus, Kev. That's a lot of kids."

"Best decision I ever made, after marryin Sandra. You'll see, someday."

Not wanting to touch that with a ten-foot pole, Declan pushed into the morgue and greeted Sandra with a kiss on the cheek. She pulled on gloves and gestured them over to the judge's body. Once again, she'd managed to secure privacy to speak with them. "Well, boys, looks like we got another."

"What do you mean?" Kevin asked.

"Judge here died of asphyxiation. Just like Lola."

"He didn't overdose."

"Found a dozen pills in his belly, yet to disintegrate."

Declan looked to Sandra. "What's goin on your official report?"

"Overdose. What else am I supposed to do?" she asked with a shrug.

"Just like his brother."

Everything in Declan stilled. "What did you just say?"

"Overdose, like his brother," Kevin said.

Declan looked back to the judge's body, his head spinning around the possibility. "Just like his brother. Sandra, did you work that case? Austin Beaumont?"

"That was what, about a year ago?"

"Sounds right. Just before Judge Beaumont announced his plans to run for congress," Kevin said.

"He announced just after his brother's death?" Declan asked.

"That's right. What? You think Austin's suicide was staged, too?"

Declan didn't answer. He looked at Sandra with eyebrows raised. She nodded. "I'll look into it."

Chapter Twenty-Two

Stepping into Sergeant Lewis' office, Declan waited for the homicide supervisor to acknowledge him. When Gordon looked up, he gestured for Declan to take a seat.

"We've got phone records back from Jackson Beaumont's phone. They show a forty-five second call made to your number just before midnight. However, his phone was not recovered from his person, nor was it located in his home. So, let me ask you this; are you certain it was Judge Beaumont's voice you heard?"

Declan sat in silence, his mind racing. If the judge's death had been a suicide, there would be no reason for his phone to be missing. If it was a murder, there was every chance the perpetrator would have taken personal property, like a phone or wallet. The fact that Lewis was asking him, in effect, to change his story, put Declan on edge.

Something was off here. He'd seen it before, had even asked Kevin about Sergeant Lewis. If he fought it now, he'd be fighting the highest levels of the force. If he agreed, he'd be helping to cover up a potential murder.

His choice now might also decide whether he keeps his job or not.

"There were two men's voices, of that much I'm positive."

"You said it was difficult to hear at first. Perhaps the voices sounded skewed? Perhaps the words did, too?"

Declan's jaw locked as he ground his teeth together. He hated this. "It's a possibility."

Lewis nodded. "The coroner's office has ruled the death a suicide. The chief himself asked me to wrap this case up. The last thing this city needs is another high-profile case. We want the public to feel safe."

"I understand."

"I knew you were a good man. You're dismissed."

Declan left, fuming. He'd follow orders to keep his job, but he'd be damned if he left it at that.

△ △ △

Sadie and Eva sat inside her parked car, staring at the brick building. Neither made to get out of the car. "Want me to come inside with you?"

Eva shook her head, but Sadie could see the trepidation there. It was difficult for Sadie to sympathize—she'd never had to start a new school. Sliding a surprise from her purse, Sadie held it out, palm up. "If you need me, I'm just a call away."

Looking up with her large, too-old eyes, Eva asked, "For me?"

"Every teenager has a smartphone, right? You'll have to set it up with a passcode and everythin, but I've programed my number, along with Seth's and my parents, and Declan, too—in case you need any of us."

Eva took the phone carefully between two fingers. Tears brimmed her eyes and it caused Sadie's heart to ache. "Thank you," Eva whispered. Taking a deep breath, she nodded decisively and opened the car door.

"I'll be right here when you're out of school," Sadie said.

With a little wave, Eva acknowledged that before joining the throng of kids walking into school. For a little while Sadie simply sat and watched her walk away, making sure she made it safely into the building. Then, she pulled into the street and headed to her shop.

An idea had struck while she'd watched Eva walk into school. A little celebration was in order. She began to plan for something fun. She'd wait until Friday, so Eva had a full week of school under her belt.

Sadie decided to keep the party small. She'd invited those Eva felt most comfortable with; Savannah, Seth, and Declan. All three agreed whole-heartedly.

Friday morning, after dropping Eva off, Sadie did some last-minute shopping. She planned to go all out with Eva's favorite foods, including pizza, grilled cheese, and chocolate ice cream with raspberries. The latter she had specially made by the local creamery, and was her last stop before dropping it all off at home.

She hurried into the ice cream shop without noticing the rusty red truck sitting in the parking lot. With the freshly made gallon in her hand, she rushed back out and nearly ran straight into Declan.

"Oh!" she said, taking a step back. When she looked up and registered what she was seeing, Sadie realized Declan was not alone. "Donna Jo. How are you?"

"Just fine, Sadie. How are you?"

Her eyes tracked Declan's hand at the small of Donna Jo's back. He moved it away as if he'd been burned. She smiled and spoke through gritted teeth. "Lovely. Sorry to interrupt... whatever this is. Better get this home before it melts."

Spinning on her heel, Sadie made it several steps before Declan called out her name. "Sadie, wait up."

She didn't. Anger and jealousy reared up in ugly waves as she fought back ridiculous tears. What right did she have to be upset? Declan had made a move, she'd rejected him. This was on her. Still... seeing him with his arm around Donna Jo woke the green-eyed monster and there was no putting him to sleep now.

"Hey, Sadie," Declan said softly, reaching out to grip her arm and stop her forward progress. "Are you okay?"

She refused to meet his gaze. "Just fine. I've gotta go."

"I'll see you tonight. Right?"

"Of course. Eva will love to have you." She spun away from him, reaching her car and calling back over her shoulder. "See you later."

Declan stared after her, confusion warring with a primal male satisfaction for which he didn't feel the least bit proud. Donna Jo approached his side. "Is she okay?"

"Yeah, yeah I think so. I should get goin, I have to put in a few hours at the station."

"Oh, all right," she said with a practiced pout. Declan didn't notice. "Thanks for the coffee."

"It was nice to catch up," he answered, walking her toward her car. When they reached the door, he evaded the inevitable awkward moment by leaning in to kiss her cheek, pulling open the driver's side at the same time. "Take care now."

She began to say something else, but he shut the door after she'd slipped inside. He waved and jogged to his truck, even more eager for the evening to arrive.

When he walked into the precinct, Kevin noticed his jovial mood straight away. "Date went well, I take it."

"Not at all."

"Care to explain yourself?"

"We just don't have anythin in common. I only went to appease my aunts."

"Not what I meant. You practically bounced in here. What happened?"

"Nothin yet. I'll let you know if it does."

Kevin knew better than to push. They had plenty to keep themselves busy. Crime never rested in this city. It was no secret between them that Declan still worked privately on both Lola Vasquez's and Jackson Beaumont's cases. Kevin just didn't know when to tell him enough was enough.

Still, this was the best mood he'd seen his partner in since he'd moved back. He wondered at it, but decided not to share it with Sandra quite yet. She'd be disappointed in the lack of details. She just didn't understand that between men, details were irrelevant.

Declan seemed to be in a hurry to leave that evening. The fact that he'd stopped off in the bathroom to tame his hair and spray on some cologne didn't get past Kevin. Oh, something was definitely going on with him. Kevin thought it was about time.

△ △ △

Sadie had managed to calm herself down after her run-in that morning. Mostly. She just kept reminding herself that the party was for and about Eva. Not her and her missed opportunity with Declan. Seth had volunteered to pick up the pizza, and both he and Declan, along with Savannah, were waiting when Sadie and Eva walked through the door.

"Surprise! Happy first week of school," Seth said, with Declan and Savannah echoing the sentiment.

Shock crossed Eva's face. "This is all for me?"

"Of course, squirt. You know I sure didn't go to school this week."

Eva looked up at Sadie, who nodded encouragingly. "We've got pizza, grilled cheese, and ice cream."

"All at the same time?"

"If you want."

Eva laughed, then walked over to pull on a string of balloons. "When did you have time to decorate?"

"This mornin. Plus, Savannah helped a lot."

"Thank you all. This is so nice."

"You deserve it, sweetie. Now, let's eat."

Sadie went into the kitchen and set the butter to sizzling in a pan while she got out plates. She knew Declan would follow her, but that didn't mean she was ready for it. "What can I take out?"

"Everythin's ready but the sandwiches," she said, loading napkins and silverware on top of the plates. "Good thing Seth brought the beverages."

"I also picked up pizza," Seth said, defending himself. He looked to Eva for back up. "I picked up the pizza."

"It's much appreciated."

Satisfied with that, Seth poured root beer for himself and Eva and sat at the table next to Savannah. "Tell me all about school."

While she filled them in, Declan tried again. "Sadie, about earlier."

"Take this, would you?" she said, handing him a bowl of chips.

"In a minute. Would you look at me?"

"This is about Eva right now, Dec. If you want to talk, we can talk later."

His eyes narrowed, but he didn't argue. He took the bowl of chips and sat beside Seth. "Is old Mr. Maxim still teachin gym?"

"Yes! How long has he been there?"

"My dad said he looked that old when *he* went there."

"Listen to you. Poor Mr. Maxim is the sweetest man alive," Sadie said.

"Yeah, he always let me sit out when I said I had *girl problems*," Savannah pitched in.

The boys groaned while Eva looked at Savannah wide-eyed. "That works?"

"You bet your bottom it does."

"Still old, though," Seth said. "How many slices you want, Eva?"

"Two, please."

"Ever had potato chip and cheese pizza?"

"No," Eva said, eyes wide. "What's that?"

Together, Declan and Seth piled chips onto their slice of pizza, adding half a sandwich on top. Eva watched with her jaw hanging open as they each took a huge bite of their concoction.

"Boys are so weird," Sadie said.

"Yeah, but that looks good. Can I try?"

"Go for it. This is your night."

Sadie still refused to look directly at Declan. She could put their personal issues aside for the night, for Eva. But if she made the mistake of meeting his gaze, she wasn't certain what would happen.

After Eva took a bite of her chip-cheese pizza, she chewed slowly before offering a smile. "It's good, but I think I like them separate better."

"Thank goodness, the girl has some sense."

They ate their fill, even as Declan and Seth dared each other to try increasingly strange and twisted combinations of food. Sadie put an end to it by bringing out the ice cream—or so she thought.

"What if you scoop up the ice cream with a chip?" Seth shrugged and tried it. Though he tried to play it off, he didn't fool Eva. "It's terrible, isn't it?"

"Yeah. I don't recommend it."

"Would anyone like some coffee?" Sadie asked.

"I'd love some," Declan said.

"Sure you didn't have enough this mornin?"

Seth and Savannah gave her a strange look, and she instantly felt stupid for letting her tongue slip. Declan gave her a lazy smile in return. "Now that you mention it, I did have some good coffee this mornin. Real sweet."

"I suppose you couldn't handle somethin stronger."

"Oh, I could handle it. But maybe the coffee couldn't handle me."

Sadie stood now, having made the mistake of looking at him head on. A tiny voice somewhere deep inside screamed at her to stop, but she couldn't seem to listen. "Is that what you think? Believe me, the coffee could handle you. But it has others to think about. Sugar cubes and milk and damn stir sticks!"

Savannah stood and gripped Sadie's arm. "I forgot, I brought a special gift for Eva! Help me get it?"

Before Sadie could protest, Savannah had carted her off to her room. Closing the door behind them, Savannah spun her friend to face her. "What the hell was that about?"

"Freakin Declan! I saw him this mornin, havin coffee with Donna Jo. Donna Jo!"

Savannah tried to keep a straight face. Tried, and failed. "It all makes perfect sense now."

"What's that supposed to mean?"

"Oh, sweetie. You are so far gone for him you're in another country. Just sleep with him already."

"What? How could you—"

"The tension between you is thicker than frozen butter. Only one way I know to solve that."

Sadie spluttered, spinning to pace away and back again. She forced herself to take deep breaths. This wasn't about her. It was about Eva. She just needed a minute to calm down and remember that.

When the women left the room so abruptly, Seth knew he had to do something. He didn't know what had triggered this extremely odd conversation, but Sadie looked madder than a wet hen and Eva had shrunk in on herself. He could strangle his sister and his best friend both for putting that look on Eva's face.

"Eva, Savannah and I cooked up a little surprise for you. How'd you like to sleep in a tree?"

"A tree?"

"A really nice tree," he said with a wink. "Savannah completely decked out the treehouse at my parents'. What do you say?"

"Okay," Eva said to Seth, eyes darting to Declan and back. "Are you mad at Sadie because of me?"

"Oh, no sweetheart, of course not. Sadie's mad at me because I'm a dumb boy."

That made Eva smile. "Are all boys dumb?"

"Afraid to say, yes. We never really grow out of it. But Sadie and I both care about you and would never ever do anythin to hurt you. Okay?"

"Okay."

"Why don't you go pack an overnight bag?" Seth suggested. "We'll be ready to go when you are."

As soon as Eva was out of earshot, Seth leaned forward and punched Declan's arm. "What the hell, man?"

"Ow, jeez. What's your problem?"

"You obviously did somethin to hurt my sister. What the hell?"

"She saw me havin coffee with Donna Jo."

"Oh." Seth understood it all perfectly. "God, you're both idiots. Figure it out."

"Seth—"

"Eva, are you ready for..." Savannah charged out of the room and made a show of looking around for Eva. "Where'd she go?"

"She's packin a bag," Seth said. "I spilled part of the beans."

"I suppose you had to. There she is! Eva, I have somethin for you."

Eva came down the stairs slowly, still judging the atmosphere. Sadie put on a bright smile to help reassure her. "For me?"

"That's right," Savannah said, pulling out a wad of purple material from a gift bag with a flourish. "This!"

Eva approached carefully, studying the mass with consternation. "It's pretty. What is it?"

Letting the material unroll, Savannah held it out for Eva to see. "A sleepin bag! We're gonna stay up late eatin junk food and lookin at the stars!"

Finally allowing a full smile to show, Eva pinched the material between her thumb and forefinger. "Really?"

"That's right! And I've got more surprises for you when we get there. We'll even let Seth hang out for a little while if you don't mind stinky boys."

Eva giggled. "I don't mind."

"Have fun, sweetie," Sadie said.

"Thank you for my party. I've never had one before."

"You're very welcome."

"Bye, Declan. I'm glad you were here."

Declan knelt so he was at eye level. "I'll always be there for you."

In a move that surprised everyone in the room, Eva wrapped her arms around Declan and gave him a brief hug. She stepped back before he could even return the gesture. Sadie's eyes filled with happy tears and she waved as Savannah led Eva out the door.

"You two clearly need to work some things out," Seth said as he followed. One again to get his point across, he added, "Figure it out."

He left, closing the door sharply behind him. Sadie turned to Declan, baffled.

Baffled, and still angry. They'd both reeled it in for Eva, but the firm line of his mouth told her he felt the same.

They stared across the room at each other for several long beats of time, neither wanting to be the first to break. Sadie finally opened her mouth to speak just as Declan marched over to close the distance.

Before she could get a word out, his mouth came down on hers, pouring all his frustrations into the kiss. His arms wrapped around her waist, dragging her against his taller form. Sadie had no choice but to wrap her fists into his shirt and hold on for dear life.

When he released her, she gasped for breath, her dazed eyes staring up at him in wonder.

"Let's get one thing straight," he said, his voice still filled with vexation. "I only went to coffee with Donna Jo because my aunts badgered me into it. I have no feelins for her whatsoever. Got it?"

"Yeah, okay." Without another word, Declan claimed her mouth again, lifting her fully off her feet. In response, Sadie wrapped her legs around his waist, oblivious to the fact that they were moving until she felt the soft give of her mattress beneath her back.

Words became useless as they explored with a desperate kind of frenzy, yanking off clothes and gripping with bruising force. Declan's lips trailed down her neck, leaving a blazing fire wherever they touched. Sadie moaned and arched into him, her brain fuzzy but for one thought; she needed him. *Needed* him.

She needed him to join them together, to ease this relentless ache. To be one. He'd taken her heart so long ago, and she'd given him her soul. Her body was the only thing she had left to give, and she did so freely.

Declan's mouth continued to drive her wild until she grasped at his arms, his back—anything to tether her to this world. She came undone, a willing sacrifice to his touch. Just when she thought she could take no more, he filled her, capturing her breath as his mouth moved back to hers.

They fit so perfectly, moving in such tandem it became difficult to tell where Sadie left off and Declan began. She teetered on the ledge, pressing herself against him so tight they were nearly sharing the same skin.

Sadie screamed as Declan pushed her over the edge, though he didn't let her savor the freefall. He immediately pushed her back up, higher and higher until she began to spiral out again. This time, she took him with her.

Chapter Twenty-Three

They lay in a tangle of limbs, breathless. Sadie's vision blurred and her heart raced. *Wow*, was all she could think.

She turned her head gingerly to the side, where Declan's eyes were on her. They shared a lazy smile, and she let out a shaky laugh. "Why didn't we do that sooner?"

He chuckled, his hand resting against her stomach. "That's a good question."

For several minutes they remained as they were, content, the silence broken only by the sound of their slowing breath. As her humming skin began to calm, Sadie suddenly felt an awkwardness descend. What did they do now?

"Um, I'm gonna get some water," Sadie said hastily, standing to wrap a robe around her naked form.

Without waiting for his reply, she moved quickly out of her room and into the kitchen. Her hand shook as she filled a glass with water and took several gulps. When she turned from the sink, Declan stood behind her, wearing only a pair of jeans that hugged his hips. She found herself staring, unable to help herself. The man was *sexy*.

Offering him the rest of the glass, she crossed her arms and racked her brain for something to say. Anything to ease over this moment. Declan finished off the water and set the glass down as he raised an eyebrow. "You look uncomfortable. What's wrong?"

Was he kidding? "I, uh—I don't really know what to do. This is sort of new for me."

"You've dated before, haven't you?" Declan asked, confused.

"A little, yes," she replied, annoyed at having to explain this. "But I've never—I mean, it's never been like *that*." Rubbing a hand across her forehead, Sadie took a deep breath and tried again. "I've only been with one other person. We dated a long time, and when we slept together, it was sweet and... gentle. I didn't know it could be like this."

Declan cupped her cheek, his hand sliding down from shoulder to wrist before gently lifting the sleeve of her robe. There were tell-tale dark smudges along her upper arm, as well as other parts of her body.

"I'm so sorry," Declan murmured, his eyes clouded. "I never meant to hurt you."

A bubble of laughter escaped as Sadie realized he'd completely misunderstood. "No, Declan, you have nothin to apologize for. Nothin. That was incredible. If anythin, I wanted more."

"And that freaks you out?"

"Yes, a little, and also—we're not exactly datin. So, where do we go from here?"

"Oh," Declan said, understanding finally lighting his eyes. "You think this was just a one-night stand for me, a way to relieve the sexual tension between us?"

Sadie shrugged self-consciously, refusing to meet his gaze. "You've never exactly been committed in a relationship before."

Absolute silence fell, and Sadie found herself terrified to look up. He would be angry, and she'd just ruined what had been the best night of her life.

"Sadie. I've never felt about anyone the way I feel about you. It's different because you're different. *We're* different." His utter calm was nearly Sadie's undoing. With damp eyes, she shook her head, though she wasn't sure what she was trying to deny. With a soft sigh, Declan gripped her upper arms gently. "Do you remember the day I found you in the treehouse in tears over Bobby Hall? You'd given him a Valentine and he'd been mean to you."

Oh, she remembered. Bobby had called her a freak. "You told me to punch him in the balls."

"You should have listened to me. The point is, I hated seein you that way. I had so much anger in me, I wanted to kill that kid. At least beat him bloody and senseless. But I didn't. I sat with you until our parents called us in."

She remembered that, too. He'd been the last person she'd wanted to see her cry, but the only person that made her feel better. "You were sweet to me. And a little harsh."

"I was fifteen. As we all know, boys are stupid. The truth was, I didn't know how to make you feel better and handle what I was feelin. What I'm tryin to say is, Sadie, I love you. I've been in love with you since before I knew what love was."

"Really?" she asked, her tone reminiscent of a kid in a candy store who'd just been handed a hundred-dollar bill. Her heart swelled to bursting.

"Really," he said with a half-smile, his eyes steady on hers. "This was not a one-time thing for me. I want you, and I want to be with you. That is, if you'll have me."

"I've been in love with you for as long as I can remember." Then, needing no more words, she framed his face and poured her feelings out in a kiss.

△ △ △

Humming a soft tune, Sadie opened her shop door, propping it with an oversized vase she'd painted with cheerful yellow flowers. She lit candles, prepped the coffee and cucumber water. The first customers came in and she greeted them with a bright smile.

"Hi, there! How can I help ya'll today?" While she looked over the hem of a sundress to ascertain if she'd be able to fix the tear in the seam, Seth, Savannah, and Eva walked in. Sadie waved and offered them another dazzling smile, and she didn't notice the knowing smirk on either face. After telling her customer she'd have the dress repaired by that afternoon, Sadie bounced over to the three. "Good mornin!"

"Back at ya," Savannah said. "I take it you had a good night?"

Two pink spots appeared on her cheeks. "It was wonderful."

Eva had wandered away to look at the new jewelry items, and Seth raised an eyebrow at her blush. "I wasn't sure if you'd be in yet."

"I still have a business to run."

"So, Declan didn't stay over?"

The blush returned. "He did."

Savannah grinned. "I take it you had a good mornin, too."

"Savannah!" Sadie admonished with a laugh. "You're terrible."

"You're welcome."

She glanced over at Eva, concerned at what the younger women thought of last night. "How was she?"

"She's good. Madeline kidnapped her for a while, last night and again this mornin. We ate tons of junk food and stayed up too late. We had fun."

"I'm glad," Sadie said with a sigh of relief.

"I'm gonna do a coffee run. Can I get you both somethin?" Savannah asked.

"You just might be the perfect woman," Seth said.

"Sorry, buddy, it's too late to sweep me off my feet."

"I could take him."

"He's a fireman, so he could probably kick your butt."

"Them's high stakes. He treat you right?"

"That he does. In fact, I meant to tell you both last night before we got sidetracked," Savannah answered, raising an eyebrow at Sadie, "we're havin an engagement party next Friday. I'd love you both to come, your parents too."

"Sadie might even have a date," Seth said with a wink.

"She'd better. Okay, I'm gonna get that coffee. Back soon."

Once they were alone, Seth crossed his arms and studied his sister. "You do look happy."

"I am. I don't know what the hell I was waitin for."

"You put Eva first. That's what a parent does."

She looked over at the teen and nodded. "I suppose you're right."

"I have some news," Seth said, gaining her attention again. "When I didn't make the cut for that international job, my name was put in a different pool and... well, I've got an interview for a travelin position."

"That's amazin! And yet I'm sensin a 'but.'"

Seth had the decency to look sheepish. "But I would be based in Minneapolis."

"Oh, Seth. That would be wonderful and truly sucky at the same time. Are you seriously considerin it?"

"That I am."

She hugged him, even as her mood plummeted. "Well, then, congratulations."

Savannah came back in with three large coffees and a hot chocolate for Eva. "Thanks, sweetheart. I'll leave you two to talk. I've got work," he added when Savannah started to pout.

"You'll be at the engagement party, though?"

"You can count on it."

He turned to leave, but Sadie reached out to squeeze his arm. "Hey, Seth? Thank you."

With a wink over his shoulder, he called out a good-bye to Eva before heading out the door. Savannah put both hands on her hips and said, "All right, tell me all about it. And I mean all. Details, sister."

"I can't do that," Sadie said, straightening an already perfect display.

"Come on, I'm a committed woman. I need to live vicariously through you."

Sadie snuck another look at the back to make sure Eva was still preoccupied. "Okay, it was amazin. But Savannah, he told me he loved me."

Her jaw dropped. "Love? With a capital L?"

"Can you believe it? I can't. I feel like I'm walkin on a cloud. Declan loves me."

"So, this is, like, serious," Savannah said, studying Sadie. "Do you love him?"

"I do. I mean, I always have, but I love who he is now, too. He's a good man."

"He better be, or he'd have me to deal with."

"Oh, trust me, there'd be a line. I'm so happy, Savannah."

"Then I'm happy for you. Now, come on. How's he look naked?"

Sadie shook her head and walked away, but not before the image came to her mind and made her pulse race.

△ △ △

When Sadie woke Sunday morning, there was the smell of bacon frying in the air. Since bacon and coffee had about the same amount of rousing effect, she stood and, wrapping her robe around her waist, went to investigate.

The scene before her was one of beauty and chaos. Eva stood at the counter popping eggs into a large silver bowl while the bacon sizzled in a pan on the stove. Remnants of mushrooms, spinach, and onion were scattered across the granite countertop and something that looked like flour had been smeared across her cheek.

"Good mornin," Sadie said.

Looking up, as she hadn't heard Sadie come out of her room, Eva shot her a wide grin. "Good mornin."

"What have we here?"

"I thought I'd make you breakfast. Madeline showed me how," she answered, picking up two eggs and smacking them together to break the shell. Sadie knew the technique well, as it was one she'd learned herself from Madeline. Eva deftly held the uncracked egg in one hand while pouring out the cracked one into the bowl. With a wink, she said, "The *southern* way."

Sadie laughed and set to making a pot of coffee. "This is lovely, Eva. Thank you. And it smells delicious."

"I tried out that pancake batter you have. They're keepin warm in the oven."

Impressed, Sadie took a peek. Some were crumbled or burned, but most were golden brown, near-perfect circles.

"They look great," Sadie said, sliding onto the counter to wait for the coffee to drip through. "Where'd all the energy come from this mornin?"

Eva shrugged, concentrating on whisking the eggs. "I slept really well last night."

"No dreams?"

"None."

Sadie's heart lifted, but she forced herself to keep her cool. "I'm glad to hear it."

When there was enough coffee to warrant a cup, Sadie poured it and added her homemade creamer for flavor. "Anythin I can help with?"

"I've got this covered. Would you set the table?"

"Happy to."

Taking down the mismatched plates she'd picked out individually, Sadie set them out along with forks and handmade cloth napkins. After pouring a glass of freshly squeezed orange juice for Eva, Sadie grabbed the plate of pancakes from the oven while Eva slid omelets onto plates.

After she retrieved the bacon, Eva joined Sadie at the table and dug in. There was butter and maple syrup for the pancakes, which Eva wasn't shy about spreading all over her plate.

"This is delicious," Sadie praised around a mouthful of egg and vegetable. "Madeline would be proud."

Eva beamed and took a bite of bacon. "She's a good teacher."

"That she is," Sadie agreed easily. What a wonderful way to start the day. There was a subject she needed to broach but was unsure how Eva would take it. Might as well dive in. "Declan was wonderin if he could take us to the movies later today, maybe grab some dinner after. How would you feel about that?"

Eva met Sadie's eyes, a rarity for the young girl. There was such a depth to the deep blue, and a heartbreaking wisdom from the trials and wrongs she'd already witnessed in her life. "Are you sure you'd want me taggin along on what is essentially your first date?"

The girl was unnervingly astute. "It's not really our first date. And even if it was, yes, absolutely. Declan is important to me. I've cared about him longer than I care to admit. But, if you don't like him for some reason, or don't feel comfortable, I want you to tell me. We're in this together, and some stinky boy won't get between us. You understand?"

Eva looked surprised by her words, and more, that she could feel how much Sadie meant them. She really would give up her happiness—give up Declan—if Eva just said the words. "I understand. And I promise, I'll tell you the truth about how I feel. Luckily, I like Declan. He's pretty cool."

Sadie turned her attention back to her food. "I'm happy to hear it. Any homework to catch up on before we go, then?"

"Some math, and I have to finish an essay before Tuesday."

Standing to clear the emptied plates, Sadie said, "Go on, I'll clean up. Thank you so much for breakfast, it was delicious."

Eva ducked her head, equal parts pleased and embarrassed by the compliment, before rushing off to her room.

Chapter Twenty-Four

As girls were wont to do, Sadie took her time in getting ready for the day. After the shower she applied oils to her skin, light fruit and flower scents that she preferred. Wrapping her hair up on top of her head, she applied makeup for a subtle look before sliding on a light blue maxi dress with a vibrant flower pattern on the hem. The dolman sleeves flowed into a deep V neckline, where she rested one of her favorite necklaces made with rose quartz.

Releasing her hair from its knot, Sadie scrunched it with some mousse for a beachy look. Satisfied with her appearance, she grabbed her small clutch and went into the living room.

Eva still worked upstairs, so Sadie took the time to pick up a few stray items in the living area before settling into her favorite chair with a book. There she stayed until she heard a knock on the front door.

Not wanting to seem too eager, she slowly placed the bookmark between the pages and stood, smoothing down her dress before walking to the door. When she opened it, she found Declan leaning casually against the frame, a spray of daisies in his hand.

"Now if that isn't the perfect picture, I don't know what is," she said with a smile. Declan reached out and yanked her against him, pressing his lips to hers with a kind of soft urgency that had her blood on a low boil in an instant. Breathless, she pulled back and blinked up at him.

"And hello to you," he grinned, releasing his hold to offer up one of two bouquets he held. "These are for you."

"Beautiful," Sadie said, accepting the flowers and stepping back to allow him entrance while she found a vase. Eva appeared at the top of the stairs, and she offered Declan a tentative smile.

"Hi, sweetheart," Declan greeted her. When she reached halfway down the stairs, he held up the second bouquet of flowers. "These are for you."

"Really?" Eva said, reaching out hesitantly. No one had ever given her flowers before. "Thank you."

Sadie grabbed a second vase, offered it to Eva. "Would you like to keep them in your room? They would be a lovely thing to see first thing in the mornin and before you go to sleep."

"Sure," Eva answered, unable to hide her excitement. Taking the vase, she ran back up the stairs to set the flowers in water.

"That was just about the sweetest thing I've ever seen," Sadie told Declan, giving in to the temptation by sliding her arms around his waist. "Thank you."

"It was my pleasure," he said, cupping her face with his hands. "Beautiful women deserve beautiful flowers."

And then his mouth pressed against hers, and all thought flew out the window.

"No PDA when a child is present," Eva announced from the staircase. She'd added a purse to complete her outfit and smiled down at the couple embraced in the living room.

They stepped apart as if they were teenagers themselves, caught by their parents. Stifling a giggle, Eva came down the rest of the way and watched with amusement as Sadie blushed.

"No promises on the PDA," Declan responded with a little-boy grin. "But I'll try to keep it to a minimum."

"I guess that'll work," Eva said, pushing her dark hair away from her face. It was growing out, Declan noted. He was sure Sadie had helped with a special lotion or oil. He didn't know much about that sort of thing, but she seemed to have a knack with it.

"Let's go, then," he said. "The movies wait for no man."

They trudged outside, stopped on the sidewalk leading to the curb. Stared at Declan's beat-up truck, with no backseat. Sadie cleared her throat. "Maybe we should take my car?"

"There're three spots in the front," Declan said, quick to defend his ride.

The girls shared a look and Sadie nodded decisively. "We'll take mine."

Knowing when he'd been outmaneuvered, Declan followed them to the driveway, chivalrously opening the driver door for Sadie and the back door for Eva. When he settled into the passenger side, he looked around and had to admit it was the better choice for comfort.

They headed to the theater, Sadie listening as he made easy small talk with Eva. He asked about school, friends she'd made. Any hobbies and interests she'd picked up since living with Sadie.

"Sadie said I could try some things with stained glass this week," Eva said.

"She's gonna join me at the shop after school, maybe man the register here and there for some extra cash. She's been sketchin out some ideas for the glass, I think they'll be beautiful." Sadie caught the beaming smile in the rearview mirror and had one to match.

"I can't wait to see your work," Declan said. "Maybe I could bring some take-out by one of the nights this week, check it out."

"Not even done with one date and already anglin for another."

"A man's gotta try."

"If it matters, I'd like that," Eva spoke up.

Declan turned to face her, his features suddenly serious. "It does. It does matter."

Something passed between the two, and Eva nodded once. Satisfied they understood each other, Declan reached over and casually linked his hand with Sadie's. He couldn't put into words how it felt to be able to hold her soft hand under his rougher one, or to kiss her when he felt a whim. For so long he'd put her in the 'do not touch' file—the 'best friend's little sister' file—that it was almost a relief just to brush his fingers against her skin.

Sadie glanced over at him and he nearly lost himself in the soft gray gaze. Right now, her eyes were light, nearly silver. He'd been witness to their darkening, when she got angry or upset. They would turn the most stunning deep gray, like a storm on the horizon. There were times—would continue to be times—when he pushed and prodded, just to witness the change.

Her lips tipped up and suddenly his gaze riveted there, distracted by their shape and the way her tongue darted out nervously to swipe along the bottom half. He knew exactly the way she would taste when he pressed his mouth to hers, when his tongue traced that same path.

But he couldn't go any further down that path, not with Eva in the backseat. Today was about the three of them, and not his wayward thoughts whenever he looked at Sadie.

So, they went to the movies. Bought abundant amounts of popcorn, and Declan and Eva opted for iced drinks that would turn their tongues and mouths bright shades of blue. Sadie laughed and snapped pictures of them with their tongues hanging out, showing off their Smurf color.

And when Declan commandeered her hand as they walked from theater to restaurant, Sadie felt herself settle. For a moment, a flash of a vision swept through her mind. The three of them, walking just like this. Eva taller, her hair longer, the shadows gone from her eyes as she tossed them a grin over her shoulder. Another little girl, just a few years old, gripping Declan's opposite hand and gazing fondly up at him as if he were the very center of her universe. The young girl had dark hair and Sadie's own stormy blue eyes. A little boy on her hip, not yet a year old, tugging at the stray ends of her blonde hair.

Sadie gasped and stumbled, caught from total embarrassment by Declan's strong grip. With an arm around her back, Declan cupped her cheek and forced her gaze to his.

"What is it? Are you all right?"

Flustered, still embarrassed, Sadie tried to wave him off. "Yes, fine."

Eva watched her curiously, not seeming concerned so much by her stumble but by the way she'd lost all color in her cheeks. Feeling the need to help, Eva reached out, placed a palm against Sadie's forearm.

A strange sense of calm washed over and through her, and Sadie looked to Eva with wide, surprised eyes. So, they shared more than eye color alone. Eva had similar gifts. It was no wonder the girl shied away from physical touch.

"Thank you," Sadie murmured, knowing what it took for Eva to touch another, to soothe. "Thank you both. I must have tripped, but I'm fine."

Declan still looked concerned, for he also noted the lack of color in her cheeks and chest. Instead of focusing on it he merely nodded, and, wrapping an arm securely around her waist, led them all to the restaurant.

They were seated immediately, as it was still early for the dinner crowd. When Sadie ordered only a water to drink, Declan stepped in. "Hot tea as well, if you will. Two for us. Eva, would you like some?"

She shook her head. "I'd like a Coke."

"What kind, darlin?"

"Dr. Pepper, please."

When the waitress left and Sadie raised her eyebrow, Declan shrugged easily. "You look to be needin a bit of a pick-me-up."

"Thanks. Tea does sound amazin."

The waitress returned shortly with the drinks and a platter of tortilla chips with salsa and guacamole that Declan had added on as well. It was a farm-to-table type of place, so the chips were made fresh with visible grains, the salsa imbued with bright green cilantro and the guacamole tossed with perfectly ripe tomatoes.

Sadie took a chip heaping with guacamole and nearly moaned in satisfaction. Avocado was truly the best all-around food, if she had any say in it.

"A little pink has returned to your cheeks," Declan said. "A welcome sight."

"The tea was a good idea, as was the instant food. What looks good for dinner, Eva?"

"The deluxe grilled cheese," she answered. "And fries."

"An excellent choice," Declan said.

The waitress reappeared then, and after Eva ordered her sandwich, Sadie a pan-seared salmon, he opted for Korean beef tacos. There was quite the array on the menu, but he'd picked the place knowing Sadie would easily be able to find something to eat.

Declan continued to watch Sadie surreptitiously, waiting for her color to fully return and the spark in her eye when she laughed. He'd known her damn near all his life and knew there was more to the bewitching woman than met the eye. He couldn't grow up in a place like Louisiana, and work for so many years in the heart of it in New Orleans, without knowing a little something about the arcane.

Not the kind with long-bearded men wearing pointy hats, but something a little earthier. Sadie had always had a special knack for understanding people, for seeing their innermost thoughts and feelings. Sometimes she would get funny feelings about a route to stay away from, or a day it was best to stay home from school. She'd been able to warn Virginia about the baby.

Over time, he'd learned to listen to the seeming nonsense, as had many others. Whether because Sadie was so in tune with her surroundings, including people, that she picked up on signs others missed—or because she held something inside her that could only be classified as mystical, magical.

He didn't know then and he didn't know now, but she'd seen something on their walk from the movies that had affected her to her core. When they had a moment alone, he intended to find out what that something was.

There was also something in the way Eva had touched her, just briefly. It had been a surprising and welcome sight, to be sure, but there was something more to it. A flicker of understanding passed between the two of them in that moment, and it made him wonder. Perhaps these two were meant to be together. Perhaps they shared more than just the haunting gray eyes he'd been in love with since he'd been a boy.

After their meal, he talked the two ladies into a round of mini golf, followed by a trip to the arcade. Eva surprised him with a good arm at basketball, beating him out two out of three times. Sadie gave him a run for his money at an old street fighter game, though he won out in the end. Then the two of them paired up against him at air hockey, and the bright bursts of giggles nearly did him in.

He could see them, the three of them, making a life of it. Spontaneous outings such as this, love and laughter floating on the air like stardust in the night. Going home, to their home. Lying beside Sadie as the evening turned to night, making love with her until morning.

Curling up on the couch as she read, music flowing gently from the old record player she favored. Eva sprawled on the floor, homework spread out before her. His hand resting protectively against a growing bump under Sadie's shirt.

Yes, he could see it all, so plain and real he yearned for it. His smile faltered as for a moment he could barely breathe. An ache rose up for that pretty little picture, and a total fear of losing it before it had even begun.

The little plastic disk flew by his frozen hand, a squeal of delight rising above the cacophony of arcade games and music, other people's laughter and conversation.

Sadie and Eva performed a happy dance, as they'd scored the winning goal.

And Declan shook himself, released the thoughts but kept that image tucked away somewhere safe. Someday, somehow, he would make that pretty little picture come true. He swore it.

Chapter Twenty-Five

Sadie and Declan sat in the little swing in her garden, a glass of wine for her and a beer for him. Eva had gone upstairs, spending some alone time before bed. The moon shone down and they listened to the happy tune of crickets for entertainment.

With his arm around her shoulders, Sadie found it easy to snuggle into Declan, borrowing his warmth. She took a sip of wine, sighed contentedly. "Thank you, for a wonderful day. Eva enjoyed it as well."

"It was my pleasure."

She hesitated, then asked, "Will you stay tonight?"

"I would love to, but do you think it's too soon? For Eva?"

"You're right," Sadie conceded. "I don't want you to be right, but you're right."

They were quiet for a while, enjoying the night, the drink, the company. Declan wasn't sure how to broach the subject, but it needed to be discussed. "About what happened earlier—you saw somethin, didn't you?"

Sadie stilled beside him, her heart hammering double time. Focusing on her glass, she tried for nonchalance. "What do you mean?"

"Sadie," Declan said firmly, taking her chin until her eyes met his. "You think I don't recognize it by now? When you see somethin none of the rest of us do?"

"We never—we never talked about it."

"No, for it was just a part of you. But things are different now, and I think it's time we did."

She searched his gaze a long while, judging if he truly wanted to know. If he could handle it. His remained steady on hers, strong. Her heart steadied, returned to its normal pace.

"All right," she said with a sigh, shifting in her seat to face him more fully. "When I make contact with another person, sometimes I get... impressions, feelins, about them. Sometimes, especially when I'm close to that person, I'll get more than that."

"Like visions?"

"That's a way of lookin at it. Some are clearer than others. Some I can tell are a possibility, some are absolute."

"And the one today?" Declan prompted after a pregnant silence. "Was it clear, absolute?"

"Yes."

"Can I know what it was?"

A strained look came over her face. "I'm not sure how you'll react."

"Because it involved me." She nodded. "Well, perhaps this will help. I had a vision of sorts, too."

"You did?" she asked, head cocked.

"I did. I looked over at you and Eva, laughin together as you beat me handily at air hockey. And suddenly I could see us, all gathered together here, in your livin room. Eva spread out on the floor with all her bookwork, you snugglin against me on the couch. My hand"—here he placed his palm against her quivering stomach—"just like this, restin over a life we'd made together."

Sadie's mouth popped open, her breath coming in short, quick little gasps. She barely managed a question through her strangled throat. "Doesn't that scare you?"

"Terrifies me. Excites me. The picture of the two of you—the three of us—put a little ache, right here." He lifted her hand to his chest, smoothed it out against his heart. Pressed her palm to the steady, rhythmic beat. "It's not that I'm ready for all that right now, or tomorrow, or even a month from now. But the fact that I know, deep down, that's where we're headed—well, nothin could make me happier."

Sadie placed her free hand now against her stomach, as Declan had done, gazed down at it with hazy eyes. When she spoke, her words were barely above a whisper. "A little girl. And later, a little boy. We were walkin down the same street as today. The little girl, she held your hand and was so in love with you. Her hair matched yours, but she had my eyes. The little boy on my hip, still in diapers. He was the spittin image of you." She lifted her eyes now, met his. Clouds swirled in their stormy depths. "Eva was taller, her hair longer. There was light in her eyes; all the shadows were gone. That, almost more than anythin, made my heart fill."

"I want that for her. I want that for all of us."

Nodding, Sadie agreed. She couldn't help but agree. "Me, too."

"She has the gift too, doesn't she?" Declan asked.

"I didn't fully realize it until today. The signs were there, I should have known, but she held herself back."

"Don't blame yourself for that. No, don't. If anythin, the fact that she felt comfortable enough with you today to show herself, that should mean the world."

Nodding again, Sadie looked at the situation in a new light. He was right, of course. But there was still a little part of her that thought she should have known. "It does. You're right, there's nothin we can do about the past. Goin forward, I'll make sure to help her, guide her. Goodness knows I could have used some of that at her age."

"Your parents?"

"They don't know. Sure, I go to church with them when they can finagle it, even believe and enjoy it a bit. But you know that's not the religion I follow. They don't know," she repeated.

"Tell me about what you believe, what you follow."

Taking a moment to think it through, Sadie began with the basics. "I've always felt connected to the elements. Earth, especially, but the others as well. Add in the strange feelins I would get every so often, and it was inevitable I looked into witchcraft. I did a lot of readin, a lot of research growin up. Came across Wiccans. Realized they'd gotten a bad rep over the years—mostly thanks to Christians tryin to take over the world—and found I connected to their followins in a way I never could, or would, with the church."

"You'll forgive my ignorance, but isn't Wicca and witchcraft the same thing?"

"Not exactly. To be a witch, a person can believe in anythin or nothin, practice for good or evil. To be a Wiccan is to also follow the rules of Paganism—the rules of nature. A balance to all things. Gods and goddesses, light and dark. Respectin the elements, followin the moon phases."

"So, a Wiccan is a witch, but a witch isn't necessarily a Wiccan?"

"That's right!" Sadie grinned, relaxed a little. "I've got a bit of an eclectic path, in that I study so many different religions and followins and keep little bits of each that speak to me. In general, I respect the elements, ask the gods and goddesses for help, and use stones and herbs for their healin properties."

"And now you'll teach Eva, allow her to choose her own path?"

"Of course. She has trouble makin physical contact with others—I did too, for a time. It's easier to read people through touch, and sometimes you can get swamped by feelins, emotions. There are ways of lessenin that. I thought she was averse to touch because of—well, other things. And while that might still be true, I think this has a lot to do with it, too."

Thinking through that, Sadie realized, as an empath, as she suspected Eva to be, any physical blows would carry with them the rage and brutality of that person's personality. The thought of what Eva had been through made her doubly sick.

Looking up at Declan, she realized his thoughts had gone in the same direction as hers. His fists had tightened, his shoulders tensed. There was a dangerous glint in his eyes.

On instinct Sadie reached up, stroked away the stark anger showing on his face. "Hey now, it's all right. She's with me now, with us. Between the two of us, we'll protect her, see to it that she blossoms into the young woman I saw in my vision today. I'll show her what it means to be in a family that loves and encourages, that understands. You'll show her what a man should be."

"It's a tough lot to swallow, bein unable to find the person responsible and show them the same kindness."

"More violence solves nothin," Sadie said, placing a hand over his.

In her world, perhaps. But Declan knew there were times that wasn't necessarily true. Knowing it was best to keep these particular thoughts to himself, he simply leaned forward, closing the gap between his lips and hers as he'd been desperate to do all damn day.

Her mouth opened with a soft sigh and he fed as a man starved. She was so responsive to him it nearly drove him mad.

His arms circled her waist, pulled her into his lap. With a laugh she shook her hair back, straddling his thighs with a sparkle in her gray eyes. "I'm not sure this swing is strong enough for this."

"If we fall, we fall together," he said before yanking her back.

She pressed close as she matched his hungry need kiss for kiss. His hands slid from her waist, brushed softly against the sides of her breasts. With a moan she arched into him, forgetting for a moment they were outdoors with Eva just upstairs.

When she pulled away again, rested her temple against his hair, he pressed his face against the delicate curve of her neck and inhaled her scent. He would never tire of the light, flowery aroma that was so wholly Sadie. She took a deep breath, sighed happily with just a tinge of frustration. He understood perfectly well her sentiment.

Lifting his head so he could look at her straight on, he asked, "Could I bring you lunch tomorrow?"

"That would be lovely," she said. "I close the shop from one to two and usually end up workin in the back."

"I'll meet you there at one o'clock, then."

"It's a date," she said, the twinkle back in her eye.

Though it was the last thing he wanted, Declan released his hold, allowed her to stand. Stood himself. "Until tomorrow."

Then, because he couldn't do otherwise, he grabbed her again, left her with something to dream of that night.

Sadie saw him out, her bones feeling like mush from his talented mouth. She stood in the doorway, a hand to her lips as if holding the taste of him there, savoring it. And once he'd disappeared down the road, finally turned and went back inside.

It was time to speak with Eva, to talk of things only the two of them understood. Making her way up the stairs, Sadie stood just outside Eva's door and knocked softly, not wanting to barge in.

"Come in," Eva called out.

Pushing open the door, Sadie found Eva curled up in her lavender chair with a book in her hands. A pretty picture, all in all. "Declan's gone home, he wanted me to tell you goodnight."

"Oh, he's not stayin?"

The directness of the question took Sadie by surprise. "No. Would it be all right with you if he did?"

Eva shrugged. "Sure. He's your boyfriend now, isn't he?"

"I suppose so," Sadie said, settling on the edge of the bed. "We didn't really speak to that, but I'm sure he wouldn't mind the title."

Raising her brows, Eva looked at Sadie with incredulity. "I don't think so either. He's totally head-over-heels for you."

With a happy laugh, Sadie dropped her chin into her hand. "As I am for him."

"You're wonderin if I'm okay with this."

"I am."

"And I am. He's a good guy."

"The best." They were quiet for a moment before Sadie broached the next subject. "Eva, earlier—when I stumbled, and you placed your hand on my arm—can we talk about that?"

The younger girl instantly closed off, her face practically shuttering with it. Hunching in on herself, she responded without making eye contact. "I don't know what you mean."

"Eva, sweetie, it's all right. There's nothin wrong with you, I promise it. I have some abilities, too, and I just want to help you with yours."

Her eyes flicked up, just for a moment. "What do you mean?"

Now Sadie held her hand out, palm up. "When I touch others, I can get a sense of their feelins, their emotions. Sometimes, I'll get more than that—things that might or could happen." Interested now, Eva looked up, met her gaze steady. Rubbed her fingers nervously against her leg. "You took away some of my pain earlier. Did you do that on purpose, or is that somethin that just happens?"

Blowing out a breath, Eva said, "Most of the time it just happens. I knew it would when I touched you, that's part of the reason I avoid bein touched."

Neither mentioned the other reason, not aloud. "If you'd like, I can teach you how to control it. How to control when it happens, or at least dim the effects. Would you like that?"

"Really?" Eva sat straight now, a twirl of hope dancing across her eyes. "Yes, I would like that very much."

With a smile, Sadie stood. "Okay, we'll start lessons tomorrow, after school and after we've finished at the shop. Sound good?"

"Yes," she answered. "Thank you, Sadie."

"Anytime, sweetheart," Sadie said, fighting against the urge to pull her into a hug. "Anytime."

Chapter Twenty-Six

After dropping Eva off at school, Sadie went straight to the shop to get some work done before the doors opened. Eventually, she would need to hire some new help. She'd already put some feelers out, but the right person would come along—she just knew it—at the right time.

Time flew as she sanded and primed a matching set of bedside tables, grabbed another cup of coffee as she unlocked the doors and pushed them open wide, enjoying the little bit of cool wind while it lasted.

After setting out the collapsible chalkboard sign that offered a cheery greeting, Sadie sank down on the stool behind the counter where she worked on small things during open hours. Sorting through a collection of stones she'd already drilled holes in, she selected a few and grabbed her pliers to do some wire wrapping. The array of jewelry Sadie kept in a display by the counter tended to move quickly, and it kept her fingers busy while she waited for customers.

Her tablet beeped and she glanced down, happy to see an online order come through. She kept that stock separate, just in case two people had an interest at the same time. Sadie rotated the stock weekly, wanting to keep everything fresh both online and in-store. Since the place currently stayed empty of customers, she went to her shelves to find the large ceramic bowl with a riot of flowers she'd hand-painted earlier that year and began to pack it for shipping.

The day went on, a few stragglers coming to browse here and there but overall low-key for a Monday. Gave her plenty of time to replenish low stock.

A few minutes to one o'clock, with the door now closed against the afternoon heat, Sadie glanced up at the happy clang of bells as someone entered. Smiled big and bright when she saw who it was, and that he carried takeout in his hand.

"My hero," she said with a dramatic sigh. "Smells delicious."

"Thank you," Declan replied, wrapping an arm around her waist to bring her in for a kiss.

"I meant the food."

"Sure you did."

Shaking her head, she went and locked the door and put up her lunch sign. Sadie invited him upstairs, to the space she'd first lived in but now used as a breakroom. The futon remained, as did a little round table painted bright turquoise, with two red wooden chairs that had a diamond design across the back in the same blue color.

"Coffee, water?" Sadie asked, taking the bags from Declan and setting out plates.

"Coffee if you have it. Cute space."

"Thanks. I'm hopin one day it'll be shared by more than just me, but..."

Her remaining thoughts were cut off as she was grabbed and spun, pressed against the counter. Declan lifted her easily and leaned close. Their tongues dueled as his wandering hands explored.

His thumbs brushed against her breasts and he reveled in her intake of breath. His hands slid up her thighs, under the sweet pink dress she wore, found her hot and ready for him. With little effort he lifted her, brought her to the couch. Blanketed her body with his.

It was fast and needy, the tension built up from the day before seeking release. They moved together with such synchronicity it was as if they'd been built for the other. He joined them with one smooth, deep thrust; felt her shudder and sigh. As he picked up the pace she met him stroke for stroke, taking even as she gave. Cried out with the sheer force of it.

Her womb clenched, her fingers gripping his shoulders. She arched back as the first wave washed over her, clung to him as it threatened to take her away. His own hoarse cry sounded like music in her ears.

They remained as they were, their breath heavy and hearts pounding. Declan eased back, looked down at her soft, relaxed features. Her eyes blinked open, hazy with satisfaction.

"On second thought," she said in a husky whisper, "havin the breakroom to ourselves is just as well." He chuckled, kissing her swollen lips because he couldn't do otherwise. When he shifted up and helped her sit, she looked around, her arms and legs still shaky. "Mm. Give me a minute, I'm not sure I can stand yet."

Declan managed it, pulled on his jeans. Handed her the dress.

Staring at it, she accepted the clothing with a wry smile. "I don't remember that comin off."

"You were distracted, understandably," Declan said before walking over to finish plating the food himself. Found the coffee, thankfully, and set it all on the table.

A little unsteady, Sadie stood, pulled on her dress. Wrapping her arms around Declan's waist, she lifted her mouth for a kiss. "You can come by for lunch anytime."

"I might just take you up on that."

Laughing, she sat down and took a bite of blackened fish tacos. There was an order of chips and salsa—one of her favorites—and he'd gotten a side of steamed broccoli for her, fries for himself. She snuck one, having a weakness for fried potato, but loved the fact that he paid attention to her way of eating. "This is all delicious, thank you again."

"You're very welcome. I have an affinity for orderin food, not so much for the cookin."

"Well, then, I think you'll have to come over for dinner. Are you free tomorrow?"

"I could move some things," he said, and she knew he was teasing her. "Can I bring anythin?"

"I wouldn't say no to a bottle of wine," she said. Then after a brief pause continued, "Eva and I spoke last night. We're gonna work on some things after we close up here, otherwise I'd invite you over tonight."

"Not to worry. This is important, plus I've got some work."

Stabbing a broccoli with her fork, Sadie watched her meal as she asked, "Would you stay over tomorrow?"

"You think Eva would be all right with that?"

"As it happens, I do. She asked why you didn't stay last night."

"She did?" Startled, Declan set down his last taco.

"She's a smart girl. She thought it was natural, seein as you are my boyfriend now." Sadie looked up at him under her long lashes, judging his reaction. He sat frozen, staring at her as if she'd grown two heads.

"Boyfriend," he finally murmured. "I hadn't thought about it, but I suppose that's what I am. That would make you my girlfriend."

Unable to fight the smile anymore, Sadie answered, "One usually follows the other."

"Sadie Nichols is my girlfriend. Huh. Has a nice ring to it, don't you think?"

"Declan Park is my boyfriend. You're right, that does sound nice."

They shared a goofy grin and finished their meals.

When Declan left, he pulled Sadie in for a toe-curling, heat-building kiss that left her dazed and stumbling for balance. The man knew how to kiss, that was for damn sure.

Flipping her sign back to OPEN, Sadie busied herself rearranging displays, selecting new items to be showcased. An older woman came in to browse, followed by a group of younger ones. The afternoon turned hectic and before she knew it, Eva walked through the doors, book bag in hand.

"Hi sweetheart, how was your day?"

"Fine," Eva answered, looking around. "What can I do to help?"

"Would you wrap up these glasses while I help the next customer?"

Eva nodded, stowed her bag behind the desk and laid the first wine glass on a large sheet of paper. Sadie smiled at the woman purchasing a dozen of her hand-painted pieces and thanked her, assuring her that Eva would have them wrapped up in no time.

Once the line dwindled a bit, Eva went around refilling the candle selection, put out some of the jewelry designs Sadie had created that morning. Tidied up a selection of pillows that had gone astray when two rambunctious kids got bored while their mom shopped.

Thank goodness it was just pillows, Sadie thought as she helped an older man finagle a side table out the front door. His wife had spotted it late last week, and wouldn't stop talking about it. He'd decided to surprise her with it this evening for their anniversary. The thought made Sadie grin, and she gifted him a pink candle called 'romance' with a wink as she'd rung him up.

At five past seven, five minutes after they officially closed, there were still three people in line to purchase items. Showing the last person out at quarter after, Sadie turned the lock and sign on the door before sinking down to the floor right there, a happy sigh on her lips. "Well now, that was quite the day. Thank goodness you came in to help."

Eva grabbed two bottles of water, handed one to Sadie and sank down crossed-legged in front of her. "No kiddin. That's great it was so busy, but man I'm wiped."

"Did you even get a snack?" Sadie asked, worried she was starving the already too-thin girl.

"A granola bar on the walk over. I'm pretty hungry now, though."

Sadie nodded, gathered her remaining strength and stood. "I'll leave the mess for the mornin. Let's get some dinner, we've still got work to do tonight."

"We don't have to—" Eva began, but Sadie shook her head firmly.

"No, I promised, and this is important. Don't worry, some proper food and we'll feel good as new."

They left together, piled into Sadie's SUV. When they reached their home, Sadie pulled out leftover stew and heated enough in a pot to feed six. Tossing together a salad for herself and toasting bread for Eva, Sadie stirred absent-mindedly, humming a bright tune as her thoughts strayed toward Declan.

She'd fallen for him as a child, and hadn't felt anywhere near the same for anyone since. Even though she'd given up on ever being more to him than his best friend's little sister, there was always that little seed of hope that had refused to die.

Now, not only were they amazing together—*amazing*—but he'd told her he loved her.

Ladling stew into two deep bowls, Sadie grinned at Eva as she set down the quick meal. Having Eva here, and Declan in her heart, she couldn't imagine being any happier.

"Oh, no," Eva said, staring at Sadie with consternation. "Has exhaustion gotten to your head? Are you gettin loopy?"

Letting out a loud chuckle, Sadie shook her head. "No, just happy. To have you, Declan. My life is just about perfect."

"Boys make girls weird," Eva decided, ripping off a chunk of bread to dunk it into the stew.

Laughing again, Sadie shrugged but had to agree. Weird, indeed.

They caught up as they ate, avoiding the subject of magic and witches for the time being. They'd get to it soon enough, and Sadie wanted to give her young charge a bit of normalcy first.

After cleaning up the little bit of mess, Sadie disappeared upstairs for a few minutes before coming back down, a small copper bowl in one hand along with other objects Eva could only guess at.

"Come on," Sadie said, leading her to the back door. "This will work better outside."

Stopping along the way to breathe in the scents of her garden, Sadie picked a few herbs to bring with before snagging a small table and moving to the center of the grass. They were well hidden here, in her little backyard paradise, between the tall wooden fence and towering trees. After setting out the objects meticulously along the tabletop, Sadie stood, hands clasped, and looked to Eva.

"First off, I guess I should explain a bit about what I believe. I'm a Wiccan. What that means, is that I believe in nature, in the balance of all things. But I also practice witchcraft." Eva's eyes widened, just slightly. Sadie understood the look and quickly moved on. "Witchcraft is not evil, as so many movies and texts would have you believe. It just is. The person who practices can use it for good or evil, like most things. All I do, I do for the good. I hope you choose the same."

"Of course," Eva said immediately. "I mean, I would rather do good."

Sadie nodded, her face serious. She knew that this girl had seen evil, had survived it. And would do anything to never face it again.

"I'm glad. You get what you put into it. Witchcraft can be practiced by anyone. We use offerins, such as these herbs. Symbols, like the candle or the pentagram. Items to represent the elements—earth, air, fire, water, and spirit." Sadie touched the herbs, lit a stick of incense and the candle, touched the water that had been placed in the copper bowl, then a silver pentagram in turn. "Earth represents the north, Air the east, Fire the south, and Water the west. Spirit is the center, the self."

Next, Sadie lifted a pretty purple stone, passed it through the incense smoke. Murmured a cleansing spell before placing it in Eva's left hand.

"Your non-dominant hand receives energy. For now, just hold the amethyst, wrap your fingers tightly around it without squeezin. Close your eyes, feel the pulse of the stone."

Eva did as Sadie instructed, taking slow breaths. After a minute her eyes popped open in surprise. "I can feel it!"

"Good," Sadie said, proud of the younger woman. "That's the stone's energy. Anythin from nature will have an energy, a pulse. Before handin it to you, I cleansed it of its previous uses, for it's yours now."

"What? Really?"

"Yes. Amethyst is a groundin stone, it will help you feel calm and balanced. It's also known for protectin against psychic attack. That includes bein swamped with other's emotions."

Marveling at the beautiful stone held in her palm, Eva stroked it reverently. "It's just like my locket."

"Your favorite color and your birthstone. It will be incredibly powerful for you. In fact, do you have your necklace with you?" Eva nodded and slipped it from her neck. She'd worn it every day since receiving it. Sadie continued, "All right, place it in your right hand. You'll use your dominant hand to transfer your energy, your wishes, into the stone."

Taking a deep breath, Sadie closed her own eyes once Eva had transferred the stone and held out her hands, palms up. "Goddess of the Moon, we seek you this night. God of the sun, lend us your might. Protect Eva from the emotions of others as she seeks her new path. Guide her into the light and save her from evil's wrath. Goddess of night, god of light, this I ask of thee. As I will, so mote it be!"

For a moment the candle shone brighter as a gust of wind blew Eva's short hair away from her face. The stones pulsed in her fist as she stared, wide-eyed, at her cousin. Sadie's head tipped down and for a moment when her eyes opened, storms swirled in the deep gray. Then, she smiled, and all that was left was a gentle hum in the air.

"The stones are imbued with power and strength. Keep them with you, they will help protect you against unwanted emotions of others, and it will also help you focus as your power grows."

"*My* power? Holy cow, Sadie, I didn't know you could do that!"

With a light smile, Sadie answered, "I didn't. You did."

Chapter Twenty-Seven

For a long time after going to bed Eva lay awake, watching the purple stone still in her fist. Her locket rested softly against her chest, where it would remain. She could feel the strength of its energy beating at her, and it was a comforting thing. Bright, steady. Too many things, and people, in her life had not been so steady, so comforting.

Sadie was different. Not just her witchy powers—and wow, did she have them. But the way she spoke to Eva as an equal, and her obvious love for her. Eva was careful not to touch others, but the love shining out of Sadie, even without physical touch, was difficult to ignore.

She slipped easily into a dreamless sleep, waking feeling fully refreshed for the first time in a long time. And for the first time ever, Eva dressed with excitement for school. There were a couple of nice kids who always said hi to her, but Eva had always been careful to keep her distance. One accidental touch and she'd be swamped with emotions that weren't hers.

Too often, she'd see and know things she should have no way of knowing. At her old school, she'd always been known as an outcast. Not just because of the bruises she tried to hide, or how many times she'd been forgotten about by her mom after an activity.

She just found it easier to stay away from everyone instead of making any kind of connection. She'd learned the hard way that even kids who acted nice to your face didn't always have nice thoughts.

Slipping the chunk of amethyst into the pocket of her jeans and touching the one around her neck in reassurance, Eva grabbed her bookbag and bounded down the stairs. Sadie greeted her with a smile as she plated scrambled eggs and toast.

"Good mornin, sweetheart. How did you sleep?"

"Really good," Eva answered with a genuine grin. "I think it worked."

"Happy to hear it. Do you have the stone with you?"

"In my pocket," she said, pulling it out as proof.

Sadie nodded. "Take it easy today, but it should help shield you against unwanted feelins."

"I will." Sadie smiled happily at the response, and the appetite. Eva wolfed down her breakfast and actually seemed eager to go to school. She bounced up from the table and hunted down her shoes. "Can we go now? We're doin that 'little buddies' program today and I need to turn in an essay before we go."

"That will be so fun. You're goin over to Westdale, right?"

"That's right. We'll be matched up with a first grader when we get there."

"I'm ready when you are."

Together they walked out to the car. Eva stayed quiet on the drive, though she still vibrated energy. When Sadie pulled up to the curb, Eva hesitated in getting out. "Can I—can I try somethin?"

"What's that, sweetheart?"

"Can I touch your arm? Without you blockin me?" Sadie nodded, held her breath. After a brief hesitation, Eva placed her palm on Sadie's forearm, her brows creased in concentration. Eva sighed in relief. "It's workin. I got nothin from you until I opened myself up."

"That's wonderful. Just remember, take it slow today. The amethyst is there to help you channel your gift, but it's not foolproof. I wouldn't recommend a group hug or anythin."

Eva shuddered dramatically. "Never."

"Have a great day, sweetie. I'll see you at the shop after school."

With a wave Eva stepped out of the car and faced the school. Realized that, for the first time in her life, she didn't have to be afraid of normal interactions with other kids. She wouldn't have to flinch away from her teachers, or find a seat by herself at lunchtime for fear of bumping elbows. Sadie had given her a brand-new lease on life.

After turning in her essay, Eva made her way to the cafeteria where the rest of the group going to the elementary school would be waiting. She stood in the back of the crowd already gathered, suddenly unsure of herself. One successful arm touch couldn't undo years of avoidance.

One girl Eva recognized from a few of her classes turned, offered a small smile. Her soft red hair, like Eva's, had been cut short but had a naturally curly wave that fell just past her chin. When the girl smiled it bunched her freckled nose and lit her mossy eyes covered by purple frames.

To Eva's surprise, the girl walked straight over and introduced herself. "Hi, I'm Megan. You're Eva, aren't you?"

"That's right."

"Pleased to meet you, official-like. We have some classes together."

"I recognize you," Eva admitted before lapsing back into silence. She realized she had no idea how to hold a conversation with someone her own age. Luckily, Megan didn't seem to have that problem.

"You're new here, aren't you? I was new at the beginnin of the year. I'm from New Orleans, what about you?"

"Baton Rouge, just a different school."

"Oh, that's cool. Do you miss your old friends?"

"I didn't really have any."

"Well, you have one now," Megan said with a grin. "Want to sit with me on the bus?"

Eva nodded as the teacher began to speak. They lined up and headed outside, where a bus waited for them to load. Megan got on first then patted the seat beside her in invitation. Taking a steadying breath, Eva stuck her hand in her pocket and wrapped her fingers around her stone before sitting, prepared to brush arms.

"I just love gettin out of school for the day, don't you? And we get to do this three more times this year. Plus, our buddies come visit us twice."

"That is nice," Eva answered.

"What kind of music do you like?"

Thrown off by the question, Eva shrugged. Megan dug into her bookbag and pulled out her phone, along with earbuds. "I've got everythin on here. I can play you my favorites and see what you like. If we have the same taste in music, we'll have to be best friends."

Best friends. Eva liked the idea of that. After plugging in the earbuds and handing one over to Eva, Megan scrolled to find the first song to play. When the drums blared over the tiny speaker, Eva jumped before settling in to listen. Halfway through she smiled tentatively over at Megan. "I like it."

"Oh, good. I would have kicked you out if you hadn't," her new friend said with a giggle.

They managed to get through three songs before the bus pulled up in front of Westdale. Eva led the way off the bus, then huddled with the rest of the group in front of the school. Thirty kids had signed up to be big brothers and sisters, to match the amount of kids in Mr. Parrish's first grade class.

Mrs. Monroe, Eva's teacher, brought the group inside. They passed by several classes in session, garnering curious glances from the kids inside. When they reached a small gymnasium, they were told to sit on a set of bleachers.

Megan slid in beside Eva, her knees bouncing with excitement. "I hope I get a cool kid. Not one that picks their nose or just wants to talk about superheroes or somethin."

"You hafta be pretty smart to get in here. They probably don't pick their nose."

"Okay, then I hope I get a girl. Boys are weird."

At that, Eva had to agree. After a few minutes, led by a tall man with a friendly smile, the first graders filed in. They sat across from Eva's group, all giggles and nervous bouncing. Mr. Parrish greeted Mrs. Monroe before raising his voice loud enough for everyone to hear.

"Welcome to Westdale, big buddies! I'm Fallon Parrish, but that's Mr. Parrish to those of you under eighteen. To start off, we'll be pairin all buddies off and you'll have a few minutes to get to know each other. After that, we'll start in on some activities we have planned." Mr. Parrish pulled out a piece of paper and began calling out names. Once both students paired off and found a spot to sit, he called out the next. "Megan Lafontaine and Molly Jo Rivard."

"I got a girl!" Megan whispered excitedly before jumping up to meet her little buddy.

Eva waited patiently for her name to be called. When they'd been dwindled down to the last handful, Mr. Parrish finally said, "Evaline Wentworth and Arabella Hoyt."

Standing, Eva stepped down to the gym floor and spotted her little buddy doing the same. Arabella had to be the most beautiful little girl Eva had ever seen. She had long, curly black hair and huge, dazzling green eyes that sparked with intelligence. Arabella's teal and white lace dress perfectly offset her dusky gold skin and Eva immediately felt underdressed.

They met in the middle where Arabella curtsied—*curtsied*—and introduced herself. "Pleased to meet you. I'm Arabella Hoyt."

"I'm Eva," she said, feeling hugely out of place. Gesturing toward the other side of the gym, she asked, "Want to sit down?"

With a regal nod, Arabella said, "Thank you kindly."

While they walked over to join the already paired buddies, Eva caught sight of Megan and Molly sitting on the floor—both wearing jeans—and laughing like they'd known each other for years. Following Arabella to a spot on the bleachers near a few other groups, Eva sat and wondered what in the world they were supposed to talk about.

"You like school?"

"Of course," Arabella replied primly. "Don't you?"

"I like learnin."

Tilting her head, Arabella searched Eva's face as if she could find the answer to the universe there. "I don't understand. You learn at school."

"Yeah, you do." Eva sighed, wishing she'd kept her mouth shut.

"But you don't like school."

"It's okay."

"You don't like the other kids?"

Eva stared at the younger girl. How'd she figure that out? "They haven't always been nice to me."

After thinking about that for a minute, Arabella smiled happily. "I'll be nice to you."

"Thanks, I guess. How old are you?"

"Six. How old are you?"

"Thirteen."

"Do you like to sew?"

"I've never really sewed. My cousin—well, she's sort of my mom now- she does."

"Sort of your mom?"

"She's adoptin me."

"What happened to your real mom?"

"She's... sick."

"What about your dad?"

"I never knew him."

Arabella pursed her lips. "Me either. I mean, I knew him when I was real little, but he died."

"I'm sorry," Eva said, feeling completely inadequate to handle this.

"It's okay. I like to sew. I made this." She smoothed down the skirt of her dress, looked proudly up at Eva. "Does your cousin-mom make clothes?"

"Sometimes. She's got a whole store of stuff she makes. I help out there sometimes. She promised to show me how to make stained glass this week."

"That sounds fun. Ms. Trudeau shows me all kinds of stuff. We've never tried stained glass before."

"Who's Ms. Trudeau?"

"She takes care of me when my mom works. She cooks and cleans the house, and always bakes me cookies."

"That sounds nice. It's a beautiful dress."

Her beaming smile returned. "Thank you."

Mr. Parrish announced their next activity, so Eva and Arabella joined the others in collecting worksheets from the teachers. They spent the morning getting to know each other, problem solving, and playing games.

Just before lunch, the first-grade students brought their older buddies to their classroom and showed them their desks. Eva wasn't at all surprised to find a perfectly neat work space, and several books that seemed too advanced for someone Arabella's age. She'd certainly proven herself to be anything but ordinary.

"Can you keep a secret?" Arabella asked after the desk tour ended.

"Sure."

"Mr. Parrish is gonna marry my mom."

"Really?" Eva asked, glancing up at the teacher. He looked older than Sadie—maybe closer to Seth and Declan's age. She wasn't much of a judge of boys, but he had a nice smile and kind eyes. "Are they datin?"

"Oh, no, they haven't met yet. But once they do, they're gonna get married."

Eva grinned at Arabella's secret plan. "I promise not to say a word."

Chapter Twenty-Eight

Picking out upbeat music for the day, Sadie opened the doors wide and began to refill stock by the checkout. Declan had spent the night again, the third time that week. Had it only been a week? Everything with him seemed so easy, so natural, it felt like he'd been in her life all along.

She still couldn't believe how well Declan and Eva got along. It had begun the moment they met, back at the Fourth of July barbecue. It seemed she had worried for nothing. Eva sat at the work table in the main room, fiddling with her latest stained-glass project. She was a natural, for sure.

A little girl burst in, her large, bright green eyes taking in every detail before latching on to Eva. With a little yelp she ran over and wrapped the surprised teen in a hug.

"Arabella, careful now. You've interrupted her work."

"Sorry!" Arabella said, stepping back with no less excitement. "Eva, this is my mama. Mama, this is Eva."

"Pleased to meet you," Eva said, standing but not getting any closer. Sadie stepped over to help smooth over any awkwardness.

"Hi there, I'm Sadie."

"You're Eva's aunt-mom.   Pleased to make your acquaintance," Arabella said, dropping into a curtsy.

"I'm Autumn, Arabella's mom. Sorry about that."

"Not at all. Eva told me all about you, Arabella. I'm so glad you got to come in today. Eva can show you around if you like. Autumn, can I get you somethin to drink?"

"Coffee? You're a godsend."

Understanding, Sadie led the way to the drink cart and poured it herself. "Cream or sugar?"

"Yes to both. This is a lovely shop. How long have you been open?"

"A few months now. Did online orders before that."

"I'm a bit envious. I couldn't sew to save my life."

"Hopefully it never comes down to that. What do you do for work?"

"I'm the Chief of Litigations for the District Attorney's office."

"Tell you what, when you need somethin sewn, you come to me. And when I need law advice, I'll come to you."

"That's a deal," Autumn said with a laugh. Sadie held out the cup of coffee, which she accepted gratefully. Their fingers brushed and Sadie's eyes went hazy.

Four women stood with her at the points of a star. Savannah and Autumn. Two others she'd yet to meet, one petite with a pixie cut, the other a dark beauty who looked strangely familiar. Power hummed in the air and shook the earth.

And then she was back in her shop, a concerned Autumn gripping her arm. "Sadie? You all right?"

She blinked Autumn back into focus and let out a long breath. The vision hadn't told her much, but the feeling stuck with her. Something was coming. "Yeah. Fine. Thanks. Just a bit dizzy for a second there."

"Come on, have a seat. Should I call a doctor?"

"No, no I'm fine. Just need a minute."

Eva'd seen what had happened. She recognized the hazy look of a vision. She bent to Arabella. "Call your mom over here. I need a minute with Sadie."

"Sure thing. Mama? Can you come look at this?"

Eva approached Sadie and smiled reassuringly at Autumn. "I'll stay with her."

"All right. I'll be right back."

When Autumn was out of earshot, Eva offered her hand. "Let me help."

"Thanks, sweetie, but I don't want you anywhere near what I just saw."

"Why? What was it?"

"I'm not sure, but it was powerful. Would you get me some tea? I think that'll help." While Eva hurried to do as asked, Sadie took deep, calming breaths. In her pocket she carried a piece of selenite, which she dug out and gripped to help cleanse her of the final remnants of evil she'd felt. The stench hadn't come from any of the women. It was more that they had been surrounded by it. Eva returned, along with Autumn and Arabella. Sadie pasted a smile on her face even as she sipped on the hot beverage. "What'd you find there?"

"This stained glass to hang in my window. Mama said I could buy it. I have my own money."

"A self-sufficient woman. Right up my alley."

Eva brought her over to the register. Autumn studied Sadie, decided her coloring looked better. "Have you thought about doin classes? Arabella has a birthday comin up, she'd love to have her friends come and make somethin like stained glass."

"That's a wonderful idea. Eva and I could put somethin together. When were you thinkin of havin the party?"

"Third weekend of September. We're still a little over a month away."

"I think that'll work just fine. Leave me your number, we'll shore up the details."

Arabella ran back to her mom and waited patiently for her to be done. "Ready to go, sweetheart?"

"We can come back, right?"

"Of course. In fact, I asked Ms. Sadie here if we could have your birthday party here."

"Really? Oh, yes, pretty please!"

"Eva and I will come up with a stained glass you and your friends can make. How's that sound?"

"Thank you, thank you!" Arabella said, wrapping her arms first around Eva's waist and then Sadie's legs. "I can't wait. I'm gonna tell all my friends."

"Let's maybe limit it to"—Autumn glanced at Sadie—"ten friends?"

When Sadie nodded, Arabella began to bounce from leg to leg. "I'll make a list as soon as I get home. This is so excitin."

"I'll see you soon, Arabella," Eva said as Autumn led them out.

"What a sweetheart," Sadie said, standing to wash out the two mugs that had been used. "I'm sorry, I should have asked first. Are you all right doin a party for her?"

"Sure, I don't mind helpin."

"If it goes well, we could start advertisin for more. You'll get half of whatever we bring in."

"Half? Really?"

"Sure. You're much better at the stained glass. I couldn't do it without you."

Eva beamed with pride as she headed back to the work table, even more determined than before to become proficient.

△ △ △

Declan spent most nights at Sadie's, and missed both her and Eva like crazy when he stayed away. He'd gone over gun awareness with Eva, since he kept his sidearm with him at all times. Sadie agreed he could take her to the shooting range if it was something Eva wanted to learn.

"It's better to know the proper way to use a weapon than to ignore it. Less chance of an accident happenin," Sadie had said. "We'll still keep it out of sight when possible, and if you ever plan on bringin more guns into the house, we'll lock them up."

And Declan had thought he couldn't love the woman more. So, on the next Saturday, he took Eva to the shooting range with him instead of her going to the shop with Sadie.

He showed her each part of a gun, how to load and unload. Which guns had safeties, and which didn't. The best stance for her size. And once he'd drilled in all the safety precautions, he let her shoot.

On her first shot she missed the target by a mile, but it only made her more determined. By the end of the day, she had sore arms and a paper target full of holes.

"Are you nervous for court this week?" Declan asked as they drove back to Sadie's.

"A little. Sadie told me my mom will be there."

Declan glanced down, saw how she chewed her lip and averted her gaze. "It's okay to be nervous about seein your mom."

"I don't want to see her," she said in a tone so low he had to strain to hear.

"It's also okay to love her and not like her."

"I don't think I love her or like her."

"That's okay too. You don't have to tell me anythin that happened to you, Eva. You don't have to tell anyone. But if you're ever wantin to talk, I hope you know I'd be more than willin to listen." She didn't say anything, but she did nod. "Would you feel better if I came to the court, too?"

"That would be nice." After a few moments of silence, she asked, "Declan? Could we do this again? After the court date, I mean."

"I'd like that." Declan realized just how much he meant that.

When he went back to the precinct on Monday, he made sure to arrange his schedule for the hearing that Thursday. He wouldn't be able to do anything but sit and watch, but he felt the need to be there for his women.

And when had that happened? They were his, just as surely as he was theirs. From the moment he'd met Eva, he'd felt that link. A protective gene had been awakened and he'd known he'd do anything for her. As for Sadie—he supposed, in a way, it had always been Sadie.

Declan didn't care much for courthouses. Of course, he didn't know any that did. He'd spent plenty of time inside them for his job, but family court had a whole different feel. Sadder, somehow. Even the empty hall left him melancholy.

He spotted Sadie and Eva walking together and went to say hello. Giving Sadie a rather chaste kiss, he smiled gently at Eva. "Did you know we are just blocks away from the best pizza in Baton Rouge?"

"We are?" Eva asked.

"It'd be a shame not to grab a slice for lunch, wouldn't you say?"

"I think that sounds wonderful," Sadie said. "I've got the shop closed for the day, and Eva's playin hooky from school."

Clara approached the group and introduced herself to Declan. "Let's go in, get settled. Eva, if the judge would like to speak with you privately, would you be all right with that?"

"Yes, ma'am." Her tone was low, her hands twisting together from nerves.

"Everythin will be all right, honey. You're sure you want to go in there?"

Eva had been given the option not to be a part of the hearing, but she had a spine of steel. "I'd like to go in. It's my future, isn't it?"

"You're right about that. Okay, let's go."

Declan waved them off, wishing he could do more. "I'll be right out here, thinkin about that boudin pizza."

Eva offered him a tight smile. Sadie squeezed his arm and kissed his cheek. He watched the door closed, then settled in to wait.

He recognized Justine when she walked by with her lawyer. Eva had too much of her for him not to know who she was. But where Eva had the smooth beauty of youth, Justine looked well past her age. Her drug addiction and rough lifestyle had not treated her well.

Other witnesses were called in as needed. Maybelle, Justine's own mother, testified to Eva's well-being—or lack thereof. The woman who had come to inspect Sadie's home came and went, as did Justine's parole officer.

As they headed into the second hour, Declan paced the hall. When the door finally opened, he watched as Justine stormed out.

He hurried over to Sadie and realized his heart was on his throat. "What's happened?"

"Justine failed her last drug test. The judge granted me continued custody."

"That means you can apply for adoption?"

"It does. We'll have a final hearin to make it official."

He looked down at Eva, whose puffy eyes were red from tears already dried. "Are you all right, sweetheart?"

"I am now."

Sadie gave him a look he understood. She'd tell him all later. Only one thing mattered right then. "I'd say it's high time for lunch."

Chapter Twenty-Nine

She's asleep?"

Sadie nodded, sinking into the couch and into Declan. She'd always been perfectly happy being independent, but she had to admit it felt nice to have someone to lean on once in a while. "She was so worn out. I hope she sleeps well."

"She's as tough as you are. I hope you know that just because she looked sad it doesn't mean she's not happy to be here."

"I know, I do. I just hate that she had to be put in the middle of all this. She did so well, Dec. Even though Justine failed her last drug test, she was sober today. Clear headed enough to fight for Eva."

"What tipped the scale?"

"The judge did ask to speak privately with Eva. He didn't want her to feel pressure from either side of it. He didn't announce what she said—he said his rulin had more to do with the failed drug test and the witness testimonies—but Eva told me in the car later. She picked me. When the judge asked her who she'd rather live with, she picked me."

Tears gathered and began to spill. Declan wrapped his arms around her and held her close. They were the most heart-breaking happy tears he'd ever witnessed. Eva had picked Sadie. She'd lost her birth mom, but gained a guardian that loved her fiercely and would provide her with everything she'd need. Still, it hadn't been easy. None of it was easy.

"Are you ready for bed?" Declan asked as the tears began to dry.

Sadie shook her head. "Can we stay here? Just a little bit longer."

They settled in, and next thing Declan knew he woke late in the night with Sadie curled up on his lap. He lifted her as easily as one would a toddler and carried her to bed. Once she snuggled into the thick blankets, he headed up the stairs to check on Eva. She slept fitfully; a purple stone clutched tightly in one fist. Sitting on the edge of the bed, he gently stroked her hair back and away from her tense, beautiful face.

"It's all right, Eva. I'm watchin over you." As he continued to speak words meant to soothe, the tension slowly began to drain from her body. When her face finally relaxed, he watched just a while longer before joining Sadie. He swore he'd do everything in his power to make sure Eva never looked so anxious again.

In the morning, Sadie dropped Eva off at school and watched her walk inside. Eva felt bad that she couldn't look as happy as she felt. As relieved as she felt. She could see how worried Sadie looked and wanted to take that anxiousness away. Megan ran over and though they walked in together, Eva still didn't feel like herself.

Eva made it through school that day in a strange sort of daze. On one hand, she had just a small remnant of the hurt that had squeezed her heart the day before. She'd expected the nightmares to come as she slept, but instead, all she remembered was the feeling of being watched over. Protected.

It wasn't that she wanted to live with her mom again. She'd meant what she said when she'd told Declan she didn't like or even love Justine anymore. Not after everything that had happened. Everything Justine had allowed to happen.

Still, she had hoped Justine would clean herself up, straighten her life out. Not for Eva, but for herself. She'd never be Eva's mama again. She'd lost that right. Eva had Sadie now. Declan, too. She'd never had a dad before. He could marry Sadie, and they could all live together.

If he wanted. Eva didn't know how Declan felt about her. But he had taken her shooting. That was fun. And he'd shown up at the court case yesterday. For her, and for Sadie.

Those thoughts had stayed with her the whole day, even as she waved goodbye to Megan and began to walk to the shop. So lost in her thoughts, Eva didn't notice the trashed, once-yellow car that had parked along her route from school to Sadie's Things. Her head had been so high in the clouds she didn't register the strung-out druggie that slipped from the driver's side and blocked her path. When she finally looked into the deranged smile and wild eyes so like her own, Eva's whole body froze even as her heart raced.

"What are you doin here?" she asked, wanting to sound confident but only coming off scared.

"I'm here for you, baby. That stupid bitch thought she could keep us apart, but she can't. No one can. Let's go. We're goin on a road trip."

"No. I'm not goin anywhere with you." Eva worked through her terror and grabbed at the phone in her pocket. If she could just call Sadie...

The phone slipped and clattered to the ground. Justine lunged as Eva scrambled. Justine won. Snatching up the phone, Justine tossed it over a fence and reached behind her back with her right hand. When Eva's eyes landed on the cool metal of a gun, all struggles ceased. "Get in the car. Let's go."

Hands held out defensively, Eva back toward the passenger side. Justine waved her in using the barrel. Through her fear, Eva forced herself to think. She recognized the type of gun. Declan had shown her one just like it. The M&P on the end of the barrel was easy enough to pick out. Smith and Wesson. Sixteen rounds, plus one in the chamber. No external safety.

She slid into the seat and watched as Justine hustled to the driver side. Even as Justine started the car and drove off, she kept the gun in her lap.

Keep thinking. Keep thinking. Eva had to find a way to contact Sadie or Declan or just the police. She had to find a way to get the gun away from Justine. Before either of those could happen, she had to get on Justine's good side. Eva had plenty of practice dealing with high Justine. Logic wouldn't work. There would be no reasoning. The only thing that had a chance was to play on her emotions.

"Where are we goin, Mama?" Eva asked quietly, keeping her tone soft and even.

"Somewhere far away, baby. Somewhere no one can bother us. You'll see. You'll see."

"Do we have enough gas, Mama?" Justine jerked her head toward the nearly empty gas gauge. Her right hand tightened on the wheel while her left rubbed the gun against her leg. Eva spoke again to distract her. "It's okay. I have some money. We can fill up and get far away."

"You have money? How much?"

"Forty dollars. You can have it, Mama. We can put some gas in. Get some snacks for the road. I'm hungry. Aren't you hungry?"

Justine's hand loosened, but still twitched. "Yeah. Snacks. Good idea, baby girl. Let's get some snacks. And gas, too."

Eva wanted to sigh in relief, but she kept it to herself. Justine pulled into a gas station several blocks from her school, the opposite direction of Sadie's shop. That was fine. She just needed a minute.

Justine made to get out, gun in hand. Eva steeled herself for backlash and spoke up. "Mama? Maybe we should leave the gun in the car. I don't want you to get in trouble in the store."

For several beats of time, Eva thought she'd resist. But then Justine gave her a jerky nod and slid the gun into the center console. After a minute Eva got out of the car and walked into the store with her. She took the money out of her backpack and handed it over. "Here, Mama. Forty dollars. I have to use the bathroom."

Justine grabbed her wrist with bruising force. "You just gonna run."

"No, Mama," Eva said, fighting through the tears that had sprung up. "I promise, I'll come right back. Will you get me those crackers I like?"

"Those cheese ones?"

"That's right. And you can get those little cookies. We could share."

"One minute, baby. You be back in one minute, or I'll come find you."

Eva nodded and hurried to the back. She slipped into the restroom to find it empty. She'd hoped there would be someone with a cell phone, but she'd come prepared just in case. Tearing out a sheet of paper from her notebook, she fumbled for a pencil and began to write a note.

Please help. My name is Eva Wentworth and I've been kidnapped. Call the police and ask for Declan Park. We're driving an old yellow car with license 874-ACJ.

Propping it against the sink, she stared at it for a moment before reaching behind her neck to pull off the long chain holding the locket from Sadie. That way, she'd know it was really Eva. She hated the thought of being without it—of being without her protection—but them finding her was more important. Setting the locket with the note, she rushed back out of the bathroom before

Justine could come looking for her. On her way out, a woman with long dark hair brushed past her. Before she could think, Eva grabbed the stranger's arm and made eye contact.

The shock of the vision rushed through her. Darkness. So much darkness. A man with a tattoo. Another woman, eyes wide with shock, collapsing to the ground, surrounded by books. More darkness.

Eva gasped and released her hold. The woman, completely baffled, gripped her shoulders with concern. "Are you okay, sweetheart?"

Blinking up at the woman, Eva realized she recognized her but couldn't figure out why. Like she'd been on television or something. "Bathroom."

"You need to go to the bathroom?"

"No. Please. Go in there. Please help." Before she could say more, Justine found her. She wrapped an arm around Eva's shoulders, squeezing like a snake.

"Ready to go, baby?"

"Yes, Mama," she replied, while using her eyes to plead with the woman.

"Ya'll have a great day," the woman said with a bright smile, edging toward the bathroom. Justine turned them around, but when Eva glanced back, the woman gave her a determined nod.

△ △ △

Declan was wrapping up paperwork when he got the call. The voice on the other end surprised him nearly as much as the message. "Detective Park, this is Inali Grayson."

"Ms. Grayson, what can I do for you?"

"Do you know an Eva Wentworth?"

His heart in his throat, Declan stood so fast his chair rolled across the room behind him. "Yes. What about her?"

"I ran into her in a gas station. She left a note in the bathroom that said she'd been kidnapped."

A string of expletives left his mouth first. A sharp pain settled in his chest. He had to focus. He had to be a cop. "Tell me everythin."

Inali explained the entire situation, and read the note word for word. When she described the locket, his heart sank. He typed the plate into the system and wasn't surprised to find it hadn't been registered in the last three years. "Did you see which direction they were headed?"

"East from here. I feel terrible. I should have done more."

"No, Inali, you did exactly the right thing. Thank you." He hung up and updated Kevin, who had overheard most of the conversation anyway. As they raced to the car, Declan made the call to Sadie at her shop while Kevin notified the missing persons division. When he heard Sadie's cheerful voice on the other end of the line, Declan was at a loss for words. What the hell was he supposed to say? "Sadie, it's Declan. I have some news about Eva."

"You're scarin me, Dec. What's goin on?"

"We believe Justine has taken her." He told her everything he knew, then asked, "Do you have any idea where Justine might go?"

He could hear Sadie taking several deep breaths. "Not her apartment. Not Maybelle's. I doubt Justine has any friends that she could run to. You know, I think Maybelle had a cabin for a while.   Not anymore, she couldn't keep up with it, but it's somewhere Justine would know and probably sittin empty."

"Do you know the address? Whereabouts?"

"Over by Lake Maurepas. Let me get a hold of Maybelle and I'll call you right back."

Kevin hit the siren and headed for highway ten. Declan kept his eyes peeled for a yellow '85 Oldsmobile with expired plates. When Sadie called back with the address, she was nearly frantic with worry. "What can I do? I need to do somethin. I need to find her."

"Kevin and I are headed that way. We've already contacted missing persons and have a notice out for the car. The best thing you can do is stay at the shop or at home, with your phone by your side in case she calls."

"Can't I track her phone? I had them set that up at the store."

"Good thinkin. Use 'find my phone' and see what you find out. I'll stay on the line."

After a minute of silence, Sadie groaned with frustration. "It's showin a block away from her school. Not movin."

"I'll still have someone check it out. Send me a screen shot, okay?"

"It's sent. Bring her back to me, Declan."

"I will. I promise. Sadie, I love you."

"I love you, too. Update me when you can."

He hung up, looked over at Kevin. Kevin seemed just as determined to bring her home safely. Declan knew they'd both do everything in their power to make that happen.

Declan became concerned when they didn't spot the Oldsmobile. They should have overtaken them by that point. No calls had come in from the patrols, either. Kevin had someone check Justine's apartment, just in case she'd been dumb enough to return there. No such luck.

A call finally came in. "This is Park."

"Detective Park, this is Jim Morgan from the Sherriff's office. You had the BOLO for an '85 Olds?"

"That's right."

"It's been spotted on highway twelve crossin sixty-three. Should we pursue?"

"Follow, but stay back. We know where she's headed." Declan gave them the address, asked for a follow up if they veered off route. To Kevin he said, "She's takin the long way. We'll beat her there."

"You said Inali thought she looked high. Probably not makin the best decisions."

"Like takin Eva? No, I'd say she's not."

"Quite the coincidence, her runnin into Inali. One of few people who would not only believe her, but also have your cell phone number."

Declan stared hard out the window. They were close now. "I don't believe in coincidence."

He called Sadie as Kevin turned off the siren and wound through the affluent lakeside neighborhood. The patrol that had checked out her phone location had found it in a lawn near the school. When he told Sadie that they were on the right track, at least some of her worry eased.

Kevin drove past the property once, slowly. It didn't look occupied at the moment, so they circled back and found a parking spot out of view from the direction Justine would be coming. With gun at his hip and cuffs in his pocket, Declan slipped from the car and moved swiftly and silently through the yard. The driveway cut off at one of two garages, with no access by vehicle to the rear of the house.

"One of us should wait at the door, the other around the side of the garage."

"I'll take the garage," Declan said. "Get her attention on you, I'll come up and grab Eva. The Sherriff's that are followin should be just minutes behind."

"They'll have notified locals, too."

"I don't care, as long as we get Eva back."

Kevin took a moment to squeeze his partner's arm. "We will. Let's go."

Declan jogged to his position to wait. Fifteen minutes went by before he heard tires against the gravel drive. He risked a look; the rusted-out Oldsmobile pulled to a stop. He saw Eva's dark bob of hair in the passenger seat. Taking deep breaths, he exercised as much patience as he could muster.

He heard a car door slam. Justine's voice. "What'd I tell ya, baby? All this, for us. We never hafta go back."

"Yes, Mama," he heard Eva reply. He recognized that tone. He'd heard it when they first met. Docile, compliant. Dispassionate. Sadie had changed that.

Kevin stepped out. Spoke loud and clear. "Justine, I'm gonna need you to step away from the girl."

Declan came around the corner, gun drawn. Justine had already grabbed Eva and yanked her close. "Who the hell are you?"

"My name's Kevin, ma'am. Let the girl go, and we'll talk about this."

"I don't think so," Justine said, reaching in her waistband and removing a pistol. Declan's heart jumped into his throat. "What's gonna happen is, you're gonna let us go."

The gun pointed at Eva's temple. Justine's twitchy finger hovered over the trigger. Kevin stepped closer; his hands held out defensively. "Tell you what, Justine. I'll let you go, but only if you take the gun away from Eva's head. Point it at me, if you feel you must. Okay?"

Justine swung her gun arm out, took aim. Declan had his own trained on her head. He inched closer, not wanting to give up his position quite yet. Justine's lip curled back. "Don't you fuckin move."

"I'm not movin, Justine. Nice n easy, now. Why don't you let Eva get in the car, and you can drive away?"

Justine shoved Eva to the side. "Do what he says, girl. Get in the car."

Eva turned, looked up. Spotted Declan and felt relief wash through her. He pointed behind him and she nodded. Justine, still trained on Kevin, risked a glance over when she didn't hear the car door open or close. With the speed of an Olympic sprinter thanks to a boost of adrenaline, Eva ran straight to Declan. Justine shouted in fury and lined up the sights with Eva's back.

She squeezed the trigger; Declan's heart sank.

Chapter Thirty

Declan watched his worst-case scenario unfold before his eyes. He'd heard people say that in situations such as these, time seemed to slow. Not for him. Time moved on, but his senses seemed to sharpen. He took in the way Eva's hair splayed out from the wind of her movement, the way her mouth began opening to scream. The specks of green in Justine's otherwise blue eyes. The chipped red nail polish on her finger as she squeezed.

At that moment, the purest of instincts kicked in. They say survival is at the base of the human spirit, but Declan realized in that moment the inaccuracy of that statement. Survival is everything, until you had a kid.

Eva was as much his child as, one day, his own flesh and blood would be. Justine had given up her rights as a mother the day she'd let the drugs take over. She had a perverse love for Eva, but not the true, pure love of a mother. He knew Sadie did. Now he knew what it meant to be a father. To love another more than himself, to place another's life before his own.

He moved without thought. His arms wrapped around the slight teen who had already been through hell and back. She deserved so much more. They hit the ground and rolled even as Kevin tackled and restrained Justine.

"Eva! Eva, are you hurt? Did she get you? Talk to me." He patted his hands against her bone-white cheeks as she lay against the hard ground. "Please, Eva, be okay."

Her eyes opened and she groaned. One hand reached up to rub a spot on the back of her head. Her mouth screwed up and she said, "Ow."

Declan felt the spot with his fingers, gentle as he was capable. There was a small bump, but no bleeding. He let out a sigh of relief. She hadn't been hit. "Oh, thank every god listenin."

"Declan," she said, struggling to sit up. "I took the bullets out."

"You—you what?"

"There were no bullets. I did what you showed me. Justine had no idea."

"You beautiful, amazin, genius child," Declan said, taking her head between his hands and kissing her forehead. "I don't know what I would have done. What Sadie would have done."

"It's all right now. I'm all right, you're all right. Kevin's all right too, isn't he?"

Declan looked up as two more vehicles pulled up in the driveway. Better late than never. "You're all right, Kev?"

"Peachy keen. Our back up here will help me out."

"Come on, sweetie. You don't need to see this."

Declan led Eva to his car as Justine got hauled into the back of a cruiser. He settled her in the backseat, digging a blanket from the trunk along with a bottle of water. When he handed her his phone, she called Sadie and endured the happy screaming and crying. He felt like doing a little bit of both, himself.

When she hung up, Declan asked her to relay what she could of the story. She told him everything, from the moment Justine

259

confronted her on the street to the minute they pulled into the drive. "I asked her to leave the gun in the car. I took out the bullets real quick and stuffed them in my backpack."

Kevin brought over her backpack and Declan found the bullets before handing it back to its owner. Leaning down, Kevin did his own inspection of Eva. "You all right, sweetheart?"

"I am now."

Kevin nodded, straightened. "The Sherriff will handle the rest. We can bring Eva home."

△ △ △

It had been a week since that awful afternoon with Justine. Sadie and Declan had both been overly protective, picking Eva up from school instead of letting her walk, and checking on her several times throughout the night. Truth was, Eva didn't mind. She liked the fact that she had someone who cared about her that much.

Sadie had cried most of that first night. Eva had cried a little bit, too. Sometimes the bad dreams would filter through even with her special dreamcatcher and protective stones—including the locket the nice lady from the gas station had returned to Declan. Sometimes in the dreams the gun hadn't been empty. Sometimes Declan died.

Those dreams made her scream in her sleep. But when she woke up, both Sadie and Declan would be there, alive and well. Sadie kept a tub of chocolate and raspberry ice cream in the freezer, just for her. Declan would eat it with her. Sometimes Sadie would sneak a bite, too.

Sometimes, her dreams included a shadowy figure of a man with a hand tattoo.

It had been exactly a week since the Justine incident when Declan picked Eva up and wanted to talk. Instead of driving to Sadie's Things or home, he asked, "Are you feelin okay with me bein around so much?"

"Sure, Declan. It's nice." Declan looked real nervous. Eva thought it was sweet. "What is it?"

"I love Sadie, Eva. Always have, always will. I'd like to marry her." Eva's heart began to pound. What did that mean for her? Would Declan want her around? He seemed to catch the anxiety flitting across her features, for he quickly backpedaled. "I'm askin you first, because I want to make sure you're fine with it. With me. I understand that marryin Sadie I won't just be gainin a wife, but a daughter."

"You see me that way?"

"More than. Eva, I couldn't have picked a more wonderful, smart, beautiful kid if I'd been given a choice. In fact, I don't want to just be Sadie's husband. I want to be your dad, if you'd like that too. I'd like to adopt you with Sadie."

Tears welled. Overwhelmed by his words and the gesture, Eva finally nodded. "I'd like that."

"Really?" A bright grin broke out across his face. "Wow. I'm gonna be a dad."

"As my first daughter-duty, I have to ask—how do you plan on askin Sadie?"

"I hadn't really thought about it. Over dinner?"

"Tonight?"

"That was the plan, as long as you agreed."

Eva shook her head with mock pity. "It's a good thing you came to me. We don't have much time."

"What did you have in mind?"

"We're gonna need flowers. Lots of flowers. And candles, but Sadie has those. A special dinner, too." She took out her notebook and began jotting things down. He had no idea what the young woman planned, but he was certain he was about to be schooled in romance.

Eva paused and glanced up. He watched her with amusement, awaiting her direction. Steeling herself for the contact, she wrapped her arms around him. It was easy with the bench seat of his pickup truck. "Thank you."

"For what?"

"Acceptin me. I never had a dad before. If I could pick anyone, it would be you, too." She sat back, and Declan had to bite his lip in order to prevent the tears from leaking. She saw, but didn't say a word. "Hope you have your wallet. We'll need it."

By the time Eva had everything she wanted, Declan felt cross-eyed. They made two stops of his choosing—first, the jeweler, where the ring he'd already picked out waited. Eva approved, so they didn't spend long there. The second was Sadie's parents' house—which also involved his own folks. Damn nosy neighbors.

James, Diana, Joe, and Madeline all stood together in the Nichols' dining room. The same place Sadie had gathered them six months earlier to announce her plan to adopt Eva. Now Declan and Eva stood together, united in their quest to ask for blessings from both sets of parents.

"I've already asked Eva's permission, but I'd like all of ya'lls blessin. I'm gonna ask Sadie to marry me."

Absolute silence reigned for several long moments. James stepped forward first, taking Declan's hand in his. "I couldn't think of a better match for my Sadie."

"Thank you, sir," Declan replied as James gave up the manly handshake in favor of a hug.

Diana added her acceptance before he turned to his own parents. His dad beamed at him while Madeline stepped forward and wrapped her arms around her only son and whispered in his ear. "It's about damn time."

△ △ △

Eva and Declan worked furiously to set up the perfect scene for his proposal. She decided it needed to be done in the garden, Sadie's favorite spot. When Sadie walked in that evening, Eva had already snuck upstairs to give them privacy—though she watched out the window.

Only one thing still bothered her. She'd found out that the woman who'd helped her in the gas station had been Inali Grayson, the governor's daughter. The vision Eva had received hadn't been just a vision—it had been Inali's memories. Not just that, but she'd recognized the tattoo man. She'd seen him before.

The night of Fourth of July, the first time Sadie took her out for ice cream after a nightmare. She hadn't told Sadie what she'd seen, but it had been the tattooed man. And he'd been talking to that judge, the one that had killed himself.

He hadn't killed himself. The tattooed man had done it.

She had to tell Declan. He may not believe her, but he had to know. She had no proof, she knew, but at least if he knew the truth he could find the evidence to prove it. She hoped.

Out the window she saw Declan get on his knee, watched as Sadie squealed and tackled him to the ground. Laughed as they hit the earth and she smothered him in kisses.

A few seconds later Sadie was on her feet, dragging Declan in her wake. They came to her room first and group hugged. Then Sadie was off to call her parents and Savannah, and Declan noticed the shadow in Eva's eyes. "This is still all right with you?"

Eva nodded, but her eyes remained wary. "It's not about that. I trust you," she told him. Then, taking a deep breath, she decided to prove just how much she meant that. "I have to tell you somethin. That night, when the girl was murdered? The man who is in jail accused of killin her?"

"Levi Jones," Declan answered, his brows drawing together in confusion of where this conversation was headed. "What about him?"

She paused a moment longer, her eyes searching Declan's gaze for a long time before finally speaking. "He didn't do it."

Epilogue

Music flowed from open windows, winging its way across the night to entice passersby to stop for a cold drink and hot beats. Located just off the bayou in downtown Baton Rouge, Gaston's had become the exclusive hot spot to rub elbows with the rich and famous.

Patrons paid exorbitant prices for immaculate service and privacy. Every employee had signed a nondisclosure on being hired, promising not to sell their stories to the media.

Below the raised stage surrounded by a wide dancefloor and VIP balconies, below the lower level where barrels of beer and whiskey awaited their turn to slake the thirst of the clientele, a man poured a perfectly aged bourbon into four glasses.

Cell phones had been left outside. Four leather chairs gathered loosely around a simple table furnished the space. Its occupants felt secure holding a conversation here, knowing the pounding music would drown out any sound.

The first man sat back and sipped his drink. "This band is really quite good."

"Found them in a dive bar makin fifty bucks a show. They just needed a little direction," said the second man. "How do you like the bourbon? Aged in white oak for thirteen years."

"It's superb," said the first man.

The third man took a sip, let it settle. "It's good, but I prefer the younger varieties."

"Are we talkin bourbon or women?"

A flash of teeth. "Both."

"Gentlemen," said the fourth man, quiet until now. "We have some issues to discuss."

The second man nodded. "That thing with Beaumont was close. You're lucky I caught it."

"Park seems to have let it go," said the first man.

"There's another that's been sniffin around." The third man swirled his drink and held the rest in suspense. "Lookin for information on Kofi."

"Who?"

"Mhina Abara."

"Who the hell is she?"

"Besides a powerful Mambo? She's the grandmother of Grayson's assistant. What's his name?"

The first man sat forward. "Jaser Parrish. He's one of the witnesses."

"He didn't see anythin."

"He must have seen somethin, otherwise why would his grandmother be puttin herself on Kofi's radar?" asked the third man. He rather enjoyed riling up the others.

"I'll look into it," said the second man, wanting to ease the tension. "Who else do we have to worry about?"

"Currie and Hoyt will be easily swayed in the trial," said the fourth man. "But we need to do somethin about Inali Grayson."

"We've already taken care of Beaumont and his so-called evidence," said the first man. "Isn't that enough?"

"She remembers more than we counted on," said the second man.

"You mean the tattoo?" asked the third. "It doesn't matter. Levi Jones is behind bars."

"It does matter. You know well as I do this stuff isn't perfect. What if she gets her true memory back?"

The fourth man swirled his drink lazily. "There's a man that can take care of it. Won't tie back to us at all."

"Who?"

"Damien Caine." The others frowned. It was a name only whispered in the shadows. A shadow himself. Assassin. "He worked well the last time."

"Kofi can handle it."

"Kofi already tried to handle it. I have as much faith in him as the rest of you, but we need a professional, someone who won't be seen. And if Damien is caught, he'll have nothin on us." They all shared a long look. The fourth man nodded with satisfaction. "I'll make the call."

Dear Reader,

Thank you so much for reading Book One of The Strangers Saga: Baton Rouge.   There will be five books in this series, continuing on with characters you've already met.

Join Rae and Jaser as they navigate love and magic in the second book of the series, available early 2020!

If you enjoyed this book, please visit Amazon or Goodreads to leave a review. It would only take a few minutes and would help spread the word. A review would be greatly appreciated!

As always, you can keep up-to-date by "liking" me on Facebook @AnaBanNovels, or check out www.anabannovels.com

Thanks again, and happy reading!

Always,

Ana

Other books by Ana Ban:

The Parker Grey Series

Young Adult/Crime Novels recommended for ages 13+

Abstraction; A Parker Grey Novel (Book 1)

Backfire; A Parker Grey Novel (Book 2)

Coercion; A Parker Grey Novel (Book 3)

Deception; A Parker Grey Novel (Book 4)

Dubious Endeavors; A Parker Grey Novella (Book 5)

Exposed; A Parker Grey Novel (Book 6)

Firestarter; A Parker Grey Novel (Book 7) (available soon)

Grownup; A Parker Grey Novel (Book 8) (available soon)

The Gifted Series

Paranormal Romance Novels recommended for ages 18+

Allure of Home: Book 1 of The Gifted Series

Immaculate: Book 2 of The Gifted Series

Night Shift: Book 3 of The Gifted Series

Stow Away: Book 4 of The Gifted Series

Reservation: Book 5 of The Gifted Series

Shadowed Soul: Book 6 of The Gifted Series

Vows at Dusk: Book 7 of The Gifted Series (with special bonus novella *After Dusk!*)

Dark Omens: Book 8 of The Gifted Series (available 2020)

The Mirror Trilogy

Crime/Police Procedural Novels recommended for ages 18+

Infiltration: Book 1 of The Mirror Trilogy

Split: Book 2 of The Mirror Trilogy

Wakening: Book 3 of The Mirror Trilogy

Coming Soon:

Murder Mystery Romance recommended for ages 18+

The Strangers Saga: Baton Rouge: Book One

The Strangers Saga: Baton Rouge: Book Two (available 2020)

Books Three–Five (available soon)